Meta Lander

The Tobacco Problem

Meta Lander

The Tobacco Problem

ISBN/EAN: 9783742811400

Manufactured in Europe, USA, Canada, Australia, Japa

Cover: Foto ©Andreas Hilbeck / pixelio.de

Manufactured and distributed by brebook publishing software
(www.brebook.com)

Meta Lander

The Tobacco Problem

THE

TOBACCO PROBLEM

BY

META LANDER

AUTHOR OF "THE BROKEN BUD," "LIGHT ON THE DARK RIVER," "MARION GRAHAM," ETC.

FIFTH EDITION, ENLARGED

BOSTON
LEE AND SHEPARD, PUBLISHERS

TO YOU,

MY YOUNG COUNTRYWOMEN,

I DEDICATE THIS BOOK,

BECAUSE THE SOLUTION OF THE TOBACCO PROBLEM
LIES VERY MUCH IN YOUR HANDS.
A CAUSE WHICH AIMS TO LIFT SO FEARFUL A
BURDEN, TO REMOVE SO TERRIBLE AN
EVIL, IS WORTHY OF YOUR WARM-
EST EFFORTS, YOUR MOST
SKILFUL ADVOCACY.

MARGARET WOODS LAWRENCE.

LINDEN HOME, MARBLEHEAD.

"I do not place my individual self in opposition to tobacco, but science, in the form of physiology and hygiene, is opposed to it; and science is the expression of God's will in the government of his work in the universe."

"Every interest of purity, dignity, and honor should lead every woman and every maiden to set her face and her whole example against everything that is of the passions, everything that is of the appetites, which leads into peril."

AUTHOR'S PREFACE TO THE FIFTH EDITION.

In bringing out the present edition of "The Tobacco Problem," I desire to say that, while I have taken tobacco for my text, I have included all other narcotics, especially those used, at first, under medical prescription and continued until the servant becomes, not only a master, but a tyrant.

I wish also to acknowledge the great kindness with which my book has been received, even by many devotees of the weed. I had hardly expected such a degree of sufferance. It is true that, outspoken as I have been, I have set down naught in malice, and have aimed to avoid unfair and unwarranted statements. Yet I am aware that it is well-nigh impossible for one with strong convictions as to the use of narcotics, to write a treatise on the subject which will not seem, perhaps to a large class, unreasonable and extravagant, if not absurd. Judging from the indications, the majority in Church and State are against me. Again and again have I been told that I injure the cause by demanding too much; that it is the abuse and not the proper use of tobacco against which I should direct my efforts.

The same charges have long been rung against

those who plead for total abstinence from intoxicating liquors. Such persons assert that temperance means "the moderate use of all these good things;" that it is really *intemperance* to insist on entire abstinence. I can only reply that in many cases the tobacco users with whom I have conversed frankly concede that the habit, however limited, is not only foolish but injurious, and that they wish themselves well rid of it.

On the other hand, not a few insist that their use of tobacco is moderate, even when physicians and friends are alarmed by their excessive indulgence. It is very hard for such smokers, perhaps indeed for smokers generally, to admit that they smoke *too much*. Is not this an evidence that the tobacco habit impairs the judicial faculty?

I have discussed this subject with more than one excellent clergyman who assert that their temperate use of the "*divine weed*" is not only harmless, but really beneficial. May I not respectfully refer back the subject to these preachers of self-denial for a fuller consideration?

That there may not be exceptions to the rule governing the habitual use of narcotics, I dare not insist. But if such exceptions exist, are they not so rare that they may almost be regarded as strengthening the general rule?

Totally apart, however, from the more or less injurious results, physical and intellectual, of the tobacco habit, arises the question whether, in an ethical view, the yielding to such a habit is worthy of one's better self — is not, indeed, a lowering of the moral tone.

Says Archdeacon Farrar: "It seems to me that, when man has so many natural wants, it is not desirable to add to them another want, which can only be regarded as artificial."

Governed by the same principle, Sir Isaac Newton refused to smoke, "because he would make no necessities for himself."

Is there not sound philosophy in what Tolstoi writes : " It is incumbent upon us, as far as in us lies, to surround ourselves and others with the conditions most favorable to that precision and clearness of thought which are so indispensable to the proper working of our consciousness ; and we should certainly refrain most scrupulously from hindering and clogging this action of consciousness by the consumption of brain-clouding stimulants and narcotics."

Is not compliance with any doubtful indulgence weakening to the moral sense? Must not continuance in such indulgence by one who admits that it is foolish and injurious, check his religious aspirations, and bring him down to a low, earthy level? Are those who make self-indulgence their law fitted as good soldiers for the real battle of life? — especially as leaders of those who are pressing by thousands into the ranks?

I desire to express my indebtedness to all those

who have strengthened my hands and cheered my heart in my difficult and often discouraging work. A few who most generously aided me at the outset — William E. Dodge, Sr., of New York, Elizur Wright of Boston, William Hyde of Ware, and President Fairchild of Berea, — have all passed to a higher field of labor. Are there any who will take their places?

I am also under obligation to many, including physicians, both in our own and other lands, for their testimonies and encouragement. Particularly would I pay my warm tribute of thanks to my good friends, Dr. John Ellis of New York and Dr. Charles C. Drysdale, senior surgeon of the Metropolitan Hospital, London, — not only for the valuable information they have given me, but for their unwearied sympathy and kindness.

Let me add that it was not at hap-hazard that this book was dedicated to my country-women, and that every year strengthens the conviction that I made no mistake in this. I have seen enough of the effects, on the one hand, not merely of the condoning, but of the self-complacent approval, of this narcotic barbarian, this insidious but desperate defier of æsthetics, by thoughtless and sometimes frivolous women, and, on the other hand, of the decided and unfaltering stand against it on the part of intelligent, conscientious women, — I have seen enough of all this to convince me a hundred times over of the potency of woman's influence in this as in other matters.

If all our women would combine in kindly but earnest and unwavering warfare against this tobacco necromancer, there is not a question but he would be slain. Think of the multitudes who would thus be forever freed from their degrading bondage !

Will the women do it?

Margaret Woods Lawrence.

Linden Home, Marblehead.

HISTORICAL SKETCH.

This society, which was born in 1848, was, I believe, the first for this cause ever known in the world. Its founder, George Trask, by a slavery to the weed of more than twenty years, was brought to the gates of death. Looking to God for help, he broke from its bondage. In his own words, "Its renunciation lifted a loathsome incubus from my soul. I came back to a normal condition of body and mind. I ran, I leaped for joy, and sometimes my gratitude to God for the return of health was so intense that I was overwhelmed and wept like a child."

In all the enthusiasm of a fresh convert, George Trask began to labor with his neighbors, and finally consecrated himself to this work, in which he continued through life, undeterred by the greatest obstacles.

In giving his experience sometime after he says:

"My clerical brethren have treated me in a style somewhat diverse. Some have heartily bid me Godspeed; some — votaries of the weed — have eyed me askance, and, I presume, wished me in Japan. Some have played the captious critic — laughed at my work, as they have laughed at all reforms while struggling for life.

"Riding out of Brattleboro one Monday morning with Rev. Dr. Pierpont, he asked me, 'What did you do yesterday?' 'I preached to Baptist friends in the morning on the text, "Whether ye eat or drink, or whatsoever ye do, do all to the glory of God," and showed them they could not glorify him by using tobacco. I addressed three Sunday-schools at noon, and showed the boys that tobacco leads to *idleness, poverty, strong drink, vice, ill health, insanity and death*. I preached to the Congregationalists in West Brattleboro in the afternoon on the text, "That which is highly esteemed among men is abomination in the sight of God," showing them that men highly esteemed tobacco, but God abhorred it. I lectured in the evening in the town hall to a noble body of young men on the destructive effects of tobacco.'

"The poet exclaimed in surprise, 'A prodigious worker!' Then musing a moment, added, 'I will give you your epitaph.' In a Hudibrastic sort of verse which I cannot repeat, he said in substance : ' "We have great men enough, philosophers enough, poets enough, geniuses enough. D. D.'s enough, L. L. D's enough. The world needs *workers. Here lies one*." This is your epitaph.'

I take a few specimens from the journal of Mr. Trask's warfare on tobacco, which he says "are the off-hand record of the rough and tumble incident to the early stages f this reform, when to assault tobacco in the shape of a smoker, chewer, snuffer or raiser, was tantamount to assaulting a hornet's nest, and we were about as likely to be stung by friend as foe."

"October 28, 1852. — On my way to the city, I have free talk with Dr. P., who affirms, 'It is an insidious evil; it injures the individual more than the community; to fight it is like fighting the miasma,' and winds up by saying, 'Brother, I wouldn't fight it another day. Take a parish, be quiet and happy the rest of your life!'

"Right in front of Tremont Temple, a clerical brother takes me by the button, and facetiously asks, 'Brother, have you got all the tobacco out of the world?' 'Not *all*, brother; to mend the world is a vast concern. Dr. P. bids me quit this reform and take a parish.' 'No, no; go on; *agitate, agitate!* It is up-hill work, but in the strength of the Lord, go on.'

"Called on Professor ——. He assures me I shall do a world of good if I do not carry matters too far. 'I chew a little,' he adds; 'if I did not, I should be as fat as a pig. The little I chew does me good. *I detest smoking;* it poisons the common air.'

"I passed to the seminary to give a lecture to the students. The first I met accosted me: 'Mr. Trask, you are too late to benefit me; I gave up tobacco three months ago.' 'You smoke, my young brother; I smell it.' 'Yes, I must smoke a little, *but I abhor chewing.*'

"At Greenfield, saw Rev. Mr. Langstroth, the Corypheus in the science of bees. He says, 'Bees are wiser than men about tobacco. One of my hives was insulted, made stupid or drunk by tobacco smoke; but when the persecutor came round again with his pipe they gave him to understand that he could not repeat the insult with impunity. They assailed him on all sides with a vengeance.'"

I give selections from some of Mr. Trask's campaigns:

"Mr. J. C., of Connecticut, in a letter, denounces me and my mission. He bids me meet him at the judgment day, and answer for the sin of preaching against tobacco on the Sabbath. I reply: '*Mr. J. C.* — *When you write again, pay your postage. George Trask.*'

"January 26. — Spirits below zero. Letter after letter, giving me not a ray of light, not a farthing of money, not a word of encouragement. One from a brother clergyman says: 'Our association criticised you and your mission in a fraternal manner, after you left us the other day. Many of us thought you ought to be a little more cautious and courteous, and thereby carry on your unpopular work in a way less offensive and with better success.' 'O God!' I cry, 'have mercy on an amateur ministry! One-third of this association, or more, sit in their chairs, chew, smoke, criticise, and imagine that a man can handle pitch and not defile his garments.'

"Called at a school in Boston to drop a word touching pernicious habits. The teacher assures me it would not be best. 'My scholars are from rich and fashionable families which smoke, and it will not do to forbid the boys to do what their fathers practise.' The Lord have mercy on genteel families and genteel schools in this city of notions!

"May 13.—On my route to Waltham. Three red cents in my treasury to hire a hall, pay my board and battle the most popular of all narcotics. God give me grit and grace.'

"Cambridge, July 20.—Commencement. A class of eighty-eight were graduated. With rare exceptions the young men were pale, lank and lean—the pitiable victims of smoke. This is Cambridge College in 1853. How was it in 1650? 'No scholar shall take tobacco, unless permitted by the president, with the consent of their parents or guardians, and on good reasons first given by a physician, and then in a sober and private manner.'

"I met an admirable woman, a clergyman's wife, who said: 'My husband preached an excellent sermon on self-denial one Sabbath, and as he came down from the pulpit I said, "Husband, that is a good sermon. Now go home, drop tobacco, and put it into practice." *He did.*' Luther says, 'The sweetest thing in the world is the heart of a pious woman.' Brother Martin, I sincerely believe it.

"A deacon in Hadley besought us not to lecture against raising tobacco, because by raising it he could give more to foreign missions. The deacon reminds me of a man in Marlboro, who said to his neighbor: 'Sir, I wish to sell you my conscience. It is just as good as brand new, for I never used it.' Tobacco fields and distilleries of liquid death belong to the same category. When, oh when, will Christian pulpits in that fat valley do their duty?

"A school-master caught his boys smoking. 'How, now!' he shouted to the first lad; 'how dare you be smoking tobacco?'

"'Sir, I am subject to headaches, and smoke takes off the pains.' 'And you? And you? And you?'

"One had a raging tooth; another colic; the third a cough.

"'Now, sirrah!' shouted the master to the last boy, 'what disorder do you smoke for?'

"Looking up in the master's face, he said in a whining tone, 'Sir, *I smoke for corns.*'"

Then follows a characteristic report:

"LADIES AND GENTLEMEN: A few friends have urged me to call you together to listen to a statement of the doings of the American Anti-Tobacco Society for the ten years of its existence, and to give you an opportunity to adopt measures to arrest an evil of great magnitude.

"This society is not rich in names; still we are

happy to present a *Board of Officers* so united in purpose, so efficient in action, so reliable, and so well looking, considering the 'wear and tear' of this decade of hard service.   The president of this society is George Trask; the vice-president, secretary, treasurer and auditor is George Trask.   The honorary body, corporate and incorporate, is the same unwearied individual—the Anti-Tobacco Apostle.

"The object of this society is to break up a death-like, prevalent stupidity in relation to the evils of tobacco, and by 'light and love' create a public conscience, which we trust in God will lead to the removal of so great a curse.   This society encounters many obstacles.   Among these is the incorrigibility of the habit it assails.   A man can give up his pastimes, his bottle, his pastor, and his politics with less ado than his quid or his pipe. If any devotee of the weed disputes this, *let him try it*.   This cause encounters scorn and derision. It has been laughed at in the church and out of it from Maine to Georgia, from Plymouth Rock to California.   We have needed temples of brass, we have needed faith in God like Abraham's to brave this tide of sarcasm.   Thank God, we have had it!

"The position of many women is unfavorable to this cause.   They think it in bad taste to rebuke husbands and sons for indulgence in this fashionable pleasure.   But they do not think it in bad taste to live day and night in apartments fumigated with this impurity; they are used to it.   They are like the Irish girl, who was advised not to marry a drunkard. She replied: *'I will; I am used to it; it will seem more like home.'*

"We have during ten years delivered more than two thousand sermons and lectures, adapted to show the pernicious effects of the poison on the bodies and souls of men. We have published a number of small books and thirty tracts on the subject. These tracts have never been modified or mollified by any committee; hence they are not perfect; they retain all the original depravity they had at the hands of their authors; I mean the respectable board of gentlemen we have named who constitute the officers of this society."

Thus all along the years, this unwearied reformer preached and prayed and wrote tracts and small books which he sowed broadcast. But in the great Boston fire a sore calamity befell him in the destruction of all his plates. I remember seeing a letter he wrote on this occasion, in which he speaks of himself as lying flat on his back, yet looking up into the sky. And with a heavenly inspired courage he instantly went to work and had the plates re-cast.

That he was never unwise in his methods, he was the last man to claim. Fighting single-handed as he did against a public idol enthroned in the highest places, it would have been a miracle had he escaped criticism. But with the most imperturbable good nature, he skillfully parried the many hard blows he received.

After a quarter of a century's incessant toil, his health gave way and for months he was a sick man. Yet his busy hands never ceased their work, his last tract being an *Appeal to the Rev. Charles Spurgeon,* of which I give the closing characteristic sentence: "The project of converting the world by the Gospel of Christ, by the power of the Holy Ghost, and by man's free agency is not a humbug, but a natural, scriptural, glorious, project eclipsing every other. The idea of converting the world whilst rum, opium, and tobacco are its masters, *is* a humbug."

It was while correcting the proofs of this tract that the Master summoned him. So on January 25, 1875, the old hero joyfully passed from the toils of earth to the higher, broader services of the heavenly kingdom.

Blessed be the memory of George Trask, one of the earliest workers in this great field — THE ONE-MAN ANTI-TOBACCO SOCIETY! .

But the good work was not to end with George Trask's mortal life.

At Cincinnati in November of the same year, 1875, at the Second Annual Convention of the Woman's Christian Temperance Union, — that wonderful society, born of the Crusades and which has grown with such marvellous rapidity,—arrangements were made for giving thorough instruction concerning alcohol and tobacco to the members of the Juvenile Union.

At the Fourth Convention in Chicago, 1877, a strong resolution was taken to oppose the use of tobacco in every form.

At the Tenth Convention in Detroit, 1883, Mrs. M. B. Reese, of Ohio, was appointed superintendent of a department of "Effort to Overthrow the Tobacco Habit."

At the Twelfth Convention in Philadelphia, 1885, this department was changed to a "Department of Narcotics," of which Mrs. Havens, of Denver, Colorado, was made superintendent.

At the Thirteenth Convention in Minneapolis, 1886, Mrs. E. B. Ingalls, of St. Louis, was appointed national superintendent of this department, the different state superintendents securing superintendents in district or local Unions. There is thus a chain of workers from the National to the smallest Union in every state.

Under the influence of this department, antitobacco literature has been widely circulated, and instruction has been given in our schools, while the District of Columbia and thirty-five states have passed laws of greater or less stringency, forbidding the sale of tobacco to minors of various ages. It is hoped eventually to have the full period of minority secured against the evil.

There are several societies now enlisted in this important reform.

THE BRITISH ANTI-TOBACCO SOCIETY.

This society was founded in London, 1853, by Thomas Reynolds, who, like George Trask, was for some years a great smoker, and who, like him, when converted, freely devoted his time and substance to the cause. And he did this so to the neglect of his own personal interests that some friend proposed as his fitting epitaph, "Here lies a man who in his great regard for things spiritual well-nigh forgot things temporal."

The organ of the society is the "Anti-Tobacco Journal," now edited by Mr. Reynolds' daughter, who, at her father's death, bravely took up his work and is still faithfully carrying it on.

THE ENGLISH ANTI-TOBACCO SOCIETY AND ANTI-NARCOTIC LEAGUE.

In November, 1867, at a conference convened in Manchester, an organization was formed, designated as the Manchester and Salford Anti-Tobacco Society, a title subsequently enlarged to its present form. The very Rev. F. Close, D.D., Dean of Carlisle, was the first president. This society seems to have been *very much alive*, if I may use the expression, many eminent men having been connected with it as working officers. Alfred E. Eccles, Esq., of Chorley, with the late Peter Spence and his son, Frank Spence, have given liberally of their time and money to the cause. Mr. Eccles, who is now president, has made a free distribution of many millions of tracts and booklets, at an expense of hundreds of pounds. The organ of the society is "The Committee's Monthly Letter to Members and Friends." It is pleasant to report that a number of branches have been formed in different parts of the kingdom.

In "The Band of Hope Chronicle," issued monthly by *The United Kingdom Band of Hope Union*, are frequently published articles, and sometimes a series of articles, upon tobacco.

A local anti-tobacco society has been established at Reading, about an hour's drive from London. And this year an attempt is being made to establish in London a national anti-tobacco society, with Dr. Drysdale as its president.

SOCIETE CONTRE L'ABUS DU TABAC.

In Paris, in 1867, M. Decroix, with the assistance of Messieurs Bourrel and Blatin, formed an association against the abuse of tobacco. On inquiring of M. Decroix why it was not named the association against tobacco, he replied that the government, which has the monopoly of the tobacco revenues, would not authorize this, and that the temperance society was restricted in the same way, — *The Society against the Abuse of Alcoholics.*

After a time, the addition of new members greatly changed this organization, and having labored in vain to bring it back to its original character, M. Decroix, in 1877, founded the present society. In 1883, the first association was dissolved, and the commission of liquidation passed over to the new society three hundred and sixty francs to be awarded in prizes, while M. Blatin left a legacy to found an annual prize of fifty francs, bearing his name.

It was with this society that the International Congress on the subject of tobacco was held during the great Paris Exposition of 1889.

The members have shown much energy in publishing and distributing valuable anti-tobacco literature. M. Decroix, the founder and president, has written a number of excellent pamphlets, among which is one of special importance on "The use of Tobacco in the Army." In this connection I cannot forbear naming a French work of over five hundred pages, by Dr. H. A. Depierris, entitled "Physiologie Sociale Les Tabac." The treatment of the subject is candid and exhaustive, and the book is interesting as well as instructive from the beginning to the end.

THE INTERNATIONAL HEALTH AND TEMPERANCE ASSOCIATION.

This society was formed in 1879, by Dr. J. H. Kellogg, of the Medical and Surgical Sanitarium, Battle Creek, Michigan. It has an anti-tobacco pledge, to which there have been nearly twenty

thousand subscribers. Dr. Kellogg has written
a number of tracts concerning the tobacco habit,
of which several hundred thousands have been sold.

THE ANTI-TOBACCO ASSOCIATION OF ST. JOHN, NEW BRUNSWICK.

Several years later, on December 6, 1887, largely
through the influence of the W. C. T. U. workers,
Mr. R. A. H. Morrow, with several others, formed
this society. Among the good results has been the
publication of a book containing "Three Prize
Essays on Tobacco," the giving up the sale by
some of the traders, and the passage of a law prohibiting its sale in any form to persons under
eighteen.

Rev. A. S. Sims has labored for some years in
this cause in Canada, but I have been unable to
get particulars of his work. And there are others
enlisted more or less prominently in the tobacco
warfare, of whom my limits preclude mention.
They are all helping to secure the final victory.

AN ANTI-TOBACCO CLUB IN TURKEY.

A cheering token of progress comes through
Mrs. Montgomery, missionary of "The Woman's
Board" in Adana, Turkey, some extracts from
whose letter I may be pardoned for giving:

"On my return to the Cilician Plain in 1887, I
carried with me a copy of 'The Tobacco Problem'
which I afterwards put into the hands of Mr.
Hagop Yeranian, at that time the Armenian Pro-

testant preacher at Tarsus, knowing him to be greatly interested in such matters. He was so impressed by the book that he immediately set about organizing an anti-tobacco club in the city of Paul's birth. In the spring of 1889, he informed me that he had secured twenty members, who were quite enthusiastic over the pledges they had made. I remember that they were of three different nationalities, Armenian, Greek, and Turkish. Two years later this preacher left Tarsus, and is now working in the Smyrna field. I have no doubt that he will start another club in the country of Paul's early labors."

THE ANTI-NARCOTIC SOCIETY OF THE PACIFIC COAST.

Dr. C. Clifford Vanderbeck, who is at the head of a sanitarium in San Francisco, called "The Hygeia," has long been deeply impressed with the terrible evils of the opium habit, which he says "has saturated our society here through and through." After many efforts by lectures and in other ways to interest the public, on December 1, 1891, he founded "The Anti-Narcotic Society of the Pacific Coast." Dr. Vanderbeck writes: "Some of the poor victims who are brought before the police judges, beg to be sent to the county jail or the House of Correction, where they cannot get their accustomed narcotic. Hitherto, with all our charities, nothing has been done for one of the most flagrant vices on this coast. But we hope, in the near future, to have an institution for the treatment and cure of the victims of the opium habit."

Some one has expressed the doubt whether the introduction of hypodermic injections, with their frequent and fearful results, is not, on the whole, proving a curse to mankind. But may not the difficulty lie in their frequent inconsiderate prescription and their sometimes reckless application? This is a matter of such grave importance that I cannot forbear summoning witnesses from the medical faculty.

Dr. Vanderbeck, in a treatise on "Narcotic Inebriety," frankly admits, "We cannot get away from the fact that we are sometimes a little careless in our use of narcotics." He quotes Dr. Charles C. Cranmer, of Saratoga, N.Y.: "I am grieved to find that physicians possessing a supposed liberal education, and knowing fully the terrible effects of the continued use of opium and morphia, prescribe the same in the most reckless manner. I use the word reckless because I am bound to believe, from actual facts before me, that the above drugs are constantly prescribed for every simple ache or pain coming under their professional care."

Dr. Vanderbeck continues : "Dr. Cranmer affirms that, within a radius of half a mile of his office, he knows of a dozen friends with the opium habit, and in the majority of them it came about from the physician's prescribing an opiate for a simple pain. He asks the profession to raise their voice against this terrible crime. On the other side of the water, we find the note of warning has been sounded as well. Dr. Minnet, of Edinburgh, reports cases of opium eating, all starting from physicians' prescriptions. . . . In using opium, the profession should always bear in mind that we might be the agent of setting the spark to the fire that may only be extinguished with life. . . . In cases of insomnia and of neuralgia we have a number of new and safe remedies that ought to lessen materially the prescribing of the direct narcotics."

In view of these facts, is it not in order to express the very earnest desire that physicians be most scrupulously considerate and cautious in making such prescriptions?

It has been suggested that a law should be enacted forbidding the sale of the instrument and the drug to any outside the medical profession, and that physicians should never commit them into the hands of patients or of any irresponsible person, but restrict their use to themselves or to an instructed nurse. Some means of limiting and controlling this practice is of vital importance.

The Right Rev. Bishop of Little Rock has recently called the attention of the Catholic Total Abstinence Union to this subject. He says : "What priest in charge of souls does not know that it is the well-nigh universal practice among physicians

of the day to administer intoxicants, morphine,
opium, etc., to their dying patients to alleviate
their pains and then send them intoxicated (or
stupefied) before their Judge, and even without
the opportunity of arranging their will or family
affairs."

MRS. HUNT'S EDUCATIONAL WORK.

There is no more grievous bondage than that in
which the narcotic despot holds his victims, and
his dominion extends to the uttermost parts of the
earth. There was a time when the warfare against
him seemed utterly hopeless; but God be thanked
that the brave hearts and unwearied hands which
have undertaken this battle have not fought in
vain. We have seen one organized army after
another rising against him, and, though the conflict has been desperate, some trophies have been
won.

Of the wonderful work accomplished by Mary
H. Hunt, it would take pages to speak adequately.
Interested in the subject of temperance as a mother,
as early as 1872, she commenced a thorough investigation which, on the formation of the W. C. T. U.,
led to her accepting the superintendency of the
Department of Scientific Temperance Instruction,
both national and international. The thrilling
story of her labors, her battles, and her victories
is too long to be told here, but can be found in
the "Brief History of the First Decade of Scien-

tific Temperance Instruction in Schools and Colleges." *

I have only room to say that, as the result of her indomitable efforts with our legislators, in thirty-six of our states, all the territories, our military and naval academies, and the Indian and colored schools under federal government, education as to the evil effects of alcoholic drinks and other narcotics is now required; thus bringing more than twelve million children under temperance education laws. And in twenty different countries interest has been awakened in the work of this education of the young. Who can predict the result when the children of every land are thoroughly instructed in the evils and the perils of the drinking and narcotic habit, and when anti-alcoholic and anti-narcotic societies girdle the whole earth?

THE ANTI-VENENEAN SOCIETY.

Although this society, in its birth, preceded by many years that of George Trask, yet as it related more prominently to the drinking than to the tobacco habit, and was moreover limited to Amherst College, the mention of it comes later. It was formed in 1830, by President Hitchcock, a pronounced temperance man, for the purpose of pledging its members during their college course against

---

* Obtained by addressing Mrs. Mary H. Hunt, Hyde Park, Mass.

the use of alcoholic drinks and of tobacco, in case they were willing to forswear that also.

It was the president's custom to invite the freshmen, on entering college, to his house, when, after a talk on the subject, he would unfold his roll and give them an opportunity to add their signatures. After a long period the society was given up to the entire control of the students, and a few years since "it died of inanition."

"At the present time," writes Professor Hitchcock, "more than twenty per cent. of our students enter college with the tobacco habit. And the only power I have against it is that men in athletic training cannot use it."

But the Anti-Venenean, otherwise Anti-Poisoning Society, deserves warm mention as being one of the earliest protests against nicotine, and also for what it accomplished through its honored founder.

I cannot resist the temptation to quote here a few passages from President Hitchcock's "*History of a Zoological Convention held in Central Africa in 1847 :*"

"After protracted discussions, as the sessions of the convention were drawing to a close, a committee appointed early in the deliberations came forward and through their chairman, the Asiatic Leopard, reported the following resolutions." Of these resolutions I can give only one :

"6. *Resolved*, that we now pledge ourselves, by touching noses, that we will entirely abstain from all beverages but water; that we nauseate the poisonous weed called tobacco; that we will discountenance their use by other animals, and that we will do all in our power to increase their use among men as the surest means of their ruin, and the only hope of preventing them from gaining the entire control of the whole animal kingdom."

REPORT FROM WEST POINT.

The history of tobacco, as connected with our National Military Academy, is of special interest. From the account kindly sent me September 16, 1892, by Col. Charles W. Larned, a professor in the Academy, the following outline is given:—

In the early days of West Point the use of tobacco was prohibited, but as, notwithstanding this, smoking was prevalent, the superintendent resolved to try the permissive course. In 1857, therefore, tobacco was given free entrance and was included among the stores issued by the commissary. The only restriction laid upon the cadets was the forbidding of smoking outside the limits of their rooms and during "call to quarters" or study hours. This regulation, however, had little influence.

"In my own day," writes Col. Larned, "which was from 1866 to 1879, the great majority were smokers, a number of my class smoking from *reveille* to *tattoo*, and not a few lighting their pipes after taps. At our social meetings during release quarters, the air was dense with smoke to a degree I have never seen equalled, not even in a smoking car. . . . I believe this habit to have been distinctly injurious to very many, and of three whose post-graduate careers were wrecked by personal habits, all smoked to inordinate excess.

"In 1881, the authorities prohibited smoking absolutely. In the discussions preceding the recommendation of this course by the Academic Board to the Secretary of War, then Lincoln, it was urged that the effect of toleration is to encourage the habit; that the effects of smoking were in most cases distinctly detrimental to study, and in many instances to health, and that many who came to the Academy without having acquired the habit were induced to form it. It was argued also that, unlike civil institutions, the Government assumes in the disciplinary code of the Military Academy direct charge of, and responsibility for, the physical and moral welfare of its students, and that it is bound in consequence not to sanction or tolerate any practice which is in any degree subversive of either.

"It has been urged by some that the effect of prohibition is to induce surreptitious violation of regulations. This objection is valid against every prohibitory regulation whatever, and applies with equal force to hazing.

"A close questioning of recent graduates and of cadets themselves substantiates the assumption that at present about half of the cadets smoke more or less, but that very few smoke to excess. My personal opinion is that on the whole the effect of prohibition is decidedly beneficial, and that, under the wise system of cumulative punishment adopted by the present superintendent, the habit is on the decline. An examination of the roster of officers now stationed at the Academy, from the superintendent, Col. John M. Wilson, who is a total abstainer as regards both liquor and tobacco, down to the junior lieutenant, shows that, out of a total of sixty-one, some twenty-six or seven either do not use tobacco, or to so slight a degree as to place them virtually on the list of abstainers. Twenty-two do not use tobacco in any form, and the majority of these graduated after the introduction of prohibition. It may be observed in this connection that the steadiness, sobriety, and studiousness of the Corps of Cadets has steadily increased of late years in a very marked degree. To what extent diminished smoking has contributed to this condition must be left to conjecture. It is fair, however, to cite these various facts as strongly favoring influences."

Equally encouraging is a letter from Capt. R. S. Pythian, superintendent United States Naval Academy, Annapolis, Md. :

"SEPT. 21st, 1892.

"I beg to state that Naval Cadets are forbidden to use or to have in their possession tobacco in any form. The regulation against the use of tobacco is enforced as rigidly as possible, and its violation is severely punished. While it must be admitted that the practice cannot be altogether broken up, even in an institution where the students are under such close observation, still the strict enforcement of the regulation produces good results by restricting the evil so far as it is possible to do so."

In this connection I quote from a letter dated September 28, 1892, from Dr. Albert L. Gihon, recently in charge of the Naval Hospital at Brooklyn :

"The views that I held, and which you did me the honor to quote in 'The Tobacco Problem,' as to the prejudicial influence of tobacco upon the growth and development of adolescents, the result of five years of close observations of cadets at the United States Naval Academy at Annapolis, Maryland, during the period of my duty in charge of the Medical Department of that institution (1875–1880), I still hold in undiminished degree.

"I am more than ever convinced that the use of tobacco by adolescents should be vigorously interdicted in every educational or other establishment in which the young are under disciplinary control, and I further believe that the sale of cigarettes, or other forms of tobacco, to minors, should be prohibited by legislation."

PREFATORY.

I HAVE carefully examined the work on Tobacco, as prepared by Mrs. Lawrence, and find in it a thorough and kindly consideration of the subject in all its relations, without prejudice, and with every desirable concession.

The book cannot fail to impress its truth upon the public mind. Its mission is in the family, the shop, the college, the pulpit, — in short, in all places of education and of training for business, and in all classes of the community.

WILLARD PARKER, M. D.

NEW YORK, May, 1882.

CONTENTS.

MORAL AND SPIRITUAL VIEW.

TOBACCO INDICTED AND TRIED.

TOBACCO.

INTRODUCTION.

Whatever benefits may be legitimately claimed for tobacco, very few will deny that the prevailing habit of using it is expensive, unwholesome, and uncleanly, if not actually demoralizing and perilous. Why, then, must it be touched so gingerly? Why must we approach it with deprecating bows and apologies, as if, after all, it was not much of an offence?

Alas! it is because this ugly brown idol is set up in high places; because it has more worshippers than any heathen god; because it is enshrined in many a heart as the dearest thing on earth. If, now and then, some fearless hand attacks it, not a few, even among those who are not its votaries, in their concern lest some good man may chance to get hit, stand ready to warn off the assailant. One is thus often reminded of the old slavery days, when many who were not practical partakers condoned the offence of such as were.

Are not those who use this narcotic in its various forms as truly slaves as were our Southern negroes? Is not its bondage as oppressive as was theirs? Are not its fetters as tightly riveted?

This tobacco-habit extends to every nation on the globe, and permeates every rank in society. The gray-haired patriarch is not too old nor the boy of twelve too young to be its willing subject. The filthiest slum and the politest society are alike pervaded by it.

It stalks defiantly through the streets, fouling the very air of heaven. It boldly sits in our legislative halls, both state and national. In spite of special arrangements to imprison it, there is no such thing as shutting it away from the tell-tale air and the whispering breeze.

Its insidious spell has so fallen on the community that multitudes seem utterly insensible to its character and its consequences. Indeed, so potent is this spell that there is now and then a woman who, instead of being disturbed by seeing her father or brother, husband or lover, among the victims, will complacently smile upon his offence and gayly decorate the symbols of his slavery.

Shall I be pronounced a fanatic, a monomaniac, for writing thus? Yea, verily. But though I am struck, I will still claim a hearing.

If you deem it audacious for a woman to attack so terrible a giant, let me plead in self-defence that, deeply moved on the subject, I was impelled to go forth, and, under cover, to fire a few shots. Through the encouragement and solicitations of many, I have been led to extend my investigations and to venture on a bolder assault. Yet in this public arraignment of tobacco, a power so high in position, so well-nigh supreme in influence, I have been painfully aware of my difficult and delicate task, and, but for the abundance of testimony against the despot, should never have gathered courage to prosecute it.

Great pains have been taken to authenticate the statements contained in these papers. And I would express my sense of obligation, not only to those able writers on the subject from whom I have gathered much of my material, but also to the various medical authorities — strangers as well as friends — to whose courtesy in response to inquiries I have been indebted in the performance of my work.

If I have written strongly, it is because I have felt deeply. But however strong the language used, — and it will be noted that the sharpest, most uncompromising passages are quotations from those much better informed on this subject than myself, — it has been far from my thought to represent the tobacco-vice as the only or the greatest vice in the world, or tobacco-votaries as sinners above all the men that dwell in Galilee. And it has been frankly, though sorrowfully, conceded that among these votaries are men of unquestioned moral and spiritual excellence.

FINANCIAL VIEW.

QUANTITY AND COST.

SOME years since, the annual production of tobacco throughout the world was estimated at four billions of pounds. This mass, if transformed into roll-tobacco two inches in diameter, would coil around the world sixty times; or, if made up into tablets, as sailors use it, would form a pile as high as an Egyptian pyramid. Allowing the cost of the unmanufactured material to be ten cents a pound, the yearly expense of this poisonous growth amounts to four hundred millions of dollars. Put into marketable shape, the annual cost reaches one thousand millions of dollars. This sum, according to careful computation, would construct two railroads round the earth, at twenty thousand dollars a mile. It would build a hundred thousand churches, each costing ten thousand dollars, or half a million of school-houses, each costing two thousand; or it would employ a million of preachers and a million teachers, at a salary of five hundred dollars.

4

What more effective, pathetic appeal to the head and the heart can be made than by these figures? Two millions of tons of tobacco annually consumed by smokers and snuffers and chewers; while from every part of the habitable globe are hands stretched out imploringly for the bread of life, which must be denied for lack of means to send it!

In Great Britain alone there are not far from three hundred thousand tobacco-shops. England prohibits the culture of the weed, that she may secure larger imports, her annual receipts amounting to forty million dollars, a greater revenue than she gets from all the gold mines of Australia.

In Austria, the duties from this source reach the same figures; while in France, where tobacco is a monopoly, they come up to sixty millions. In most countries official statements show that it costs more than bread.

In the United States, we find, from the Internal Revenue Report, that above ninety-five million pounds of manufactured tobacco and one billion three hundred million cigars are used in one year, at an expense of two hundred and fifty millions of dollars, while the taxes have amounted to forty millions.

In the city of New York above seventy-five millions of cigars are annually consumed, and at a cost of more than nine millions of dollars — enough cigars to build a wall from the Empire City to Albany.

An English firm has compiled a table showing that in forty years the amount of tobacco manufactured has been more than doubled.

J. J. H. Gregory, of Marblehead, Mass., ascertained as the result of careful inquiry that there were sold in that place about eight hundred thousand cigars, fourteen thousand pounds of tobacco for chewing or smoking in pipes, and about four hundred pounds of snuff; and all that in a town of only six thousand inhabitants (in 1850)!

In Syracuse, the leading city of Central New York, twenty-seven millions of cigars were manufactured during the year 1881.

How often will a man go through life without owning a house, when the money he expends on this narcotic, if put on interest, would be ample for the purchase of one! How many a family is cramped for the necessaries of life because the husband and father will not give up his cigar! And how many a man, reduced to beggary, holds on to his pipe!

Wives there are not a few who are obliged to sacrifice their artistic tastes to this juggernaut. Books, music, pictures, excursions with the children to the seaside or the mountains, a thousand and one little refinements and brighteners of the dull routine of life — all are swallowed up by his rapacious maw. No matter what self-denials the patient wife and mother may endure, provided the husband is not robbed of his cigar.

Suppose a young mechanic, whose earnings are

very small, expends five cents a day for tobacco. Instead of this let him invest the money at compound interest. The amount in ten years will be $240.54; in twenty years, $671.30; in thirty years, $1,442.77.

"Twenty years ago," remarked a gentleman, "on finding how much money I was wasting upon tobacco, I stopped using it, yearly depositing the amount thus saved. When it had accumulated to three thousand dollars I built with it a house, which I call my smoke-house."

Said an inveterate smoker: "Twenty thousand dollars falls short of what I have spent for tobacco."

But we have not yet done with figures. In a single Western town $3,098 were expended for tobacco, and for the support of churches and schools only $2,712.

A Methodist pastor states that, while his whole society expended in a year only $841 for the support of the gospel and other church and mission work, sixty-seven of his church members during the same time spent $845 for tobacco.

At a Methodist Episcopal Conference held in Massachusetts, Bishop Harris expressed the opinion that "the Methodist Church spends more for chewing and smoking than it gives toward converting the world."

It has been estimated that the smokers and chewers among the preachers and members of the Cincinnati Conference alone expend annually over \$180,000 for tobacco, while there are many instances where from five to ten members of a circuit spend more for this weed than their whole circuit gives for all the church charities combined.

It was estimated from the internal revenue tax paid in the fourth district of Michigan, one of six internal revenue districts, that the tobacco used in that district must have cost the consumers \$1,500,000 in one year, — about ten times the cost of supporting the University of Michigan and the students therein for the same time.

From the *Independent* we learn that a single New Haven firm sells one hundred and twenty thousand cigarettes a month to Yale students, or for the ten months of the year, when they are in town, one million two hundred thousand, at an average expense of about eight thousand dollars a year.

There are many religious (?) communities which spend an aggregate of from five hundred to one thousand dollars every year for this drug that cannot afford the expense of a minister.

Three hundred dollars a year for tobacco, and three dollars for Bible, tract, and mission purposes. Eighty dollars for tobacco, and twenty-five cents for home missions. Yet these are but samples of almost numberless cases.

In a Southern Presbyterian paper a correspondent states that "in a town of five thousand inhabitants, in North Carolina, seventy-five thousand dollars' worth of snuff is sold every year." He also affirms that in any Southern State where the negroes compose half the population, "the snuff which is sold amounts annually to more than the cost of all the farming implements of every kind, including cotton-gins, cotton-presses, steam engines for farm use, horse-powers, and all sorts of mechanical tools." In conclusion, he says: "I stand prepared with Chalmers' challenge, 'Give me your pinches of snuff' and I will support the church.' Give me your tobacco, cigars, and snuff, and I will support the whole Southern church, and do it handsomely."

It is stated by Rev. Mr. Evans, formerly president of Hedding College, Abington, Ill., that the people of that city and vicinity have, in the course of twenty-four years, paid eighty thousand dollars to Abington and Hedding Colleges, while in the city itself twenty thousand dollars are expended every year for tobacco. "This great Christian nation," he affirms, "pays annually forty millions for its religion, and two hundred millions for its tobacco;" adding, "we make an estimate within the limits of the facts, when we say that this community, city, and country pay as much for tobacco as they do for their religion and education combined."

Said the late President Wayland: "The American Board, an institution of world-wide benevolence, and which collects its funds from all the Northern States, does not receive annually as much as is expended for cigars in the single city of New

York ! " What a record to appear on the heavenly ledger !

COST FROM FIRES.

The destruction of property from fires occasioned by throwing away the ends of cigars, or matches used in lighting them, comes properly under the financial head.

It is stated by Dr. Ritchie that in London fifty-three fires occurred in one year as the result of smoking. He adds: " I have more than once seen a carpenter under a London station light his pipe and cast the half-burnt match among the shavings."

From the throwing down of a cigar, or a match used in lighting it, the Bateman Hotel in Pittsburg, Penn., took fire and was destroyed. The son of the proprietor was fatally burned, while the wife and four daughters perished in the flames.

What shall we say to the setting on fire of a forest near Lowell, Mass., by ministerial cigars? to the burning of several buildings in Fall River from juvenile cigars and matches? to the consuming of a church in Chicago from a carpenter's pipe? and to the destruction of three millions' worth of property in one of our cities from a half-smoked cigar which a young man threw down?

So infatuated are the devotees of the weed that, in spite of the strictest regulations, workmen sometimes persist in smoking even amid the most dangerous surroundings.

In a single day pipes and matches were found

in the pockets of fifty-eight workmen as they were just entering the powder works at Hounslow.

The blowing up of a powder-magazine in Mexico, and many houses near by, with the destruction of seventy lives, was caused by the dropping of a lighted cigar.

After the Blantyre explosion in 1879, resulting in the death of twenty-eight persons, the inspector of mines found matches and partly smoked pipes lying near the bodies.

It was from a match thrown down by a smoking plumber that the Harpers' printing establishment took fire, consuming five blocks, at a loss of about a million of dollars, and throwing nearly two thousand people out of work.

By a spark dropped from a pipe a dreadful fire was kindled in Williamsburg, destroying three vessels and six buildings, with the lives of three persons.

Says an insurance agent : "One third or more of all the fires in my circuit have originated from matches and pipes. Fires in England and America are being kindled with alarming frequency by smokers casting about their firebrands or half-burnt matches."

From the reports of various journals as to the burning of the mail-car on the New York Central Railroad, there seems scarcely a doubt that it was owing to the smoking habit. Does not common prudence require the absolute interdiction of cigars by all employed in the postal department during the hours when they are engaged in this service?

An account lies before me of an appalling fire in a crowded circus in Russia, where the side exits were nailed up and the doors of the main entrance, which opened inward, were kept closed by the pressure of the frantic throng. Parents threw their children into the ring, and then, as the flames increased, leaped after them, the scorched and maddened horses also plunging into the area, and, in their frenzy, trampling people to death. And the cause of this terrific fire, in which about three hundred perished, is stated to have been a cigarette thrown carelessly among the straw.

LAWS LIMITING USE.

We find from " Chambers' Encyclopædia " that in Great Britain sailors are generally limited to chewing, smoking at sea being prohibited, or greatly restricted from danger of fire.

To a certain extent, the laws in some parts of our own country have been cognizant of this danger. In 1818 the following Acts were passed in the metropolis of New England.

" Every person who shall smoke, or have in his or her possession any lighted pipe or cigar in any street, lane, or passage-way, or on any wharf, in said city, shall forfeit and pay, for each and every offence, the sum of two dollars."

" And, further, if any person shall have in his or her possession, in any ropewalk, or barn, or stable, any fire, lighted pipe or cigar, the person so offending shall forfeit and pay, for each offence, a sum not exceeding one hundred dollars, nor less than twenty dollars."

The first of these Acts was never enforced, and having remained on the statute-book a dead letter for more than sixty years, in 1880 it was repealed.

The second, which is a law necessary to safety, is still in force in Boston, and *ought* to be in every city, town, and hamlet throughout the land, simply as contemplating protection against fire.

CULTURE.

Much might be said under the financial head as to the culture of this weed, but space allows only a few words.

"The tobacco plant," writes one, "is a great exhauster. Whether raised north or south, on the banks of the Danube or the Connecticut, it is all the same. It is a huge glutton, which, consuming all about it, like Homer's glutton of old, cries: ' *More! Give me more!* '"

Another: "A gum issues from green tobacco that covers everything it comes in contact with. We met recently a troop of men, fresh from the tobacco-field, who might pass for Hottentots. They looked as if they always burrowed in the ground, and in hands and face, as well as dress, were the color of woodchucks."

Dr. Humphrey: "What shall we say to raising tobacco — a narcotic plant which no brute will eat, which affords no nutriment, which every stomach loathes till cruelly drugged into submission, which stupefies the brain, shatters the nerves, destroys the coats of the stomach, creates an insatiable thirst for stimulants, and prepares the system for fatal diseases?"

Prof. Brewer: "The sole advantage is that an individual may grow rich from raising it. But what one man gains is obtained at the cost of his son and his son's son."

Jefferson: "It is a culture productive of infinite wretchedness."

Gen. John H. Cooke, of Virginia: "Tobacco exhausts the land beyond all other crops. As proof of this, every homestead, from the Atlantic border to the head of tide water, is a mournful monument. It has been the besom of destruction which has swept over this once fertile region."

Says a traveller: "The old tobacco-lands of Maryland and Virginia are an eyesore, odious 'barrens,' looking as though blasted by some genius of evil."

There are those who claim that the land can be kept in good condition by the free use of fertilizers. But the experience of many years furnishes evidence that this crop ultimately exhausts the soil, and that, in consequence, its culture is deprecated by the better class of agriculturists.

Tobacco-raising consumes the greater part of the year. The seed is planted about the middle of April, and in two or three months the shoots are transplanted or *set*, which process occupies several weeks. Besides the older members of the family, the little boys and girls work in the fields, thus becoming familiar with the weed from their earliest childhood.

In September the plants are cut, and, after lying some hours in the sun, are hung under cover to be cured. When the winter thaw occurs, they are taken to a room where the leaves are stripped from the stalk and packed in bundles, and then handled one by one, to be arranged in grades, or *sorted*, not being carried to market, however, until April. Thus, throughout the year, tobacco is the great subject of conversation, and, as it is an uncertain crop, the mind is kept in an absorbed, anxious condition till it is delivered, when the processes are again started. Meantime, other crops are mostly neglected.

This culture is greatly on the increase. Among other regions, the beautiful Onondaga valley in New York State is becoming more and more devoted to it. The reports from this valley as to its unfavorable effect upon the health are clear and decisive. Nor is this strange when we learn that the stripping rooms are kept at a high temperature and without ventilation. Thus the strippers who work here for several months every year are breathing the noxious vapor from morning till night. Physicians assert that in this way many cases of tobacco-poisoning occur. One instance is given of an infant whose death ensued in consequence, the mother admitting that she had taken the cradle into the room so that while at work she might care for her child.

That the physical effects are due solely to the poisoned atmosphere created is evident from the fact that many who raise tobacco do not use it, some even considering this to be wrong. The great argument is : — " If I don't raise it, somebody else will, and I might as well make the money as anybody else." What must be the influence of such reasoning upon the conscience! It is not surprising that ministers should consider the effect on the moral and spiritual health to be no less unfavorable than on the physical. It was the remark of one not a professing Christian, —"A revival need never be expected where everybody is raising tobacco." There are clergymen that have had experience in this line who feel that the time a minister spends in a tobacco-region is virtually wasted.

A pastor who is laboring in the Onondaga valley says: "Although I came into the place without knowledge on this subject, and entirely unprejudiced, yet my observation has satisfied me that tobacco-raising injures the farms, impairs the health, dulls the intellect, and blunts the moral and religious sensibilities."

And what shall be said of cultivating this exhauster of the soil, this foulest, most destructive of poisons in the beautiful Connecticut valley, the land of the Pilgrims? A cruel matricide, which Christian hands, alas! join in perpetrating.

On this subject, a gentleman of large experience writes: "The raising of tobacco has *cursed* our fair valley. Hatfield, for instance, some twenty years ago the richest town in the State according to its population, early entered into the craze for gain through tobacco-raising. As a result nearly everyone has failed financially. But far worse, — our farmers, who once declared, 'I would cut off my right hand rather than engage in such business,' seeing their neighbors — at the outset — growing rich, gradually choked conscience and became absorbed in the traffic. This has demoralized the people and paralyzed the church. The spiritual death resting upon our valley may to a great extent be traced to this cause."

Before me is a letter from Bishop Huntington of Central New York, dated June, 1884, and bearing on the same point: " While my old homestead in Hadley, Mass., lies on the Connecticut River, where the alluvial soil is particularly favorable for profitable tobacco crops, I have never allowed a plant of it to be raised on the farm. There is an extraordinary fact connected with the culture there, which is attested by intelligent residents of the town. Since 1855 enormous harvests of tobacco have been raised and carried off every year, — hundreds of thousands of pounds. Yet, by the working of some mysterious law, not one dollar can be found to show for it in all the property investments or scenery of the entire population."

When there was some querying whether so singular an assertion would be accepted, he replied: "My statement was, I believe, literally and indisputably true, that the farmers of Old Hadley have, for a quarter of a century, been planting, raising, and gathering tobacco as the principal crop of the soil; yet that there is in the whole town not one visible sign of improvement, enrichment, thrift, or prosperity to show for it. In all these respects the town, from end to end and side to side, has lost rather than gained. It is not strange that you are perplexed by a fact so paradoxical. So am I. The mystery has sometimes struck me as containing a silent judgment of God on the abuse of his ground."

Alluding to some natural explanations that might be suggested, he adds : "These only partially account for a blight so persistent and universal."

From the Boston *Transcript* we learn that enough Connecticut tobacco has been produced in a single year to make nine hundred millions of cigars !

Most eloquently writes Prof. Bascom : " Take the land, the sunshine, the rain which God gives you, and set them all at work to grow tobacco; throw this, as your product, into the world's market; buy with it bread, clothing, and shelter, books for yourselves, instruction for your children, consideration in the community, and perchance the gospel of grace ; pay ever and everywhere, for the good you get, tobacco, only tobacco — tobacco, that nourishes no man, clothes no man, instructs no man, purifies no man, blesses no man ; tobacco, that begets inordinate and loathsome appetite and disease and degradation, that impoverishes and debases thousands and adds incalculably to the burden of evil the world bears; but call not this exchange honest trade, or this gnawing at the root of social well-being getting an honest livelihood. Think of God's justice, the honesty he requires, and cover not your sin with a lie. Turn not His earth and air, given to minister to the sustenance and joy of man, into a narcotic, deadening life and poisoning its current, and then traffic with this for your own good."

OTHER TOBACCO COSTS.

Still another point deserves consideration. Besides the hours that many spend on tobacco, from which, to say the least, they get no benefit, is the fact that the narcotic, by diminishing their force, tends to lessen the value of their remaining time.

Moreover, it is estimated by many medical men that the victims of this weed, on an average, cut short their life about one quarter. Thus, from an average life of forty-five to fifty, about ten or twelve are sacrificed to this evil-doer.

Nor is this all. In order to make a fair estimate of what this drug costs the country, we ought to visit our almshouses and houses of correction, our reform schools, insane asylums, jails, and penitentiaries, to which poverty, disease, and crime, resulting from the tobacco-fiend, with intemperance following in its wake, bring hundreds and thousands. For the support of all these we are taxed, and that doubly, since we are also assessed to supply many of them with the very poison that brought them there.

In the old snuff-taking days a senatorial snuff-box was kept on the stand of the Vice-President for the use of our legislators! The annual report of the expense of our National Senate still contains the item of snuff, which has always been furnished at the expense of government, and which may, not improperly, be reckoned among tobacco-costs.

YORKTOWN BILL.

But although in respect to this form of tobacco, there may be some diminution, we have small cause for self-gratulation. Examine the bill for "rum and cigars" which were furnished to the Centennial Commission on their trip to Yorktown, by order of the congressional committee. In the list of items we find set down, among the large variety of liquors : —

3200 Reina Cigars	$400.00
3600 Concha Cigars	594.00
2000 Londres Cigars	340.00
1500 Domestic Cigars	120.00
17 pounds Gravely Tobacco	11.20
1 gross Fine Cut	9.00
1000 Lone Fisherman Cigarettes	6.00
1000 Richmond Gem Cigarettes	6.50

The cost of this convivial provision was nearly seven thousand dollars, and all at the expense of the people.

What a picture! The old pagan bacchanals over again in this grand Republic in the year of our Lord 1881!

There are Congressmen who urge in defence of this course that if we entertain visitors from abroad we must entertain them according to their own customs. Must we, then, provide dog-meat for our Chinese guests, and share it with them? Let us not plead that national hospitality required this at our hands — not, certainly, till we have forgotten the disgraceful arrangements in connection with the funeral *cortége* of our lamented Garfield.

TOBACCO CENSUS.

The United States census of the tobacco crop for 1880 is truly a disheartening document. With the honorable exceptions of Colorado and Wyoming, Montana and Utah, all the States and Territories are implicated in this business. The number of acres devoted to the weed throughout the country was 638,841. The number of pounds raised was nearly 500,000,000, — bringing a vast revenue of gold and silver to the government coffers, and an equally vast revenue of penury, wretchedness, and shame to countless homes and hearts.

During the year 1882 more than three thousand millions of cigars and six hundred millions of cigarettes were manufactured in our country, showing an advance in both together, over the preceding year, of three hundred millions.

In the city of New York twenty thousand per-

sons are engaged in the cigar manufacture, a number of them being American women.   "The hands
in a single factory consume three million cigars a
year, saving the tobacco out of their allotment and
rolling and filling the cigars for themselves."

The tobacco manufacturers urge a reduction of
the tobacco tax, to promote their own moneyed interests, and for the same reason oppose its aboli-
tion ; while members of Congress *advocate* its abo-
lition in order to cheapen the article.   In strange
contrast with these attempts we find that King
James I. of England raised the tobacco tax from
twopence a pound to six shillings and tenpence.
To do this, as he did, without the consent of Parliament, was an unwarranted act ; yet the legislation was in the right direction, while ours, should
these unwise attempts succeed, would be in the
wrong.   Until the happy day arrives when this manufacture shall be prohibited by our national government, may we be saved from any disastrous
congressional acts that shall make the poison still
freer to the community !

NICOTINE POISONING; EXPERIMENTS; FACTS.

IT is upon the effects of the tobacco-habit on body and mind that this whole question hinges. And these effects must be determined by the opinions of medical and scientific men, founded on experience and observation, with such facts as corroborate them. It has therefore been deemed important to treat this point with great fulness, and to summon many witnesses as to the various diseases, bodily and mental, charged to the account of the weed.

A chemical examination of a tobacco-leaf shows its surface dotted with minute glands, which contain an oil found in no other plant, the proportion of this oil being seven per cent of the whole weight of the leaf. This oil is nicotine. It is this nicotine — one of the subtlest of poisons — that determines the strength of tobacco. Physicians who have studied its effects thus sum them up:

"Nicotine primarily lowers the circulation,

23

quickens the respiration, and excites the muscular system; but its ultimate effect is general exhaustion. As administered in even the minutest doses, the results are alarming, and in a larger quantity will occasion a man's death in from two to five minutes."

W. A. Axon asserts in the "Popular Science Monthly" that "the nicotine in one cigar, if extracted and administered in a pure state, would suffice to kill two men."

The Indians used to poison their arrows by dipping them into nicotine, convulsions and often death being the results of these arrow wounds.

In a paper upon Tobacco, read before a Sanitary Convention in Michigan in 1883, Lemuel Clute, Esq., a lawyer, quotes freely from a work on poisons, by Dr. Taylor, in which many diseases are attributed to the use of the weed. He says: "I have cited thus fully from Taylor on Poisons, because he is a recognized authority in courts, and no one can charge him with being a temperance fanatic. The principles he has gathered and discussed in his book are constantly referred to, and are largely the guide of our judges in passing upon the questions of the liberty, life, and death of our citizens."

Brodie, Queen Victoria's physician, made several experiments with nicotine, applying it to the tongues of a mouse, a squirrel, and a dog, death being produced in every instance. A frog placed in a receiver containing a drop of nicotine in a little water will die in a few hours. Franklin found that if the oil floating on the surface of water, when a stream of tobacco-smoke has passed through it, is applied to the tongue of a cat, it shortly causes death. Put on a cat's tongue one drop of nicotine, and in spite of its " seven lives," it *instantly* writhes in convulsions, and dies.

Set an open bottle containing a small quantity of this oil under an inverted jar. Place a mouse or a rat under the jar, taking care that the fresh air is not excluded. Death presently follows, simply from the animal's breathing the poisoned atmosphere. And this same tobacco-laden atmosphere is that which we find everywhere, and from which there is no escape.

Put a tobacco victim into a hot bath ; let him remain there till a free perspiration takes place ; then drop a fly into the water, and instant death ensues.

Hold white paper over tobacco-smoke, and when the cigar is consumed, scrape the condensed smoke from the paper and put a very small amount on the tongue of a cat; in a few minutes it will die of paralysis.

Pack a tobacco votary in a wet sheet, and when he is taken out the whole room is filled with the odor. No wonder that wolves, buzzards, and cannibals retreat in disgust from the flesh of such a man !

Among the animals denominated irrational it is asserted that none can use the weed except the loathsome tobacco-worm and the rock-goat of

Africa. Of the latter, the smell is so offensive that every other animal instinctively shuns it.

At Dartmouth Park, England, an old wooden pipe was given to a three-year-old to blow soap-bubbles with, the pipe being first carefully washed out. The boy was taken ill, and died in three days, his death, according to medical evidence, being caused by the nicotine which he had sucked in while blowing bubbles.

The daughter of a tobacco merchant, from simply sleeping in a chamber where a large quantity of the weed had been rasped, died soon after in frightful convulsions.

A child picked up a quid that had been thrown on the floor, and, taking it for a raisin, put it into her mouth, dying of the poison the same day.

Bocarme, of Belgium, was murdered in two minutes and a half by a little nicotine. A very moderate quantity introduced into the system, or even applying the moistened leaves over the stomach, has suddenly extinguished life. Indeed, so thoroughly does tobacco poison the blood that, according to the testimony of a physician to a dispensary in St. Giles, " leeches are instantly killed by the blood of smokers; so suddenly that they drop off dead immediately when they are applied."

In this view, we cannot wonder that it is pronounced perilous for a delicate person to sleep in the chamber with a habitual smoker.

Medical journals report the poisoning of babes from sharing the bed of a tobacco father, and even from being in the room where he smoked; and infant deaths have occurred from no other cause. Says Dr. Trall: "Many an infant has been killed outright in its cradle by the tobacco-smoke with which a thoughtless father filled an unventilated room."

Not a few physicians regard much of the invalidism, and also the positive ill-health of women, as due to the poisoned atmosphere created around them by the smoking members of their household.

A gentleman in a Saratoga hotel said to a doctor: "See that portly man yonder smoking like a volcano; he stands the racket; smoking don't kill him." "No, but he is killing his wife. See her by his side, pale, shrivelled, tremulous, sinking into the grave. So far as health is concerned, she might about as well have wedded a cask of tobacco."

A French journal reports the case of a farmer who, with two companions, smoked one evening in a chamber where a young man was asleep. When, at midnight, the visitors withdrew, the farmer found the youth insensible. A doctor was summoned, but all efforts for his restoration were fruitless. At the *post mortem* it was pronounced that he had died of congestion of the brain, caused by the respiration of tobacco-smoke during sleep.

Tobacco commences its dreadful work in the factories, the operatives inhaling its dust and absorbing its poison, so that, according to the doctors, "it takes only four years to kill off the worker." Dr. Kostral, physician to the royal tobacco factory in Moravia, reports that, of a hundred boys entering the works, seventy-two fell sick during the first six months, while deaths frequently occur there from the nicotine poisoning.

Three or four women, after drinking fresh coffee, were seriously affected with faintness, vertigo, nausea, convulsions, and loss of consciousness. It was discovered that the coffee-beans had been picked out from the store-sweepings, consisting principally of tobacco leaves, among which the coffee had got mixed and lay for a time exposed to the rain.

A squadron of hussars hid tobacco leaves in their breasts for smuggling purposes. Every man of them was seized with headache, vertigo, and vomiting. Soldiers have sometimes purposely disabled themselves for war by applying these leaves to the pit of the arm, thus inducing alarming symptoms.

A Frenchman living near Paris, having cleaned his pipe with a knife, but neglecting to wipe it, subsequently happened to cut one of his fingers. The wound was so slight that he thought nothing of it. A few hours later, however, the finger grew painful and swelled, the inflammation rapidly spreading through the arm. Doctors were summoned, but the case remained a mystery till, in answer to inquiries, the enigma was explained. All remedies proved ineffectual, and the man's condition grew so alarming, that he was taken to the hospital, where the arm was amputated as the only chance of saving his life.

CONSIDERED MEDICALLY, THIS WEED RANKS AMONG THE DEADLIEST POISONS.

This must be a very sick world to require nearly as much medicine as food. Though the scientific men who have charge of the public and private health very seldom prescribe tobacco, they all admit that it is a powerful medicinal agent. As a poison, it stands next to strychnine. Its method of cure is by partially killing.

In a late treatise on Physiology it is stated: "Tobacco produces remarkable effects on the system, whether it be taken into the stomach, or applied to portions of the body from which the skin has been removed. In the latter instance it is absorbed into the blood, and its use is attended with great danger, sometimes with death."

Brodie: "It powerfully controls the action of the heart and arteries, producing invariably a weak, tremulous pulse, with all the apparent symptoms of approaching death."

Another physician: "If we wish at any time to prostrate the powers of life in the most sudden and awful manner, we have but to administer a dose of tobacco and our object is accomplished."

"The effect on the heart is not caused by direct action, but by paralyzing the minute vessels which form the batteries of the nervous system. The heart, freed from their control, increases the rapidity of its strokes, with an apparent accession, but real waste of force."

According to Dr. Druhen's testimony, "a boy of fourteen, who smoked fifteen cents' worth of tobacco for the toothache, fell down senseless and died the same day."

It was formerly used as an emetic, from its prompt action, all the powers of the system rallying to expel the enemy. A poultice of tobacco placed on the stomach of a child dying with croup caused deathly nausea and instant vomiting. The physician, who arrived shortly after, admitted that it had saved the child's life, but pronounced it to be an exceedingly dangerous, and often fatal, remedy.

No one will deny that tobacco is a drug. And it is an axiom among physicians — whoever among them practically may disregard it, — that *no drug should ever be taken in health*.

From Dr. Stillé's *Therapeutics and Materia Medica* we learn that "tobacco as a therapeutic agent, belongs to the same class with belladonna, alcohol, and opium, but that its use is restricted within comparatively narrow limits, because of the distressing symptoms which, even in moderate doses, it occasions; the risk of fatal consequences; and the uncertainty in regard to the degree of its influence upon individuals."

Dr. Grimshaw: "It is believed by all judicious practitioners too dangerous to be employed as a medicine. The benefits, as a remedy, do not counterbalance the risk of using it. Yet so *insidious* are its effects, that very few have regarded it as swelling the bills of mortality.   It is, never-theless, true that multitudes are carried to the grave every year by tobacco alone."

Dr. Clay: " I have been called to children writhing in horrid convulsions from having the de-coction of tobacco applied for the scald head, and I have always experienced great difficulty in re-storing them; three instances, in my own recollec-tion, were attended with fatal results."

Dr. Newell, a Boston practitioner : " Small doses of the oil of tobacco administered to a dog for a few weeks cause marasmus and a withering of the spinal cord.   The dog soon drags the hind legs, sheds his hair, sloughs off the eyelids, becomes blind, and dies.   Thus it is seen that nicotine is one of the most deadly poisons, its fatal results being produced in less time than any other poison except prussic acid."

In confirmation of this, it is asserted by M. Or-fila, president of the Paris Medical Academy, that " Tobacco is the most subtile poison known to the chemist, except the deadly prussic acid."

A prominent tobacco manufacturer declares that nothing ever goes into tobacco so deleterious to the constitution as tobacco itself.

That its legitimate results are not invariably man-ifested is owing to the marvellous power in the human system to tolerate poison taken gradually. It is with tobacco as with laudanum, opium, ar-senic, whiskey, and other liquors, to the use of which a man may, by degrees, habituate himself, so that he can take it with seeming impunity ; yet it is none the less a poison, slowly, it may be, but surely, impairing the organism and inducing diseases which strike at the life forces. And the victim may be quite sure that nature will, in the end, reassert herself, and exact a bitter atonement for all such infractions of her wholesome laws.

" The effect of tobacco on the glandular system is not less evil than on the nervous. If there is any tuberculous tendency, this enemy searches it out, excites it, and sends its victim to the grave by rapid stages. Whatever weak spot there is in the constitution, this insidious thief creeps into, mining and sapping about it until the fabric crumbles into dust. In some stages of its action, it excites the passions abnormally, and later they are deadened as unnaturally."

A promising young man of fine constitution and correct habits, with the single exception of smoking, was found dead in his bed. Examination showed the blood in one lung completely black from the disintegrating effects of tobacco. According to the doctors it was this which killed him.

Such are the characteristics of tobacco, making its prescription permissible only in the extremest cases, and with the utmost caution. Yet this most powerful, most fatal of all drugs it is which has come to be regarded by thousands as a daily necessity — more to them than meat, or drink, or any earthly good.

Writes Dr. Solly, for many years the medical

examiner of various English life insurance offices :
" The profession have no idea of the ignorance of
the public regarding the nature of tobacco.   Even
intelligent, well-educated men stare in astonishment
when you tell them that it is one of the most
powerful poisons.   Now, is this right? Has the
medical profession done its duty? Ought we not,
as a body, to have told the public that, of all our
poisons, it is the most insidious, uncertain, and,
in full doses, the most deadly?

" What a blessing it would have been to mankind if all men had shrunk from this plague of the
brain as did the first Napoleon! One inhalation
was enough. In disgust, he exclaimed, ' Oh, the
swine! my stomach turns.'

" In the course of my practice I have met with
many who, like myself, have abandoned smoking.
I have never found one who does not assert most
positively that he has been in better health since,
and that his intellectual activity has increased. I
may be mistaken, but I believe that our greatest
men, statesmen, lawyers, warriors, physicians,
and surgeons, have either not been smokers, or, if
smokers, that they have died prematurely."

EFFECTS ON CHILDREN AND YOUNG MEN; LOWER-
ING SCHOLARSHIP.

Dr. Willard Parker: "Tobacco is ruinous in
our schools and colleges, dwarfing body and
mind."

Dr. Ferguson: "I believe that no one who

smokes tobacco before the bodily powers are developed ever makes a strong, vigorous man."

Prof. Richard McSherry, president of the Baltimore Academy of Medicine: "The effect of tobacco on schoolboys is so marked as not to be open for discussion.

From " Lessons on the Human Body:" "Tobacco, like alcohol, and for nearly the same reasons, injures the brain, deranges the entire nervous system, spoils the appetite for wholesome food, lowers the life forces, injures the lungs and heart, and depresses the spirits. When indulged in by young persons, it saps the foundation of health and dwarfs the body and mind."

Dr. B. W. Richardson: " The effects of this agent, often severe even on those who have attained to manhood, are specially injurious to the young. In these the habit of smoking causes impairment of growth, premature manhood, and physical prostration."

A superintendent of education in Vermont gives the case of a boy of fourteen who fell unaccountably behind his class. The incapacity thus evinced in one naturally bright was a puzzle to his teachers. At last he sickened and died, when it was found that he was killed by tobacco, to which he was in the habit of helping himself privately from his father's store.

At an examination for admission to the Free College of New York, out of nine hundred girls, six hundred and sixty, or seventy-one per cent, passed, while only forty-eight per cent of the boys could enter, the difference being ascribed to the stupefying effect of tobacco.

A prominent teacher in Syracuse writes : " After long experience, I have come to the conclusion that many boys from all departments of the public schools become incapable of prolonged mental effort, and are lacking in refinement and in interest and attention to school duties, in consequence of the use of tobacco, and that very many of the failures in promotion from year to year are due to the same cause."

The testimony on this point, both as to our own and foreign countries, is clear and overwhelming. Statistics obtained from European institutions show that lads whose standing had been good before they began to smoke or chew were invariably found, after they became addicted to either habit, to fall below the school average.

In 1862 the Emperor Louis Napoleon, learning that paralysis and insanity had increased with the increase of the tobacco revenue, ordered an examination of the schools and colleges, and finding that the average standing in both scholarship and character was lower among those who used the weed than among the abstainers, issued an edict forbidding its use in all the national institutions.

The investigation of the public schools of France by medical and scientific men has been very thorough. M. Bertillon reported some of the results in the *Union Médicale*. Facts as to the Polytechnic

School in Paris are given in the *Dublin Medical Press:* "It is shown that smokers have proved themselves, in the various competitive examinations, far inferior to others. Not only in the examinations on entering the school are they in a lower rank, but in the various ordeals of the year the average rank of the smoker has constantly fallen."

Science and Health contains the translation of a report on this subject by Dr. Constan, one of the medical men employed in the investigations spoken of, and which covered the ground from 1876 to 1880. He says: "Our inquiries have extended to three groups of educational establishments, viz.: primary, secondary, and higher, or special schools. Whether the use of tobacco is entirely prohibited, or only indulged in surreptitiously, or on going-out days, or permitted under certain restrictions, and consequently more largely practised, the figures show that it affects the quality of the studies in a constant ratio, and this influence is more marked in the different establishments where tobacco is more extensively used."

Dr. Constan gives statistics with regard to the grammar schools of Douai, St. Quentin, and Chambéry, the primary and the higher normal schools of Douai, with the military school at the same place, and also that at Saumur. The general results in all these schools are substantially the same as those in the Polytechnic School at Paris. Still more striking results are given as to the Naval School at

Brest, where the students were allowed to smoke half an hour every morning and evening. After one year's study, eight smokers so fell in their rank that they "lost between them one hundred and twenty-three places."

Dr. Constan thus concludes his article: "The depressing action of tobacco on the intellectual development is, therefore, beyond question. Its influence clogs all the intellectual faculties, and especially the memory. It is greater in proportion to the youth of the individual and the facilities allowed him for smoking."

It having been thus clearly established that the students who do not smoke outrank those who do, and that the scholarship of the smokers steadily deteriorates as the smoking continues, we are not surprised to learn that the Minister of Public Instruction issued a circular to the various teachers in all the schools of every grade, forbidding tobacco as injurious to physical and intellectual development. Indeed, so much anxiety is felt concerning the decreasing stature of the French — some of the most eminent scientists ascribing it to tobacco — that the question of prohibiting this drug to all classes of children and youth is under consideration.

It is pleasant to state that the Council of Berne in Switzerland has issued such a prohibition to boys under fifteen.

A report by the Medical Department of the United States Naval Academy at Annapolis, Md., enu-

merates the following as the result of the use of
tobacco in the school : —

" Functional derangement of the digestive, circulatory, and nervous systems, manifesting themselves in the form of headache, confusion of intellect, loss of memory, impaired power of attention,
lassitude, indisposition to muscular effort, nausea,
want of appetite, dyspepsia, palpitation, tremu-
lousness, disturbed sleep, impaired vision, etc.,
any one of which materially lessens the capacity
for study and application.

" The Board are of opinion, therefore, that the
regulations against the use of tobacco in any form
cannot be too stringent."

The *New York Times* rebukes Commodore Parker for allowing naval students to chew and smoke,
notwithstanding the expressed opinion of the
Board ; charging that it was done " with an impress
of ignorance not creditable to the commanding officer."   It goes on to say : " The boy who smokes
cigars or chews tobacco poisons himself, and the
teacher who does not know this is not fit to be
trusted with the charge and government of boys.
He who permissively encourages boys to smoke or
chew is a corrupter of youth."

Justice to Commodore Parker, however, requires
the admission that he conferred with a prominent
physician, claiming that it was almost impossible
effectually to prohibit the practice, and concluding
that, on the whole, it was better to allow the boys to
smoke under regulations than to punish them constantly for violation of rules.

The first general order of the superintendent succeeding Commodore Parker forbade the use of tobacco in every form. Unfortunately, however, the habit is such a tyrant that, "in spite of the system of daily inspection, strict bounds, military punishment, and the fact that all supplies are bought from the Post Commissary, it is not entirely suppressed." Such is the testimony of a graduate, now a professor in one of our colleges.

The classes in Yale College are graded according to their scholarship, the best scholars being in the first division, and the poorest in the fourth. From the *Yale Courant* we learn that in the first division only twenty-five per cent use tobacco; in the second, forty-eight; in the third, seventy, and in the lowest, eighty-five.

It is asserted that during the last fifty years no devotee of the weed has graduated from Harvard at the head of his class, although above eighty-three per cent of the students are addicted to its use.

We also learn that in Oxford and Cambridge, England, nine tenths of the first-class men are non-smokers.

It is humiliating to state that at Amherst College the average number of tobacco-users among the students for the last fourteen years has been nearly twenty-nine per cent, while in one of the graduating classes at Princeton it was fifty per cent.

In addressing the graduating law class of the Wisconsin State University, ex-Senator Doolittle remarked : —

" I verily believe that the mental force, power of labor, and endurance of our profession is decreased at least twenty-five per cent by the use of tobacco. Its poisonous and narcotic effects reduce the power of the vital organs and tend to paralyze them, while the useless consumption of time and money takes away twenty-five per cent of the working hours, if it does not consume the same amount of the earnings."

With very few exceptions, medical and scientific men are in substantial agreement as to the effect of tobacco on the intellect; indeed, I have yet to hear of the first one that has expressed himself at all on the subject who is not explicit in his declaration of its injurious influence on the physical and mental powers of the young.

Prof. Lizars of Edinburgh enumerates a fearful catalogue of diseases which he proves to be the result of tobacco, adding: "It is painful to contemplate how many promising youths must be stunted in their growth and enfeebled in their minds before they arrive at manhood."

What an advance in intellectual and moral power should we behold if our young men could be induced to follow the example of Sir Isaac Newton, who refused to smoke "because he would make no necessities for himself;" a sentiment worthy to be engraved over the doors of every college and school-house in the land. Dr. Depierris, a French physician, in his excellent treatise on tobacco, exclaims, "How sad it is to behold so many fine intellects, well cultivated, full of vitality, and striving with enthusiasm towards the heights of human knowledge, withered in the barrenness of narcotism, and sinking into premature death."

Wrote President Nott of Union College : "The lives of some and the health of many have been destroyed by persisting, in despite of counsels, in the use of this poisonous narcotic, which, next to intoxicating liquors, is, in my opinion, more destructive to the health of the youth in our country than any other agent."

A prominent physician testifies : "I never observed such pallid faces and so many marks of declining health, nor ever knew so many hectical habits and consumptive affections as of late years ; and I trace this alarming inroad on *young constitutions* principally to the pernicious custom of smoking cigars."

Even *the organ of the tobacco trade* is forced to admit that "few things could be more pernicious for boys, growing youths, and persons of unformed constitution than the use of tobacco in any of its forms," — a truly significant confession.

In Germany the mischief done to growing boys has been found so great that the government has ordered the police to forbid lads under sixteen from smoking in the street. The Swiss canton of Schaffhausen has also issued a law prohibiting boys under fifteen from using tobacco, either on the streets or at home. On *our* streets we behold a vast and ever-increasing number of young Americans who evidently consider smoking essential to manliness.   And, alas, our police have no orders to forbid it.

For a gleam of dawning light, however, we will thank God and take courage.   We catch this gleam in an act of the New Jersey legislature on this subject, entitled " An act prohibiting the sale of cigarettes or tobacco in any of its forms to minors." And now " every person who sells the narcotic in any form to a boy or girl under sixteen years of age is liable to a penalty of twenty dollars for each and every offence."

HARD BREAKING-IN.

How emphatically nature protests against this alien, almost every tobacco-user can testify.   I give but a single instance.

In a neighborhood of smoking boys, Dio Lewis made an experiment on a lad who had never used the weed, giving him a pill of plug-tobacco to chew.   Instantly, before he had swallowed a particle, he grew fearfully sick, became pale as death, while a cold sweat crept over him, and soon, in the midst of violent retchings, he had to be carried into the open air.

Yet what pains are taken and what obstacles conquered in forming the habit!   A lady met on the street a three-year-old with a black stick in his mouth.   She begged him to throw it away, promising him a nice present if he would ; but he held on to his stick, asserting that he " liked smoking and meant to smoke himself when big enough."

Boys sometimes break themselves into this vice by rolling up tea or ground coffee in papers, and smoking them as cigarettes.

Neal Dow graphically describes the early processes: "At the very first the use of tobacco is a dreadful disgust. It is even worse than this. It inflicts upon its future victim a nausea, a retching, a vomiting, a headache, to which the horrors of seasickness are not to be compared. There is the blue upper lip, the livid, ghastly hue of the face, the eye like that of a dead fish, the limbs limp and powerless, a violent and painful vomiting, every symptom of death, which it would soon be in reality if the unutterable horror of the suffering did not compel the poor fool to postpone the attempt to become a man in that way. Here endeth the first lesson. The silly youth resolves always that he will never touch tobacco again, and holds to his purpose until he has entirely recovered from the effects of the first lesson. Then he sees other youngsters like himself who have succeeded in conquering their disgust at tobacco. They have done it. Why not he? They laugh at him as white-livered; they assure him that the worst of it will be over in a few days, or, at most, in a few weeks. They strut through the streets or in other public places so grandly; they have such a manly way with them; there is such a grace in their style of holding the cigar between finger and thumb, and striking off the ashes with the little finger. When they put the cigar into their mouths again, it is with such a flourish, and their heads are thrown back, a little on one side, with so much self-consciousness, their eyes at the same moment cast slily right and left, to see who observes and admires them! Ah! this is quite irresistible, and our poor, foolish youngster goes off behind the barn, or into some other out-of-the-way place, and takes the second lesson. All this is carefully concealed from the parents, so the tobacco-pupil must go to bed before supper, under pretence of headache. Pretence? It is no sham. He has a racking and splitting headache, with the return of dreadful nausea. In a few weeks, more or less, our youngster has learned to smoke or chew, as the case may be."

All this painstaking and all this suffering voluntarily endured to make himself the slave of a terrible tyrant! "He little knows that a god more cunning than all the heathen divinities put together has bound him in his spell, and that he is in for a whole life of unspeakable abominations."

CIGARETTES.

Something should be said as to cigarette-smoking, which is becoming so prevalent, and which is thought by many to be quite harmless. A physician, who had strong suspicions on the subject, for his own satisfaction had a cigarette analyzed. The tobacco was found to be strongly impregnated with opium, while the wrapper, warranted to be rice-paper, proved to be common paper whitened with arsenic. Thus the cigarette subtlety combines a threefold deadly bane, proving in the end, per-chance, as fatal to the unwary as the poisoned garment of Nessus to the unsuspecting Hercules.

A chemist in New York city, who also had his own suspicions, purchased from prominent dealers a dozen packages of the highest-priced cigarettes. These he sent for analysis to an eminent chemist in another State, and was astounded by his report of the quantity of opium found in these standard brands.

Dr. Lewis A. Sayre pronounces cigarettes to be worse for boys than pipes or cigars, and paper cigarettes to be worse than tobacco cigarettes, perhaps because the paper absorbs more of the nicotine ; that they lead to a nervous trembling of the hands, and, if used excessively, affect the memory.

Dr. Hammond bears testimony to " the ill effects of cigarettes in the production of facial neuralgia, insomnia, nervous dyspepsia, sciatica, and an in-disposition to mental exertion."

In a city school a bright lad of thirteen became dull and fitful, and troubled with nervous twitch-ings. His condition at length compelling him to be withdrawn from his studies, he was found to be a smoker of cigarettes. When asked why he did not give them up, he replied with tears that he had often tried to do so, but could not.

The following is from a public journal: "Parkham Adams, aged fourteen, a student in the University of Tennessee, is dying. He smoked forty cigarettes, and inhaled the smoke on a wager."

A young man exhibited symptoms of heart-disease, the pulsations sometimes almost ceasing, and again so accelerated that he could scarcely catch his breath, and seemed on the point of dying. On consulting a doctor, he was told that all these symptoms came from the use of cigarettes, and on banishing them his health was soon restored.

Says an eminent doctor: "We look upon the cigarette as a leading demoralization of the last twenty-five years."

From the Philadelphia *Times* we learn that several leading physicians in that city "unanimously condemn cigarette-smoking as one of the vilest and most destructive evils that ever befell the youth of any country;" declaring that "its direct tendency is a deterioration of the race." One of these physicians affirms that within a single week he had two patients who had been made blind by cigarettes, while he knew several other cases of the same kind.

There are in the city of New York a good many "cigar-butt grubbers," as they are termed, that is, boys and girls who scour the streets for stumps and half-burnt cigars, which are dried and then sold to be used in making cigarettes. A religious weekly of that city is responsible for the following account: A ragged eight-year-old Italian boy, bareheaded and barefooted, was brought before one of the city justices on the charge of vagrancy. The officer who arrested him stated that he had found the boy picking up cigar stumps from the streets and gutters, showing the justice a basket half full of such stumps, water-soaked and covered with mud. "What do you do with these?" asked his Honor. "I sell them to a man for ten cents a pound, and they are used for making cigarettes."

The statements of the representative of a large Southern tobacco house, given on the authority of the New York *Tribune*, will not be questioned. He asserts that "the extent to which drugs are used in cigarettes is appalling," and that "Havana flavoring" is sold everywhere and by the thousand barrels. This is prepared from the tonka-bean, which contains a deadly poison. Cigarette wrappers are in some cases made from the filthy scrapings of rag-pickers, arsenic being often used in the bleaching process, while combustion develops the oil of creosote.

Tobacconists report that cigarettes are coming to overshadow all other branches of the business; and it is stated officially that the revenue of our government has gained by several millions from their increased use. As helping to account for this increase, we also learn that "ladies, in growing numbers, habitually use cigarettes."

A teacher of long experience remarks: "I think

that at least seven out of every ten boys smoke by the time they are fourteen years old."

On a winter's day may be seen skating on the lake in Central Park, New York, thousands of children, girls as well as boys, most of them puffing cigarettes bought at a restaurant close by for a penny apiece. Indeed, one can hardly walk the streets without meeting small boys with discarded stumps of cigars or cigarettes in their mouths. No wonder that Dr. Rush should have exclaimed: "One cannot witness this sight without anticipating such a depreciation of our posterity in health and character as can scarcely be contemplated without pain and horror."

TOBACCO AND DRINKING.

It is tobacco in some form which perhaps more than any other cause leads to the dram-shop. An English physician states that he examined the breath of thirty smoking boys between the ages of nine and fifteen. In twenty-two of them he found various disorders of a serious nature, and "more or less marked taste *for strong drink,*" a taste generated by tobacco. His prescriptions had little effect till smoking was given up, when health returned. It is also said that when smoking was abandoned the boys recovered. These facts are stated on the authority of the *British Medical Journal*.

A French physician, who had studied the effects of smoking on thirty-eight boys between nine and fifteen, gives as the result that twenty-seven presented marked symptoms of nicotine poisoning; twenty-three, serious derangement of the intellectual faculties, and *a strong appetite for alcoholic drinks;* three, heart disease; eight, decided deterioration of the blood; twelve, frequent nosebleed; ten, disturbed sleep; and four, ulceration of the mouth in its mucous membrane.

Says Decaisne, an eminent Paris doctor: "Among children from nine to fifteen who were examined, smoking undoubtedly caused palpitation, intermittent pulse, and chloro-anæmia.   Besides this, the children showed impaired intelligence, became lazy and stupid, and *were disposed to take alcoholic stimulants.*"

Even the very name has by some one been ingeniously traced to the god of drunkenness, *Τω Βαχχω.* Indeed, " so inseparable an attendant is drinking on smoking," says Adam Clarke, " that in some places the same word expresses both acts. Thus, *peend*, in the Bengalee language, signifies to drink and to smoke."

Dr. Rush affirms that " Smoking and chewing tobacco, by rendering water and other simple liquids insipid to the taste, dispose very much to the stronger stimulus of ardent spirits; hence, the practice of smoking cigars has been followed by the use of brandy and water as a common drink."

The following is from a brief treatise on Narcotics : —

" When introduced into the system in small

quantities, by smoking, chewing, or snuffing, tobacco acts as a narcotic, and produces, for the
time, a calm feeling of mind and body, a state of
mild stupor and repose. This condition changes
to one of nervous restlessness and a general feeling
of muscular weakness when its habitual use is
temporarily interrupted. The body and mind feel
in need of stimulation, and there is great danger
that a resort to alcohol may be had. The use of
alcohol is frequently induced by that of tobacco."

Out of six hundred in the State prison at Auburn, New York, sent there for crimes committed
through strong drink, five hundred testified that
it was tobacco which led them to intemperance.

Dr. Logee, of Oxford, Ohio, relates that he once
heard Mr. Trask offer fifty dollars to any intemperate man who had not been a tobacco-user; and
that he himself has frequently made the offer of
fifty or a hundred dollars to any hard drinker who
would prove that he had never been a smoker or
a chewer. Not a man, however, has ever claimed
the money.

" Show me a drunkard that does n't use tobacco,"
said Horace Greeley, " and I will show you a white
blackbird."

George Trask pronounces the weed " Satan's
fuel for the drinking appetites."

" The professors in the University and High
School at Ann Arbor, Michigan, who have had a
long experience among thousands of young men,
regard tobacco as having a worse effect than even

liquor, affirming that more young men break down
in body and mind and finally go astray as a result
of smoking than of drinking, while the former
often leads to the latter." In this view concur
Dr. Parker, Dr. Rush, and a multitude of medical
men.

Dr. Cowan affirms that " the exceptions are very
rare, when a user of tobacco in any of its forms
is not ultimately led to use alcoholic liquors; and
that, next to transmitted tendencies, the use of
tobacco is the great cause of both moderate and
excessive alcoholic drinking."

MANUFACTURE OF CHEWING-TOBACCO.

For the following account I am indebted to a
Quaker friend, David Tatum, of Cleveland, Ohio,
who visited some of the largest establishments in
Virginia.

" When the tobacco is brought into the factory
and carefully sorted, it is dipped in a solution of
licorice and sugar, and passed between rollers
which press it through the leaves, while the sur-
plus juice runs back into the solution in which it
was dipped. It is then dried; after which it is
put into boxes about four feet long, and two deep,
each layer of leaves being dusted with powdered
licorice and *thoroughly sprinkled with rum* till the
box is filled, then it is covered, and allowed to remain a few days until it becomes well soaked with
the licorice and rum, and ready to work up for
market."

CIGAR-MAKING.

The New York *Tribune* informs us that five eighths of the cigars sold in the metropolis are made in east-side tenements by Bohemian families, the work being done in the room where they eat and sleep. The tobacco, wet and spread on the floor, is trodden down by the family while about their domestic employment. In the morning, damp and dirty, it is stripped from the stems by the children, the women making the fillers, and the men rolling and finishing at the rate of seven hundred a day. A choice foreign brand is affixed, and they are ready to go forth on their errand of destruction. Day and night these children exist — not live — in this dreadful atmosphere. Will not the Society for the Prevention of Cruelty to Children interfere in their behalf ?

A German smoker in New York, while using a razor, slightly cut his lip. In a few days the wound assumed the appearance of an ulcer, which the medical attendant knew to be scrofulous. The whole lower lip became affected with a repulsive outgrowth, while the gums were greatly swollen, and the teeth loose, ready to drop out. Learning where the German purchased his cigars, the doctor called at the tenement. The mystery was solved. The man was finishing, "with a lick and a stick" a bundle of fresh leaves, while on his lip was a scrofulous sore. His son, too, working by his side, had a similar sore. Nor was this instance exceptional, the doctor stating that such cases are of frequent occurrence.

In the Bellevue Hospital there were recently fifty patients suffering from one of the most fearful and incurable of maladies, contracted from cigars manufactured in tenement houses, by diseased persons, the finishing touch being given by the teeth and tongue. Among the physicians who have traced several similar cases to this source may be named Dr. L. Duncan Bulkley, of New York.

Let the sons of Esculapius who recommend cigars for their tranquillizing influence enlighten their patients with the fact that, at one time, just after thousands of cigars had been turned loose upon the world, their *makers* were discovered to be pitted with the small-pox.

We learn from the public journals that in San Francisco a hundred and ninety-five cases of leprosy have been traced by the physicians of that city to the smoking of cigarettes manufactured by Chinese lepers.

Mr. R. L. Carpenter: "It is stated that an immense quantity of cheap European tobacco is shipped to Cuba, to be made up and exported as Havana cigars. The Act of Parliament against the adulteration of tobacco informs us of various noxious articles used by unscrupulous manufacturers. Some, however, are comparatively innocent, — such as sawdust, peat, and seaweed, — so that the workman's bad tobacco may not be as poisonous as his neighbor's best Virginia. When I was in Baltimore I went into the great tobacco warehouses; a pig was wandering about, and seemed quite at home there; the leaves were being pulled by unwashed negroes without pocket-handkerchiefs. But those who do not object to poison cannot be expected to mind dirt."

The following list of the various articles used in flavoring tobacco was procured from the manufacturers : —

Sugar, honey, orange peel, lemon peel, mace, cloves, spices of all kinds, vanilla, licorice, valerian, tonka-bean, opiates, laudanum, Spanish wine, Santa Cruz rum, liquor of all sorts.

When opiates are used, a solution is sprinkled on the tobacco before manufacturing. Spices are sprinkled on the tops of the cigars after packing, to give a pleasant odor to the box, and to destroy any rank flavor from poor tobacco.

It is asserted that a manufactory in the city of Syracuse makes a favorite and increasingly popular brand of cigars by soaking the tobacco leaves in opium. Even smokers testify that there is no doubt on this point.

PROPERTIES AND EFFECTS OF TOBACCO.

In a treatise on the injurious effects of tobacco, even when used moderately, Dr. Grimshaw, in order to confirm his statements, quotes freely from some of " the most learned medical authorities, men who were not engaged in a reform movement,

who were unconnected with any society, temperate or total abstinent, and were therefore mere
recorders of facts, and propagators of truth."

Dr. Harris, physician to the New York city dispensary: "The properties and effects of tobacco
are of a curiously mixed character. Its power or
property of stimulation is strangely interwoven
with its more important and predominating one of
sedation or depression. This complex and double
action is peculiarly adapted to the work of fascinating and misleading those who submit themselves to its influence.

"It titillates the nerves and exhilarates the feelings, while it obtunds and stupefies the sensibility,
and partially suspends the process of life. The
appetite which it creates is a *never-ending gnawing* that will not be denied; and under the most
specious guise of *absolute physical necessity*, it
hides its insatiate and cruel demands. Its sedative influence acts as a damper to the bustling
excitability which the nervous system acquires
from deficient or excessive action; while at the
same time it affords fresh and fascinating excitement that for a long time makes one forgetful of
weariness, and promises to relieve the tedium of
life. There is no other substance known that can
induce such complex and various effects; but the
ultimate results are invariably the same. Its disastrous influences upon the functions of the nervous system and the action of the heart are felt
throughout every tissue of the body; the blood

moves sluggishly, and as it stagnates in delicate organs, foundation is laid for every form of disease, while at the same time the poison of the drug is diffused through every tissue of the living frame, benumbing and impairing all the powers of life, so that the system is at once more liable to disease and less able to endure its consequences and resist its power."

Dr. Logee: "Being a narcotic stimulant it breaks down the nervous system, raising the user above his natural level, only, by inevitable reaction, to depress him below it."

Dr. B. W. Richardson: "The extreme symptoms induced by tobacco smoke are intensely severe, and the idea that tobacco is a narcotic like opium or chloroform is entirely disproved by them. Its action is as an irritant upon the motor parts of the nervous system, not as a narcotic upon the sensational."

Dr. Marshall Hall: "The smoker *cannot escape* the poison of tobacco. It gets into his blood, travels the whole round of his system, interferes with the heart's action and the general circulation, and affects every organ and fibre of the frame."

Dr. J. C. Jackson: "I have long entertained the opinion that tobacco is really more deleterious in its effects than are alcoholic drinks. I have settled myself thoroughly in the conviction that no habit of the American people is so destructive to their physical vigor, and their moral character."

"We are accused of killing patients with calomel," remarks a physician; "but a thousand are killed by tobacco to one by calomel."

Solly, surgeon of St. Thomas' Hospital, London: "I know of no single vice which does so much harm as smoking. It soothes the excited nervous system at the time to render it more irritable and more feeble ultimately."

Dr. R. W. Pease of Syracuse: "There can be but one opinion among physicians, and that is, the use of so powerful a *narcotic stimulant* must be hurtful, not only to the nervous system, but especially to the circulatory organs, chiefly the heart, causing, first, functional disturbance, and finally, organic disease of that organ. In short, I am firmly convinced that tobacco is doing more mischief to the physical condition of our people than alcohol in all its forms."

Dr. Drysdale: "Nicotine enters the body by the stomach, the lungs, and the skin; and its effects are uniform by whatever gate it enters."

Strong testimony on this subject is presented by Dr. Pidduck, physician to a dispensary in St. Giles. It appears in the London *Lancet* for 1857, which embodies the results of the investigations as to the use of tobacco by prominent physicians, including Dr. Taylor, the great English surgeon and author. All are agreed that it is a poison for both brain and heart, producing paralysis, apoplexy, and heart disease, and also in the conviction that it sows the seeds of various other maladies.

It is estimated by German physicians that of the deaths occurring in that country among men between eighteen and thirty-five years of age, one half die from the effects of this drug. They unequivocally assert that "tobacco burns out the blood, the teeth, the eyes, and the brain."

Dr. Wright: "I believe it to be the great antagonist of the nervous system, especially in its relations to the organs of sense, of reproduction, and of digestion."

Dr. Harris: "At the New York City dispensary, more cases of constitutional, chronic, and functional diseases are treated than at any other institution in America, more than fifty thousand patients being annually prescribed for. Of the male adult patients affected by such diseases who have come under my care at the dispensary, I have found that nearly nine tenths of the whole number were habitual tobacco-mongers. In no small proportion of these it has been perfectly evident that tobacco had an important influence upon the cause and continuance of these maladies."

Decaisne: "Tobacco-smoking often causes an intermittent pulse. Out of eighty-one smokers examined, twenty-three presented an intermittent pulse, independent of any *cardiac lesion*. This intermittency disappeared when smoking was abandoned."

Blatin relates that "a young medical student, after smoking a single pipe, fell into a frightful state, the heart becoming nearly motionless, the

chest constricted, breathing painful, limbs contracted, pupils insensible, one contracted, the other
dilated. These symptoms lasted four days."

Tyrrell: "The tobacco habit is one of those
pleasant vices which the just gods make instru-
ments to scourge us, destroying the very principle
of manhood."

Abernethy: "Smoking stupefies all the senses
and all the faculties, by slow but enduring intoxi-
cation, into dull obliviousness."

Prof. Miller, of Edinburgh: "As medical men
we know that smoking injures the whole organism,
and puts a man's stomach and whole frame out of
order. The effects of narcotics, mental and bodily,
I can fairly testify, are nothing but evil; and I
stand in a position of giving an experienced as
well as an impartial observation."

"In our country," says one, "it is no uncommon
circumstance to hear of inquests on the bodies of
smokers, especially youths, the ordinary verdict
being "Died from extreme tobacco-smoking."
In a single death-certificate of a New York
physician, we read: "Four died of poisoning
from tobacco."

"I have no hesitation in averring," writes one
of the most able and experienced temperance ad-
vocates, "that, gigantic as are the evils arising
from the use of strong drink, those of using
tobacco exceed them."

Dr. Twitchell, of Keene, N. H., expresses substantially the same opinion.

If additional testimony were desirable, a long and goodly array of medical names, both in our own country and in Europe, might be cited. All the medical schools as such, allopathic, hydropathic, homœopathic, with the various specialists, unite in their testimony as to the disastrous effects of tobacco, whether for smoking, chewing, or snuffing; nor is this strange when it is the appalling verdict of a college of physicians that twenty thousand in our own land die annually from this poison. The only wonder is how any doctor can fail to throw the whole weight of his influence against this practice.

EXPERIENCES OF LITERARY MEN.

A volume by A. Arthur Reade, entitled "Study and Stimulants," contains the experiences of many literary men in regard to stimulants, From these I select but a few cases, and such as relate only to tobacco.

Among those who advocate its use are Edison, Wilkie Collins, and Anthony Trollope. The latter, however, admits that, finding it was injuring him, he gave it up for two years, when he resumed smoking, substituting, however, for "three large cigars daily three very small ones; and so far as I can tell," he adds, "without any effect."

Among the total abstainers on principle from tobacco, as well as from spirits and wine, are Dr. Allibone, the Duke of Argyle, Robert and William Chambers, George W. Childs, Prof. Fairbairn, Cardinal Newman, Keshub Chunder Sen, and M. Barthelemy St. Hilaire.

Of Gladstone it is affirmed that he "detests smoking."

Darwin: "I have taken snuff all my life, and regret that I ever acquired the habit."

Ernst Haeckel: "I have never smoked."

Philip Gilbert Hamerton: "I shall certainly never resume smoking. I never use any stimulants whatever when writing, and believe the use of them to be most pernicious; indeed, I have seen terrible results from them. When a writer feels dull, the best stimulant is fresh air."

W. D. Howells: "I never use tobacco, except in a very rare, self-defensive cigarette, where a great many other people are smoking."

"John Ruskin entirely abhors the practice of smoking, his dislike of it being mainly based on the belief that a cigar or pipe will often make a man content to be idle for any length of time."

Charles Reade: "I tried to smoke five or six times, but it always made me heavy and rather sick; therefore, as it costs money, I spurned it. I have seen many people the worse for it. I never saw anybody perceptibly the better for it."

The case of the distinguished French savant, the Abbé Moigno, editor of the *Journal du Monde*, is very striking. Temperate in his general habits, he became conscious of injury from his excessive use of snuff, many times giving it up only to resume it again. He was a noted linguist, knowing by heart some fifteen hundred root words in various languages; but, under the influence of the narcotic, these were all dropping from his memory. He felt this to be so great a trial that he finally renounced the habit. He writes: "It was the commencement of a veritable resurrection of health, mind, and memory, and the army of words that had run away has gradually returned."

The following item is taken from another source. Algernon Charles Swinburne, wandering one day from room to room at the Art Club, in the vain search for a clear atmosphere where he could write, at last exclaimed in poetic indignation: "James the First was a knave, a tyrant, a fool, a liar, a coward; but I love him, I worship him, because he slit the throat of that blackguard Raleigh, who invented this filthy smoking."

MEDICAL INCONSISTENCIES.

Of a physician who is not only indifferent to this great evil, but who himself makes use of the drug, what shall be said? His tell-tale breath as he bends over his suffering patient, the very smell of his garments to one for whose recovery God's pure air is a first necessity, — what can be urged in his defence? Said a refined and highly intelligent woman, "I would never employ a physician who used tobacco."

But whatever rights the doctors may claim so far as their own use of the weed is concerned, what plea can be made for those who prescribe this poison for a patient, and thus, for a mere temporary soothing effect, bring him into a bondage entailing evils beyond computation to himself and family? A certain physician recommended the chewing of tobacco to a man as the only thing to secure him against a fever to which he was exposed in the case of one of his family. But what of *a woman?* How about said man's wife and daughter, who, from being more constantly in the sick room, were far more exposed? Were their lives of less value than his? Why did n't the doctor prescribe it for them also?

I know a man of fine intellect and high moral character who had come to a ripe maturity without touching the filthy weed. He is attacked with whooping cough. A wise (?) doctor recommends smoking to quiet the paroxysms of the cough, and himself brings and presents the first cigar to the patient — *his very best medical prescription.* Does he offer one to the woman, suffering from similar paroxysms, and with less strength to bear them? And the children with their fearful coughing fits, — does he bring a cigar for their relief? The poor baby, too, who grows black and all but dies in the struggle for breath ! It is too *young* to smoke? Why not, then, teach the little coughing sister this fine art, and let her smoke in the baby's face? Does not any doctor know that under any such ill-omened spell the tender infant would speedily pine away and die?

But what of the husband and father after his

first and second and third cigar? Why, grand man though he is, — a man, too, of great strength of character, — he becomes an inveterate smoker. And though, with his fine constitution, the ill effects on his health may not at once be obvious, yet, like many another tobacco user, he may be suddenly stricken down with apoplexy or heart disease, when the doctors, perhaps, will pronounce judgment that he died from the effects of smoking.

Then who can tell what injury this loving father may not have entailed on his children by the sure, retributive law of heredity? And what if his boys aspire to a cigar? Shall their smoking father forbid them, holding himself up in *terrorem?*

A minister of rare qualities of head and heart, but of delicate organization and highly nervous temperament, who had unfortunately learned to smoke, consults his trusted physician. What a grand opportunity for helping the man to knock off his fetters! Does he seize the occasion? Why, instead, he tells him that *moderate* smoking, "just a little," will not only not injure, but will help him — will quiet his excited nerves! So the minister's wife, who knows he is the very last man who *ought* to smoke, and who sees that it is only confirming his unfavorable symptoms, is obliged, as she sees the fetters tightening, to hide her anxiety and her sorrow in her own heart.

Now, how can we account for such a course on the part of the accredited guardians of health?

Sometimes it may, without doubt, be explained on the ground of inconsideration. A physician, having recommended one of his patients to smoke, gave as his only reason that, as the patient was old and deaf and infirm, he thought *smoking might be a little amusement for him!*

A young clergyman in feeble health was directed by his medical adviser to smoke. Some doubt being expressed on the subject, the case was referred to an old physician, who indorsed the smoking prescription. It seems this wise old doctor, twenty years before, had recommended the same thing to another minister. The results had proved so disastrous that his attendant felt constrained to write to the veteran physician, asking information as to the medical value of tobacco, which had led to the prescriptions. His answer was: "I have not paid sufficient attention to the subject of smoking to make my opinion of the slightest value." How, then, did he dare indorse such a practice?

THE LATE DR. WILLARD PARKER'S VIEWS.

In reporting a lecture on Tobacco, given to the students of Union Theological Seminary by Dr. Willard Parker, to whom I have already referred, the New York *Observer* remarks: "Dr. Parker is a physician whose fame is not bounded by the metropolis or the nation. There is no higher authority than he in the line of his profession."

From this report, and from other printed matter

on this subject by Dr. Parker, the following passages are taken : —

"It is now many years since my attention was called to the insidious, but positively destructive effects of tobacco on the human system. I have seen a great deal of its influence upon those who use it and work in it. Cigar and snuff manufacturers have come under my care in hospitals and in private practice; and such persons cannot recover soon and in a healthy manner from cases of injury or fever. They are more apt to die in epidemics and more prone to apoplexy and paralysis. The same is true, also, of those who smoke or chew much."

"The use of this weed is particularly injurious to studious men of sedentary habits. The odor infects their clothing, study, and books, so that they live and breathe in a noxious atmosphere. The poison is slow, but in the second or third decade its virus becomes manifest. The words of the wise man, 'Because sentence against an evil work is not executed speedily, therefore the heart of the sons of men is fully set in them to do evil,' are strikingly applicable to those who indulge in this pernicious habit. There have died in New York within a few years three excellent clergymen, all of whom might now have been alive had they not used tobacco. The duty of abstaining from the slow killing of one's self by this poison is as clear as the duty of not cutting one's throat."

"Tobacco is doing more harm in the world than

rum.   It is destroying our race, and it is sure to destroy the farms producing it also, as it has done some of the best land in Virginia."

ILLUSTRATIONS.

A man, distinguished for scholarship, but, unfortunately, equally distinguished for inordinate smoking, paid the penalty in a manifest retarding of his mental movements — his thoughts and words coming so slowly as to be painful to the listener. This clogging of the intellect his physician unhesitatingly attributed to tobacco.

A smoking club of three young men came to its end within two years of its formation, all its members having smoked themselves to death.

A striking account, well authenticated, is given concerning a man in Detroit, of fine constitution and regular and temperate habits, except in the one matter of cigars. For thirty years he had smoked with seeming impunity. *But the day of reckoning came at last!* He complained one night of feeling unwell, and from that moment a gradual numbness stole over him. First his sight left him, next his tongue was paralyzed; then he lost the power of moving his head. Thus member after member was clutched and held as in a vise, till he lay sightless and motionless, helpless — alive, yet dead. One sense alone was untouched, — that of hearing; and he exhausted himself in frantic efforts to reply to the questions put to him. For a little time he rallied, but his constitution, undermined by the narcotic, had lost all recuperative power. He lay for a fortnight, a most pitiable object, and then sank — as all his doctors agreed — a victim of tobacco.

In speaking of Senator Carpenter, the brilliant friend of General Grant, Rev. Mr. Marsh, who has written vigorously on the tobacco habit, remarks: "He died, his system a pitiful wreck, when, as far as years went, he ought to have been in the prime of his power. An acquaintance writes of him, 'Died of smoking twenty cigars a day.'"

Lorenzo and Siro Delmonico, the famous New York caterers, were among the innumerable tobacco victims. Of the latter, Dr. Wood, who had attended him for a long time, testified, "I have known him to smoke as many as a hundred cigars a day. He was completely saturated with nicotine, and the question of his death was only one of time. He used the very strongest cigars, made expressly for him in Havana, and he was perpetually smoking. The disease this produced was called emphysema, — a morbid enlargement of the lung cells, and caused fits of coughing which sometimes nearly strangled him. He had been many years under medical treatment, frequently changing his physician, but never his practice, although often warned of its perils." From a midnight revel Delmonico went to his house, and the next morning was found dead upon the floor.

A prominent and highly esteemed citizen of Syracuse, N. Y., died suddenly of paralysis of the heart, attributed by his family physician to "the too free use of tobacco." He had repeatedly been warned against his habit of excessive smoking, and he had moderated his indulgence, coming down from twenty daily cigars to five. But he could not break his fetters, and he fell, conquered by the destroyer.

TOBACCO DISEASES.

From an able work entitled *Diseases of Modern Life*, by Dr. Richardson, an eminent English physician, I copy the following : —

"Smoking produces disturbances *in the blood*, causing undue fluidity and change in the red corpuscles; in the *stomach* giving rise to debility, nausea, and in extreme cases, vomiting; in the *mucous membrane of the mouth*, causing enlargement and soreness of the tonsils, smokers' sore throat, etc.; in the *heart*, producing debility of that organ, and irregular action; in the *bronchial surface of the lungs*, when that is already irritable, sustaining irritation and increasing cough; in the *organs of sense*, causing, in the extreme degree, dilatation of the pupils of the eye, confusion of vision, bright lines, luminous or cobweb specks, and long retention of images on the retina; with other and analogous symptoms affecting the ear, viz., inability to define sounds clearly, and the occurrence of a sharp ringing sound, like a whistle or a bell; in the *brain*, impairing the activity of that organ; in the *volitional, and in the sympa-*

thetic or organic nerves, leading to paralysis in them."

"This does not leave very much of a man," remarks Mr. Marsh, "but his hair and his bones."

Justice requires the admission that Dr. Richardson regards the diseases induced by this weed as functional and not organic, so that the suspension of its use not unfrequently removes the disease. But he goes on to say, "In the confirmed smoker there is a constant functional disturbance. . . . On the ground of these functional disturbances an argument may be used which cuts sharply because it goes right home. . . . Why should a million of men be living with stomachs that only partially digest, hearts that labor unnaturally, and blood that is not fully oxidized?"

Concerning the alleged influence of tobacco on the hearing, Stillé says that it causes " a buzzing and ringing in the ears, and even hallucinations of this sense."

In his essay on " The Effects of the Abuse of Tobacco," read before the American Institute of Homœopathy, in June, 1884, Dr. T. F. Allen writes, "Much less is known or has been reported concerning the action of tobacco on the ear than on the eye. Sufficient, however, is known to enable us to state that two distinct affections are produced. One, an impairment of the auditory nerve, recognized by a roaring sound, and diminished acuteness of hearing; . . . the other, a chronic catarrhal, inflammation of the middle ear, associated with an angina of the throat. The mucous membrane of the Eustachian tube becomes swollen, and the tube closed; the drum becomes red, thickened, and retracted. With these catarrhal symptoms are noticed roaring in the ears."

Physicians also assert that the use of tobacco tends to injure the voice, rendering it coarse, tremulous, and husky. On this point Dr. Russell, who, for forty years was a professor of Elocution, remarks : " As to the effect of the habitual use of tobacco on the quality and character of the voice, I know it to be injurious in proportion to the extent to which it is carried. Snuff-taking destroys the natural sound, and the pure ring of healthy human utterance. It deadens the voice, and by impairing its clear resonance, mars the distinctness of articulation. Smoking creates a reedy, burning sound, which hinders purity of tone, and renders the voice more or less grating to the ear. Chewing, by its exhausting effect on the salivary glands, causes the quality of the voice to become dry, hard, and bitter."

Dr. Newell, of Boston : "Tobacco has eleven special centres of action in the human system, the chief of which are the heart, eyes, spinal cord, genitalia, lungs, and the circulation. I have seen nicotine lower the circulation and lessen the respiratory powers; wither or paralyze the motor column of the spinal cord, produce atrophy of the retina and blindness. It produces mental aberrations, low spirits, irresolution, the most dismal

hypochondria and insomnia, and sometimes, after
the victim has retired, frightful shocks, likened to
a discharge of electricity. Impregnate fresh-drawn
blood with nicotine, and at once it acquires a dark
hue, while the microscope shows the red corpuscles undergoing rapid disintegration," a phenome-
non which is styled crenation.

On this point, another medical man states that,
where the tobacco habit has been of long standing,
the ratio of degenerated corpuscles to healthy ones
is often as one in twenty-five or thirty, and sometimes comes to be as one in ten.   A wealthy amateur who had been selecting a microscope at an
optician's, left on the slide a drop of his own blood
which he had used as a test.   As he was leaving
the office with a cigar in his mouth, the professor
of microscopy in one of our medical colleges,
happening in, glanced at the slide, moving it to and
fro, and then made a rapid computation.   The
optician looked on with surprise, remarking, " that
gentleman is one of our best customers, he buys
more heavily than half a dozen professors."   "And
this is a drop of his blood?" inquired the man of
science.   The purveyor of lenses assented.   "Very
well," replied the professor, "tell your best cus-
tomer, if you can without impertinence, that unless
he stops smoking at once he has not many months
to live."   But he did not stop.   A few weeks
later he went to Europe, thinking a sea voyage
might recruit his wasted energies.   In a few weeks
more his death was announced by telegraph from

Paris, where the doctors styled his disease a general breaking up.

According to good medical authority, there are more than fifty diseases — some say eighty-seven — which spring from tobacco, or are greatly intensified by its use. Among these are paralysis and apoplexy.

TOBACCO-AMAUROSIS ; COLOR-BLINDNESS.

Stillé maintains that smoking "renders the vision weak and uncertain, causing objects to appear nebulous, or creates *muscæ volitantes* and similar objective phenomena," adding that "in numerous instances it has produced amaurosis."

Chisholm, in his report *On the Poisonous Effect of Tobacco on the Eyesight*, states that " in the past few years he had treated thirty-five cases of amaurosis, directly traceable to the use of tobacco, by smoking, in every case but one."

McSherry : " When the sight fails with smokers, and no appreciable change of structure can be found in the eye, tobacco-poisoning may be assumed. The assumption is converted into certainty by the fact that appropriate remedies fail entirely while the habit of smoking is continued. In rare cases the susceptibility is so great that the smoking of a single cigar a day will produce it."

Dr. Drysdale, in *Tobacco and the Diseases it Produces:* " In one week I saw in the Royal London Ophthalmic Hospital two cases of tobacco-amaurosis in young men under thirty. The first had chewed continually; and the other smoked one ounce of shag tobacco daily. Both were completely and irretrievably blind. Lichel of Paris found some cases of blindness easily cured by cessation from tobacco."

Dr. George Crichett a distinguished London oculist, says he is "constantly consulted for blindness occasioned solely by great smoking."

Dr. T. F. Allen: "We find here the characteristic physiological action of the drug, namely, a persistent contraction of the blood-vessels, producing an anæmia of the nerve structure. This contraction is like a persistent cramp, and may pass off on ceasing to use the drug; but if it continue, malnutrition, and slow degeneration of the nerves is sure to take place."

Dr. Allen gives confirmatory opinions and testimonies from nine or ten eminent physicians, while he frankly admits that there are some who differ from them as to the influence of tobacco.

Dr. Perry, a highly educated physician of Colchester, Illinois, was an excessive smoker and chewer, sometimes in three days using not far from a pound of plug tobacco. As the result, he is totally blind.

In a medical journal, among other similar instances, one is given of a man about forty-two, a smoker of many years, whose eyesight was gradually failing. After two months' cessation from the habit, his vision was restored. But the ardent votary of the weed — refusing to ascribe his difficulty to its true cause, because, forsooth, he had smoked so long without any bad effects — returned to his idol. In a few weeks, however, the recurrence of his trouble convinced him, though much against his will, that it was entirely owing to tobacco.

A distinguished English physician states that "out of thirty-seven patients suffering from amaurosis, twenty-three were inveterate smokers."

A highly intelligent man in Vermont, a confirmed smoker, found that his sight was gradually leaving him. Being a great reader he felt the trial keenly, and was quite willing to follow the total abstinent counsel of his physician, when his sight slowly returned.

A general freight-agent in Indiana, from excessive smoking, found his vision growing dim; but, disregarding the expostulations of his friends and the entreaties of his wife, he held on to his cigar. One day, on lifting a great weight, the heavy strain went to the weakened optic nerve, and he became blind. He immediately abandoned smoking, and put himself under the care of a physician. It was too late, however, and, full of the keenest self-reproach, he caused this account to be published as a warning to others.

It is affirmed, on medical testimony, that *color-blindness* is often caused by the tobacco habit. A well-known public lecturer made the following statement : —

" A leading oculist of the United States asserted before a Science Congress, in one of our cities, that he had examined the eyes of twelve thousand of the boys and girls of that city; that he found four per cent of the boys color-blind, while but ten girls were thus affected. The boys could tell black from white, but they could not tell blue from green, or the different shades of various colors. 'I find,' said he, 'the average boy of twelve with a cigarette in his mouth, which is dipped in nicotine.' "

Notwithstanding the source from which it came, the audience received the statement with such incredulity, that the oculist requested and received permission to bring his science-test to bear on the spot. These were men, not boys; women, not girls; and not four, but ten per cent of the men were color-blind; while not a woman was thus affected.

When we consider that the safety of our trains, with their hundreds and thousands of passengers, is often dependent on the instant and accurate rendering of signals, — the color of a light or of a flag, — we can easily see how utterly such a defect in the vision disqualifies one for this service.

A thorough and annual examination of all these employés would seem indispensable to public safety.

DELIRIUM TREMENS.

That most terrible of diseases, delirium tremens, which was formerly regarded as due only to alcohol, is now, by Dr. Abraham Spoor and other learned doctors, ascribed largely "to the exasperating agency of tobacco upon the human nerves and organism."

One of the resident medical officers of St. Thomas' Hospital, London, reports three cases of delirium tremens induced by tobacco smoke.

I know of a Southern tobacco-grower who, by excessive smoking, is reduced to a deplorable condition. He falls into the deepest gloom, breaking forth in the night into frightful ravings, and threatening his wife with murder. To what a life of wretchedness and terror has he thus doomed her !

A mechanic, standing high in a temperance lodge, was subject to fearful sufferings, his whole family being at times called to his bedside at midnight to witness what seemed his dying agonies. In one of these dreadful paroxysms a doctor was summoned. "Do you use strong drinks? " " No." "Do you belong to the Sons of Temperance?" " Yes." " I supposed you did; you use tobacco. This is a tobacco fit; this is delirium tremens. Drop tobacco, or tobacco will drop you." He did drop it, and has known nothing of delirium tremens since.

HEART DISEASE ; SMOKER'S CANCER.

The physician of an insurance company, after examining a certain applicant, reported against issuing him a policy on the ground of his having what the doctors call "tobacco-heart."

Dr. Townson, another physician to insurance companies, stated that nearly every one of those whom he had rejected had an affection of the heart from excessive smoking.

Dr. E. Smith found that after smoking eleven minutes his pulse had risen from seventy-four to a hundred and twelve beats. Another physician, who counted his pulse every five minutes during an hour's smoking, computed that it had beat a thousand times in excess.

Dr. Magruder, Medical Examiner of the United States Navy, affirms that " one out of every hundred applicants for enlistment is rejected because of irritable heart, arising from tobacco-poisoning."

According to official statement, " Thousands in our civil war were discharged from the army on account of heart-disease, owing largely to the use of tobacco."

Dr. Bowditch, formerly chairman of the State Board of Health, and one of the most eminent physicians in Boston, considers tobacco nearly as dangerous and deadly as alcohol, and pronounces a man with a " tobacco heart" as badly off as a drunkard.

Dr. Twitchell: " The sedative effect of tobacco upon the brain is so great that it often requires an act of the will to stimulate the involuntary muscles to action, so that when sleep arrests this will-power these muscles cease to act, the breathing stops, and the person is found dead in his bed, — ' from heart-disease ' say his friends, but in reality from tobacco-paralysis of the heart and muscles of inspiration."

Dr. Corson relates the case of a smoker who, having suffered greatly for seven years, was one day seized with intense pain in the chest, a gasping for breath, and a sensation as if a crowbar were pressed tightly against his breast and then twisted in a knot round the heart, which would cease beating and then leap wildly, the heart being found to miss every fourth beat. For twenty-seven years, similar, though milder, attacks continued, sometimes two or three times a day. He grew thin and pale as a ghost. At length he gave up tobacco, and in a few weeks the paroxysms ceased, he grew stout and hearty, and for twenty years has enjoyed excellent health.

Mr. Carpenter: "The smoker's sore throat, and diseases of the tongue and gums are notorious."

Lip and tongue cancers are not infrequent results of continuous smoking. Of the latter Dr. Lizars gives some terrible instances. One of the victims he describes as "writhing in agony, unable to speak or swallow, his tongue having mouldered quite away."

We learn from the public journals that Senator Hill's cancer was the result of smoking, "the nicotine being absorbed by a blister on the tongue."

Catelain, "the Parisian Delmonico," died of what is called the smoker's cancer. He had the unenviable distinction of being regarded as the greatest smoker in the world, his daily allowance for thirty years being twenty of the largest cigars, the whole expense being estimated at from forty to fifty thousand dollars.

We are told of a Western clergyman, an excessive smoker, who, dying of this same disease, expressed submission to the will of God " who had decreed his death in that particular manner." He may have been a good man, and sincere in his ignorance, but *ought* he not to have known that he was neither more nor less than a suicide?

IMPAIRED MUSCULAR FORCE.

There is a fact well known to the medical profession which speaks volumes. It is that tobacco-using surgeons are unable to perform any nice operation, unless the nerves, unstrung by the narcotic, are first steadied by some powerful drug or alcoholic stimulant.

Some physicians maintain that a smoker cannot be a successful oculist, as firmness of nerve is one of the essentials in the treatment of so delicate an organ as the eye.

An impairing of the muscular force is often seen in the tremulous hand-writing of the tobacco-votary. So significant is this, that applicants for the situation of book-keeper have sometimes been rejected because of the habit thus indicated. That there is the same betrayal of the habit in drawing, we find in a letter of Medical Inspector Gorgas, who writes to the superintendent of the Naval Academy at Annapolis: "The professor of draw-

ing informs me that he has observed among the
smokers an impaired power of muscular control,
which has retarded their progress and proficiency
in this branch."

Dr. Gihon also says : " The defective muscular
co-ordination occasioned by this drug is remarkably
illustrated by the fact — which I learn from Professor
Oliver, head of the department of drawing — that
he can invariably recognize the user of tobacco by
his tremulous hand in manipulating the pencil, and
by his " absolute inability to draw a clean, straight
line."

It is well understood that, in the regimen of
athletes, pugilists, and oarsmen in preparation for
boat-races, no rule is more rigid than that which
prescribes an utter abstaining from all forms of
tobacco ; and this solely because of its enervating
influence on the nerves and muscles. Says Parton,
" No smoker who has ever trained severely for a
race, or a game, or a fight needs to be told that
smoking reduces the tone of the system and
diminishes all the forces of his body. He *knows*
it."

Dr. W. F. Carver, the famous marksman, says :
" I have never tasted intoxicating drinks, nor do I
use tobacco in any form."

An Ohio gentleman tells me of a brother of
great nerve, who had been an excellent shot. He
became a smoker, and meeting him after a long
separation, the brother found him with trembling
hands and shattered nerves. On challenging him

to a shooting match as of old, he accepted. He could not even aim straight, still less could he hit a mark, however near. The virtue had all gone out of him. He made up his mind to stop short, but his sufferings were pitiable, the miserable slave continually fumbling in his pockets after the longed-for weed.

Mr. Hanlan, the victor of the international boat-race, said before he left England : " In my opinion, the best physical performances can only be secured through the absolute abstinence from alcohol and tobacco. This is my rule. In fact, I believe that the use of liquor and tobacco has a most injurious effect upon the system of an athlete, by irritating the vitals and consequently weakening the system."

Does not the same reasoning apply even more strongly to the soldier? No man, surely, has greater need of unflinching nerve and never-failing endurance. For no man is the best possible physical condition of more supreme importance. The Duke of Wellington complained of the excessive use of tobacco by his soldiers, and attempted to restrain it. Another distinguished English officer, Gen. Markham, was so convinced of the injurious effects of this drug, that he neither smoked himself nor allowed any of his personal staff to do so.

Mr. Meadows tells us, in the British *Quarterly Review*, that, in China, " the soldier who smokes tobacco is bambooed."

In a letter to Dr. Lizars, Mr. Anton writes : " I am convinced that a soldier who is an inveterate smoker is incapable to level his musket with precision and without shaking his hand, so as to take steady aim. I recall instances of nervous trepidation which rendered many a brave man useless as a marksman or musketeer."

Corroborating this statement is a quotation from Mr. O'Flaherty, who says that "he has known men who, previous to their using tobacco, could send a bullet through the target at eight hundred yards' distance; but who, after they had become smokers and chewers, became so nervous that they could scarcely send one into a hay-stack at a hundred yards' distance."

During our civil war, a large number of the diseases in the soldiers' hospitals were attributed, in a great degree, to the inordinate use of this drug, which was often sent to them through the mistaken kindness and sympathy of distant friends. And many a man is now a miserable slave to the tyrant, who took his first lessons in that same war.

SHATTERED NERVES; INSANITY.

There are eminent physicians to whom almost every day brings fresh confirmation of the fact that nervous and brain diseases are not infrequently caused by the tobacco habit.

Prof. Kirke, in *Nerves and Narcotics:* " You see a man weary, and yet restless. By means of the narcotic this nervous irritation is subdued. The supply of vital force from the organic centres to the motor nerves is so much lessened that the irritating movement in them ceases. This gives a sense of relief to the person affected. He is not aware that the benefit is purchased at a very serious cost. He has not only lessened the supply of vital force for the time being, but has done a very considerable amount of injury to his vital system. He has, in fact, poisoned the springs of life within him. As soon as these nerves rally from the lowering effect of the narcotic, the irritation returns, and the narcotic is called for anew. Fresh injury is inflicted for the sake of the ease desired. This goes on till the vital centres, if at all delicate, totally fail to give supply to the motor nerves, and paralysis begins. Yet the man goes on indulging in the so-called luxury of the narcotic."

Dr. Allen: "Many smokers, naturally bold and resolute, lose their fortitude, become unable to bear pain, are nervous in the society of others, and even afraid of being left alone at night."

Dr. Lizars: "I have invariably found that patients addicted to smoking became cowardly, and deficient in manly fortitude to undergo any surgical operation, however trifling."

Dr. Brodie: "The earliest symptoms are manifested in the derangement of the nervous system. Almost the worst case of neuralgia that ever came under my observation was that of a gentleman who consulted the late Dr. Bright and myself. The pains were universal and never absent, but during the night they were specially intense, so as almost wholly to prevent sleep. Neither the patient himself nor his medical attendants had any doubt that the disease was to be attributed to his habit of smoking, on the discontinuance of which he gradually recovered."

Another physician : " The natural vibration between excessive action of the brain and corresponding depression, caused by tobacco, is mental unbalancing and overthrow. Memory is weakened, the perceptions are blunted, cowardice is engendered, the power of the will enervated, and insanity is the result."

From a long array of nervous cases by distinguished physicians, I have gathered the following symptoms : — great mental depression, weakness of voluntary muscles, neuralgia local and general, trembling, vertigo, difficulty in standing steadily or moving directly, shaking palsy, convulsions, uncontrollable nervous tremors, a cataleptic condition, hysterics, twitching of the flexor muscles of the whole body, palpitation, movements and gesticulations like St. Vitus' dance, startings from sleep, insomnia, epileptic fits, choking sensations, rush of blood to the head, cramps, numbness, paralysis, shocks in the epigastrium like electricity.

In almost every case a suspension of the tobacco-habit brought relief, while with a return to it the symptoms came back.

We learn that Mr. Andreas Hofer, who was grandson of the Tyrolean patriot shot by order of

Napoleon I., and who was long a member of the Austrian Parliament, has become insane from his excessive use of tobacco.

An Ohio friend tells me of a young man in business whose excessive smoking and chewing so broke him down mentally and morally that it was necessary to dismiss him from the firm of of which he was a member. In the course of a year, about eight thousand dollars, awarded him as his share of the profits, were all squandered. The father, from fear of personal violence, was compelled to place him in an insane asylum. His single chance for recovery was entire abstinence; yet the father, in his blind fondness, with his own hand supplied him with cigars, and the doctors did not interfere!

A young man promised his father that he would abstain from smoking till he was twenty-one. That time had no sooner arrived than he set himself to learn, and though nature made a fierce revolt, and he suffered terribly in the process, he persevered till he succeeded, when his health broke down and he became a confirmed epileptic. Well does Lord Bacon say: — "To smoke is a secret delight, serving to steal away men's brains," and another: "Tobacco carries but a thin edge of enjoyment ahead, and a blunt edge of dull stupidity and crackling sorrow and nervous derangement behind."

A member of the Paris Academy of Medicine: " Statistics show that in exact proportion with the increased consumption of tobacco is the increase of diseases in the nervous centres, — insanity, general paralysis, paraplegia, and certain cancerous affections."

At a meeting of the Medical and Chirurgical Society of London, Dr. Webster read a paper on the *Statistics and Morbid Anatomy of Mental Diseases*, in which he cites the great use of tobacco as prominent among the causes, supporting his opinion from statistics as to insanity in Germany.

Strong testimony on this subject follows from various institutions for the insane. From the Superintendent of the Pennsylvania Insane Hospital: "The earlier boys begin to use tobacco, the more strongly marked are its effects upon the nerves and brain." From a report by Dr. Kirkbride of this Hospital: "Six cases of insanity were clearly attributable to the use of tobacco."

From Dr. Harlow, at the head of the Maine Insane Asylum: " The pernicious effect of tobacco on the brain and nervous system is obvious to all who are called to treat the insane."

From the Superintendent of the New York Insane Asylum: "Tobacco has done more to precipitate mind into the vortex of insanity than spirituous liquors."

From Dr. Bancroft, for many years at the head of the Insane Asylum, Concord, New Hampshire: "I have known several cases of insanity most unquestionably produced by the use of tobacco without other complicating causes, and which have been cured by the suspension of the habit; while the number in which it was prominent among the causes is much larger."

From Dr. Woodward, of the Insane Asylum at Worcester, Massachusetts: "That tobacco produces insanity I am fully confident. Its influence upon the brain and nervous system is hardly less than that of alcohol, and, if excessively used, is equally injurious."

At one time, eight cases of insanity from tobacco were found in this Asylum.

According to the New York *World*, "in nine cases out of eleven, where insanity has resulted from inebriation, the primary cause was smoking." This journal also gives the number of patients in insane asylums, under treatment for "confirmed inebriation resulting in insanity," whose use of tobacco had led them to intemperance.

In Bloomingdale Asylum, out of	100	87
In Flatbush Asylum, out of	64	49
In Trenton Asylum, out of	50	48
In Columbus Asylum, out of	74	62

From a French publication, we learn that the increase of insanity in France has kept pace with the increase of the revenue from tobacco. In presenting to the Academy of Science the statistics which prove this assertion, M. Jolly remarks,— that "the immoderate use of tobacco produces an affection of the spinal marrow and a weakness of the brain which causes madness."

In speaking of mania as a result of using tobacco,

Dr. Lizars of Edinburgh gives an account of two brothers connected with a family where there was no tendency to insanity, who, through this narcotic, lost their reason and committed suicide.

He also relates the case of a gentleman of thirty-five who drank, smoked, and chewed, till attacked by fits resembling epilepsy, when he was taken to an insane retreat. He gave up drink, but no improvement occurred till he abandoned tobacco, when the fits ceased and sanity returned.

TOBACCO-HEREDITY.

A leading physician in one of our largest cities, in speaking of those who had indulged in the use of tobacco for years with seeming impunity, adds: " But I have never known a habitual tobacco user whose children, born after he had long used it, did not have deranged nervous systems and sometimes evidently weak minds. Shattered nervous systems for generations to come may be the result of this indulgence."

It is claimed by some doctors that the effects of tobacco on posterity are even greater than those of alcohol; that it destroys more vital force, and thus saps the very foundations, transmitting a tendency to disease. Sometimes, the dreadful appetite itself is entailed upon the child.

Dr. Hall : "The parent whose blood and secretions are saturated with tobacco, and whose brain and nervous system are narcotized by it, must transmit to his child elements of a distempered body and erratic mind ; a deranged condition of organic atoms, which elevates the animalism of future being at the expense of the moral and intellectual nature."

Brodie: "This is a sin which afflicts the third and fourth generation."

Spain is one vast tobacco shop, which fact is said to account largely for the degeneracy of the nation. So long ago as the sixteenth century, the sultan Amarath inflicted severe punishment on those who used tobacco, from its known effects in deteriorating and depleting the population. In a report of the Medical Director of the United States Navy, we find the following testimony on the same point : "The pernicious effect of tobacco on the generative function is authoritatively asserted by Acton, who declared, — 'I am quite sure that excessive smokers, if very young, never acquire, and, if older, rapidly lose, their normal virile powers.'"

A good man, unconscious of the wrong he was doing, smoked for many a year, often suffering intensely, but without understanding the cause. A tract on the subject, which fell into his hands, brought him needed light and led him to give up tobacco. This prolonged his life, but the change came too late for his son, who, as a consequence of his father's habit, inherits an impaired constitution. A life-long sufferer on this account, he is untiring in his efforts to convince others of the great evil of the tobacco habit, declaring that he is "before Richmond on this question until the King of Battles gives him an honorable discharge."

"I can point you," says a physician, "to two families right under my eye, where in each case there is a nest of little children rendered idiots by the tobacco habits of their parents."

A doctor found among the patients at an infirmary a young man suffering from tobacco symptoms. "What will you say to this case?" inquired a medical friend; "the youth has never chewed, smoked, or taken snuff." "His father did it for him," replied the doctor. Turning to the father the question was asked, "How long have you smoked?" "These-five-and twenty years." "Have you ever smoked an ounce of tobacco a day?" "Yes, many times."

Dr. Richardson : "If a community of youths of both sexes, whose progenitors were finely formed and powerful, were to be trained to the early practice of smoking, and if marriage were to be confined to the smokers, an apparently new, and a physically inferior, race of men and women would be bred."

Dr. Cowan : "Of all the harm done by the use of tobacco, the greater harm and the mightiest wrong is that of transmitting, to the unborn, the appetite for the filthy, disease-creating, misery-engendering drug."

A business man who was an excessive smoker, but whose work was mostly in the open air, had no consciousness of injurious effects. Of his two sons, however, one had paroxysms of insanity, and the other drunkenness. The mother was a healthy woman, and no trace of insanity or of drinking habits could be found in the family on either side; so that, by good medical authority, the condition of the sons was attributed to the use of tobacco by the father.

Of two Reverend D.D.'s who were inordinate users of tobacco, the children of one were dissipated and intemperate, while those of the other suffered every form of pain and agony, resulting from weak and disordered nerves. In both cases, the evil was pronounced hereditary, — the result of the selfish indulgence of the fathers.

"The men of the West," writes one, "are not only filling themselves with this horrid poison, but in numberless ways are transmitting the deadly influence to their offspring. How any man who knows that the condition of the parent influences, for good or ill, his offspring, can become the father of children while his system is so dominated by this powerful narcotic that abstinence for twenty-four hours nearly sets him crazy, I cannot conceive."

Says the *Journal of Science and Health*, "There are Christians and temperance men who are trying to redeem the world from sin and drunkenness, yet who are begetting children so depraved in their physical organization that their desire for stimulants it is almost impossible for them to resist."

An authentic account is given of the child of an inveterate smoker, a mere infant, whose stomach rejected food, and who was pining away for lack of nourishment. To quiet it, the father held a cigar between its lips. The babe greedily sucked it, and by means of the stimulus was able to take food. But this tobacco, for which it inherited so unnatural a craving, proved a necessity. It could not get on without it. I hardly need add that under its influence the child gradually became dwarfed and idiotic. " The fathers have eaten sour grapes, and the children's teeth are set on edge." Are we doomed, in the future, to have a race of idiots?

One of our public journals gives the account of a four-year-old who inherited the narcotic appetite, cigars being "*necessarily* given from infancy to keep him quiet." This continued, till he came to smoke twenty stoga cigars a day, and then cry for more. Spinal disease setting in, he was taken to a surgical institute. When the doctors took away his cigars, "the child kicked and howled like a maniac."

A physician relates the case of a smoker whose children " were cursed from their birth. His idiotic boy would scoop up the loathsome ashes scraped from his father's pipe and eat them with avidity ! "

Surely Dr. Pidduck is justified in his assertion in *The Lancet* of 1856, that " in no instance is the sin of the father more strikingly visited upon his children than the sin of tobacco-smoking." He adds, — " The enervation, the hypochondriasis, the hysteria, the insanity, the dwarfish deformities, the consumption, the suffering lives and early deaths of the children of inveterate smokers, bear ample testimony to the feebleness and unsoundness of the constitution transmitted by this pernicious habit."

A man of fine abilities, a member of one of the learned professions, had early formed the habit of both smoking and chewing. It grew upon him till it had gained a complete mastery. His child was diseased from infancy, had terrible convulsions, became deformed and idiotic. The father suffered from entire nervous derangement, and finally sank into a decline. It was a bitter harvest that he reaped for his indulgence, — the ruin of himself and child. " Oh, if I could only live my life over," he exclaimed, " I would never touch the weed. Would that I could warn every boy and every young man against this dreadful evil ! "

Alas ! this Havana cloud on the horizon, is it not a very dreadful one ?

SURGEON-GENERAL'S REPORT.

In the Report of the Surgeon-General of the United States Army for 1881, Dr. Albert L. Gihon, senior medical officer of the Naval Academy at Annapolis, Md., is referred to, as having made a special study of the physical development of applicants for admission to that institution, and also of the cadets at stated intervals. Dr. Gihon's report to the surgeon-general contains a graphic portraiture of the effects of tobacco, more especially on the young. Some extracts from this report will make a fitting close of this chapter.

"Unquestionably the most important matter in the health history of the students at this academy is that relating to the use of tobacco. I have urged upon the superintendent, as my last official utterance, the fact, of the truth of which five years' experience as health-officer of this station has satisfied me, that, beyond all other things, the future health and usefulness of the lads educated at this school require the absolute interdiction of tobacco.

"In this opinion I have been sustained, not only by all my colleagues, but by all other sanitarians in military and civil life whose views I have been able to learn; while I know it to be the belief of the officer who is to succeed me in the charge of this department, and who was one of the Board of Medical Officers which, in 1875, reported that 'the regulations against the use of tobacco in any form could not be too stringent.' Since then, three successive annual Boards of Visitors have indorsed the prohibition of tobacco, as a wise sanitary provision; and the last of these Boards, on being informed that the regulation against its use was not then in operation (June, 1879), emphatically recommended that ' its strict enforcement be at once restored.'

"With a sense of the serious responsibility which devolves on the sanitary officer of this establishment, conscious that the bodily welfare and happiness of these young men and of their future offspring may be permanently influenced by this vicious indulgence, I have most earnestly advised that the strongest efforts of the authorities of the academy shall be directed towards the prevention of this pernicious, indefensible, and wholly unnecessary habit.

"By the continued excitation of the optic nerve, tobacco produces amaurosis,—a fact demonstrated by Wordsworth, Mackenzie, Hutchinson, Sichel, and Chisholm.

"I have myself several times rejected candidates for admission into the academy on account of defective vision, who confessed to the premature use of tobacco, one of them from the age of seven.

"The irregularity in the heart's action, which tobacco causes, is one of its most conspicuous effects. Candidates are annually rejected for cardiac disturbances, who have subsequently admitted the use of tobacco; and the annual physical examinations of cadets reveal a large number of irritable hearts ('tobacco hearts') among boys, who had no such trouble when they entered the school. Among the applicants for enlistment as apprentices in the navy during the year 1879, ten in a thousand were rejected for functional lesions of the heart, indicating tobacco-poisoning.

"Finally, the antidotal effect of tobacco makes drinking of stimulating liquors the natural consequence of smoking."

"While it is indisputably the fact that a large number of the cadets have learned to smoke before admission to the academy, its compulsory inhibition during their academic career will be of incalculable benefit to them, as well as to all others who now unfortunately acquire the habit here through the example of their schoolmates. It is almost impossible for the cadets, however young, — and some enter at fourteen, — to avoid contracting the habit, if his room-mate indulges ; and the extent of this indulgence was instanced by one of the officers in charge, who told me that some of the rooms were so foul and offensive that it was unpleasant to enter them. The medical officer of the day was, not long since, called late at night to attend a cadet in a state of extreme prostration caused by tobacco ; and, although himself a smoker, he declared the atmosphere of the room to be repulsively stifling from tobacco smoke. I have seen youths, fresh from graduation from this school, go on board ships smoking rank, blackened pipes that would have nauseated many an adult.

"That the user of tobacco is incapable of concentrated mental effort is demonstrated by the fact told me by a member of the Academic Board, that cadets have complained of their inability to apply themselves to study and attain the class-standing they desired on account of the excessive smoking in their rooms, in which they were compelled to indulge.

"An agent that has mischievously been represented to be innocuous only because of the remarkable tolerance exhibited by a few individuals, and is actually capable of such potent evil; which, through its sedative effect upon the circulation, creates a thirst for alcoholic stimulation; which, by its depressing and disturbing effect upon the nerve centres, increases sexual propensities, and induces secret practices, while permanently imperilling virile power; which determines functional disease of the heart; which impairs vision, blunts the memory, and interferes with mental effort and application, — ought, in my opinion as a sanitary officer, at whatever cost of vigilance, to be rigidly interdicted."

Writes Rev. Dr. J. W. Chickering: "The Nicotine plant is poisoning the life-springs of coming generations; sowing the seeds of more bodily diseases than even strong drink, — so say careful observers of physical causes and effects; while those in charge of asylums for the insane, for idiots and feeble-minded persons, trace mental and moral, as well as physical, effects to the same source. Add to this the filthiness of these habits and the selfish disregard to the comfort of others, so generally characteristic of the tobacco habit, and it becomes a profound mystery how any conscientious, patriotic, and Christian man can contribute to the hundreds of millions annually spent, and to the pernicious example constantly presented in this direction."

TOBACCO BENEFITS.

ARE there no benefits, you will ask, resulting
from the use of tobacco?

I have alluded to the security it affords against
being devoured by wolves, buzzards, and cannibals,
of which advantage its defenders are at liberty to
make the most.

It is useful in destroying sheep-ticks and any
creature that molests man. The vapor of tobacco-
juice has been tested in France with great success
as an insect-destroyer in hothouses, effectually
disposing of thrips, scales, and slugs. It also
scares away moths, carpet-bugs, and other vermin,
and thus preserves furs and woollens.

By excluding ladies from festive breakfast and
dinner parties, it withdraws from gentlemen a
disagreeable restraint.

An acquaintance argues that smoking tends to
round off sharp, doctrinal edges, and thus to

mellow one's theology; instancing an eminent Western divine who has become a total abstainer, and who, he says, grows more and more conservative and afraid of progress. He claims that if this divine had continued to smoke, the extreme blueness of his dogmas would have passed off in the blue vapor of his cigar!

Still another benefit, according to a doctor of divinity whose long experience entitles him to implicit credit, is that the habit gives to a man "a sense of deep humiliation of which his unpartaking brethren can know very little."

"If any one smokes to overcome a bad smell," says Russell Lant Carpenter, — "he only adds to the nuisance; the ashes and smoke are two dirts the more."

PROTECTING AGAINST MALARIA AND TYPHOID.

There are those who plead that tobacco is a safeguard against malarial diseases.

Dr. Solly makes answer, — "I dispute the alleged benefits of even moderate tobacco-smoking as a preventive of damp or malaria."

In a city daily appears the following item of consolation for lovers of the weed: "A Virginia physician says he has never known an habitual consumer of tobacco to have typhoid fever."

A Massachusetts doctor reports the case of "an habitual consumer" who has had typhoid every summer for five years. Dr. H. J. Cate, of Saratoga, knows "an habitual consumer" who "for a series of years, has had an annual attack of this fever." Another physician, living in a mining country where all use the weed, affirms that he could report hundreds of similar cases. Indeed, so far from tobacco's being a protection against such diseases, it is the opinion of many eminent doctors that, by enfeebling the system, it renders men more susceptible to this as well as other diseases.

AIDING DIGESTION.

Dr. Alcott : "I have never known a dozen tobacco-users — my acquaintance has extended to thousands — whose digestive organs were not in the end more or less impaired by it."

Dr. Grimshaw : "Tobacco is injurious by depressing the nervous powers, by injuring the salivary glands, and by creating an undue secretion of saliva."

Dr. Harris of the New York Dispensary : — "The functions of digestion and nutrition are impaired; and though, in some cases, tobacco may for a time appear to relieve irritability of the stomach, it eventually cripples and almost destroys the digestive powers."

QUIETING THE NERVES.

The answer to this plea is found in the evidences which have been adduced to prove that, however soothing may be its temporary influence, the ultimate effect is the exhaustion and shattering of the nervous system.

AN ANTISEPTIC; PRESERVING OF THE TEETH.

" Tobacco-smoke is not a vile, noxious exhalation," declares someone. " It does not contaminate the air, but tends to purify it. It is an antiseptic principle, taking up and destroying poisons in the air."

As to the remarkable negative assertion in the above passage, let it be referred to those whose senses have not been impaired by the use of the weed. Just what the writer means by terming tobacco-smoke " a principle " one can only guess. But what of the benefit he claims?

It has been my great aim to prove that tobacco in all its forms— snuffing, chewing, and smoking, — is poisonous. If the proofs are not convincing, let them be challenged. But I make my appeal to Cæsar.

As to preserving the teeth, the claim was utterly denied by Dr. Warren, of Boston, who asserted that it was positively injurious to them.

In order to treat this subject with entire candor, I have written to a good number of eminent dentists. From their uniformly kind and courteous replies I will quote several passages, giving the names when at liberty to do so.

Dr. French, of Rochester, New York, while himself a smoker, and claiming that tobacco is antiseptic, states, in the *Odontographic Journal*, that a physician for whom he was operating called his attention to certain teeth which were decayed at the neck of the roots, and which he asserted to be caused by tobacco, as that was where he always carried the weed.

Another gentleman, having the same difficulty pointed out, said to Dr. French, "That is where I used to carry my tobacco; I have used it for forty years, but have quit now."

"I may add," continues Dr. F., "that I have smoked for thirty years, and the upper tooth where I always hold my cigar lost its vitality five or six years ago, but the lower one is perfectly sound. A friend who is an inveterate smoker has lost entirely, by gradual crumbling, the upper tooth where he held his cigar, while the lower one is all right."

"In regard to the beneficial tendencies, there is nothing which the use of the brush and proper dentifrice would not accomplish."

"The salivary and mucous glands are debilitated, and the gums and other soft tissues of the mouth are irritated, inflamed, and debased by the over-stimulation of the constant use of tobacco."

Dr. Barrett, of Buffalo: "Tobacco is undoubtedly antiseptic in the mouth, but I am inclined to think that the remedy is worse than the disease. I am given to smoking myself, but it keeps the mouth in an unhealthy condition."

Dr. Barnes, of New York: "Chewing tobacco removes particles of food, and smoking often adds a coating over softened portions, thereby rendering them less liable to caries. But we have plenty of remedies more cleanly and wholesome." Dr. B. names a case where smoking prevented toothache, but gives the smoker's remark that the effect was bad, as it stupefied the nerve, thus giving him no warning of danger, the breaking of the teeth being his first knowledge of trouble. Dr. B. adds, " To my mind, the disadvantages greatly overwhelm the advantages."

Dr. Lillebrown, of Boston : " Tobacco chewing, by causing a free flow of saliva, washes the teeth. But no benefit can even secondarily compensate for the uncleanness of the habit."

Dr. J. Foster Flagg, of Philadelphia : " Indirectly tobacco is, I think, advantageous to the teeth in cases of rapid decay, especially when complicated with pulpsensitivity. But the disadvantages inseparably associated with its use, are of such magnitude as to make with me, the advice or even *permission* to employ it, a matter of grave moment and *intense reluctance.*"

Dr. Chandler, of the Dental Department in Harvard University : " I am no believer in the preservative qualities of tobacco upon the teeth. On the contrary, in so far as the use of it injures the health, and thereby vitiates the oral secretions, it must be directly injurious. There is no doubt, however, that smoking in excess, and perhaps also chewing, blunts the sensitiveness of the teeth both directly and indirectly, by its stupefying properties, so that they can be worked upon with less pain ; but I consider this no compensation for the nastiness consequent upon indulgence in the vile habit."

The remainder of the extracts from letters on this point are by physicians, not dentists.

Dr. Heitzman, of New York: "Being a hearty smoker myself, I can assure you that tobacco smoke has no beneficial effect upon the teeth. In my case, it did not work as a disinfectant." Dr. H. is candid enough to pronounce smoking "a vicious though delightful habit."

Dr. T. F. Allen, of New York: "The statement that tobacco is antiseptic, is I think, simply ridiculous. There is no doubt that creosote, or rather the products of combustion in smoking, have an antiseptic effect; but the same effect would be produced by burning paper, cabbage-leaves, or anything else of the sort."

Dr. Cate, of Lakewood: "No authority on sanitation or disinfection, whether medical or non-medical, classes tobacco among disinfectants, or antiseptics, or protectives in any mode or degree; and those who have written most, and most vigorously, against the use of tobacco, are physicians. Tobacco is, confessedly on all hands, not only a drug, but a very powerful narcotic. And there is a universal law that the use of any drug in *health* is always mischievous.

"It is the doctrine of the day that ferments are not only accompanied but caused by minute organisms, and that any agent killing these, or their spores, will remove or prevent fermentation. As tobacco is a narcotic poison, it will certainly destroy these organisms or their germs. So will kerosene, carbolic acid, and other strong acids. But no one regards these things as wholesome when taken into the system. The effect sought is local, and only their local use is justifiable. The perspiration of old tobacco users is so saturated with nicotine that it will destroy the life of flies precisely by the same poisonous properties by which it destroys fungi in the secretions of the mouth; and there is no more wisdom in poisoning the whole body in order to destroy caries fungi of the teeth than there would be in setting up our bodies as manufactories of fly-poison to destroy flies in our rooms. Any fungicide can unquestionably be used more efficiently as well as harmlessly with the brush and by rinsing the mouth than when taken into the stomach and lungs. I believe that no physiologist can, or does deduce from the general laws of health and disease any conclusion but that the use of tobacco in every form is mischievous."

HELPFUL STIMULANT.

In regard to the arguments of those who have raised the lance in defence of tobacco as a helpful stimulant, quoting Dr. Anstie and his followers, I have taken pains to consult many wise ones, and will report from high authority a brief reply to this defence.

"Physiologists and the medical profession generally accept as axioms the principles that in small doses all the narcotics represented by opium, tobacco, the deadly nightshade, strychnine, and other similar drugs, are stimulants, not tonics, that is, in these small doses, they increase the rate of action, or living, without adding to the strength or means of living; that the decree of stimulation varies in different members of the group of narcotics, it being very slight and transient in tobacco, the 'soothing,' or narcotic effect being the result usually sought and speedily reached; that the assertion that 'food and stimulus are equally indispensable' is a monstrous fallacy; that any drug stimulation in health is unnecessary and mischievous; that all such stimulation is followed by a gradual loss of healthful vigor in the tissues and the organs involved; and that while these effects may accumulate slowly, the aggregate results of many years of even moderate indulgence is almost invariably seen in broken health and lessened efficiency, as well as in the presence of positive disease."

In reply to the claim that tobacco stimulates the mental powers, Dr. Harris writes: "A moderate indulgence *may*, for a brief period, enliven the imagination, accelerate the thoughts, and give a pleasing sense of intellectual vigor, but, under such unnatural stimulus, the intellect works neither reliably nor safely; and the reaction and stupor which necessarily succeed, more than counterbalance the largest measure even of apparent gain. And he who resorts to such expedients will soon find that not only has he been fascinated and deceived, but that he has literally sold himself into a physical and mental *bondage,* from which escape is almost impossible."

CHECKING WASTE OF TISSUE.

As to anything more in favor of tobacco, justice requires me to admit that I have learned of still one other benefit. It is that " by checking molecular waste of tissue, that is, by retarding organic metamorphosis, the adult is able to maintain his physical integrity." This very effect, however, is admitted to be " detrimental to the adolescent, since it retards that progressive cell-change upon which the advanced development of the body depends."

I am not wise enough to apprehend the whole force of this argument, though I should have supposed that anything which retards nature's processes would, except in abnormal cases, prove in the end a loss rather than a gain. We learn from physiologists that rapid waste and repair of tissues are a natural result of action, and the best condition of health ; while suspension is unnatural and in violation of hygienic laws. It is this fact that renders exercise and open air life so desirable ; that sends invalids and worn-out people in such throngs to the seaside, the mountains and the woods. Except in cases of famine, therefore, any obstruction to the removal of effete matter would seem an injury rather than a benefit.

The claim of gain on the score of economy, from

less food being required by this checking of the waste of tissue, reminds one of Mr. Squeer's custom in Dotheboys Hall of dosing his boys every morning with sulphur and treacle, in order to limit their capacity for eating.

We find it complacently stated in the public prints that, "as the result of investigations recently made, the professors of the University of Jena affirm that moderate quantities of this weed may be used with beneficial effects; that in the German army soldiers in active service are very properly furnished with smoking tobacco, because smoking enables them to endure severe fatigue upon smaller nutrition and with greater alacrity and confidence than would otherwise be the case." The ultimate influence of tobacco upon the muscular force has been already considered, "the greater alacrity and confidence" being but transient effects of the narcotic, as they are also of brandy and whiskey.

Dr. Richardson: "If smoking sustains the system longer without food, it does it by reducing the activity of all the organs, and therewith the organic power."

In answer to inquiries, Dr. John Ellis writes: "I suppose, without any reasonable doubt, that tobacco, like opium and some other substances, does actually retard the waste, and thereby the nourishment of the tissues; but this is really one of the chief objections against its use, for it is exactly *what we do not want to do*, since the health and strength depend on, or are intimately associated with, the regularity and rapidity of this metamorphosis of the tissues."

Dr. Willard Parker, from whom I have already quoted so freely, asserts that there is no occasion for this talked-of arrest of waste, except for the starving, and affirms that free waste and renewal are among the most essential hygienic conditions. "Where the processes of waste and of repairs are maintained in balance," he says, "the system is in its normal state, or in health. Disturb the balance, and disease commences. Every system is worked by force, and this is the one cause of waste. Diminish waste, and you diminish force. The work of all poisons is to diminish force. Now, if tobacco diminishes waste, it is because it diminishes force, and so far marches toward death. Let us have no more of such sophistry."

In conversing on the subject, Dr. Parker made use of an illustration which I will give in my own words: I have a house which will accommodate five persons. Every day I take in five and every day send out the same number, and the house is in good condition. But I take in five and send out three, and the condition is disturbed. I take in five more, but must push aside the two dead to make room for the incoming five. I now send out two, and have three more dead to pile up with the former two. How long will the dwelling be inhabitable? It is already a sick-house. The dead who are retained are not only no addition to the strength of the house, but are a positive obstruction, a source of disease and death.

In the same strain Dr. Cate writes: "If the change is no more rapid than in health, it is a physiological, not a diseased process; it is one of a chain of interlinked and interdepending processes which cannot be interfered with without upsetting the beautifully contrived balance, and leading to mischievous results. Every physiologist knows that the use and wear exactly correspond; that you cannot diminish one without diminishing the other. All narcotics diminish the energy of all the functions of every organ. They lessen the vigor and amount of the work done, and exactly to this extent diminish the waste. Going beyond certain narrow limits, the result is far worse, — they act so powerfully on every organ and function that the derangement amounts to disease, the power of doing healthy work is lost, and not only the waste, but repair is decidedly diminished. The difficulty after youth is not that waste is unduly active, but that repair is too little so. It follows that, instead of diminishing waste by diminishing through narcotics the energy of brain and body, and hence the amount of work done, the increase of the reparative energy is the needed power in advancing years.

"Every physiologist accepts the law that with every thought, with every emotion, with every throb of the heart, with every movement of a muscle, with every step in the process of digestion, there is waste of tissue in exact and inevitable correlation to the amount of work done; and this

waste can only be diminished by diminishing action
or production. It is like the consumption of fuel
and the production of heat. It is easy to diminish
the draft of the furnace or engine, and so the consumption of fuel; but the production of heat is
diminished in the same proportion. This is precisely what is done to the functions of the body
by narcotics, including tobacco. They lower the
vigor and energy of every organ, and so its production, and in the same degree the waste.

"I believe this is the correct statement of the
action of tobacco in the much talked-of relation
to waste : that from the *scientific* standpoint these
conclusions are inevitable ; and that from the *medical*, the experience of ninety-nine out of a hundred
of the profession clearly affirms their truth."

I am aware that Dr. Tanner's endurance under
his long fast is accounted for by the sustaining
virtues of tissue. And the same advantage, resulting, it is said, from the use of tobacco—that it
tends to prevent the destruction of tissue—is
urged for the use of wine and spirits. To this,
as argued in the *Saturday Review*, Punch responds :—

> "Oh, thanks, dear *Review*, for that comforting creed,
>   For joining with temperance-humbug the issue ;
> In Johnson and Webster in future we'll read
>   For 'drinking,' 'preventing destruction of tissue.'

> "O Daniel in judgment! for teaching that word
>   You cannot conceive what good fortune we wish you.
> *Punch* fills up a bumper, the downy old bird,
>   And 'prevents,' in your honor, 'destruction of tissue.'"

BENEFITING ADULTS.

A well-known physician, *himself a smoker*, while he pronounces tobacco "highly injurious to persons whose nervous systems are not developed, or to women, who naturally have more delicate nervous organizations than men," avows that he believes it is beneficial to most adults.

Another physician of high standing, himself *a non-smoker*, affirms that, at the very least, three fourths of the profession are against this view of said doctor; that his utterances, as reported, amount to two arguments: First, that, using it himself, he justifies its use; second, that there is in adult life a comparative tolerance of all narcotics, but that it is only a question of more or less poisonous influence. He adds that the very assertions made to defend its use are significant,— "cigarettes are more mischievous than cigars;" "the effect of tobacco is much worse on young men than on adults;" "chewing has a far more deleterious influence on the digestive system than smoking," and other similar expressions.

There is in these arguments of smokers something passing one's comprehension.

"Tobacco, by exciting the secretions of saliva, excites the secretions of gastric juice;" ergo, "used after dinner, it promotes the digestion of the adult."

"Tobacco, by exciting unnaturally the secretions of saliva, impairs the digestion of the young."

The boy of our age does not accept this logic. He cannot comprehend why that which is of such service to the adult should be so injurious to him.

It would be interesting to know at what precise point this remarkable change occurs in the digestive organs, to draw a definite line between a boy and a man. Does the change take place in the substance of the organs, or their form, or what? One is tempted to ask the question, which I trust is not irreverent, Can one who avowedly indulges in the nightly smoking of "five or six moderately strong cigars," and declares that he is a "wiser, better, and happier man for it," can such an one, even though both medical and scientific, be presumed to judge impartially?

At one stage a poison, and at another a promoter of *wisdom, morality, and happiness!* Surely, it is of the utmost importance to learn the exact moment when the peril ceases and the advantage begins.

Now, is there not a sort of *obfuscation* in such reasoning that only tobacco-fumes could occasion? According to Dr. Cate, the non-smoking physician just quoted, the stimulation to the secretion of saliva and gastric juice is a strong argument *against* tobacco, and as really so for adults as for youth. He goes on, — " The sight and taste of food and the act of eating are physiological stimulants to the glands concerned in digestion, exactly fitted to the sufficient performance of this office ; and the assertion that these glands need stimulation in health by tobacco or any other drug is a monstrous and mischievous fallacy."

We may therefore infer that the way in which tobacco aids the digestion is just as brandy and whiskey do it, — that is, by narcotizing and deadening the pangs of a dyspeptic stomach, only, in the end, however, to make it more and more incapable of its proper work.

The most zealous defenders of tobacco admit that *some* adults are poisoned by it. But how are men to decide whether it is a blessing or a bane, till they have tried it? And alas! by the time they have got over the disagreeable introduction and made a fair acquaintance, the spell is on them. By that time they will be slow to admit that its effect is injurious; and, even if convinced of this, what about breaking the spell? Has it been found so easy that you can conscientiously advise your adult friend, or brother, or son, to make the experiment?

But even should it be admitted that that which is disastrous to most might *possibly* bring to a very few some small gain, the question arises, — when the good proposed is so uncertain and so slight, and the evils are so great, and often so fatal, and when all are agreed that the habit should not be formed in youth, does it pay to form it in mature life? It is, unfortunately, a habit that will not stand still, but rather makes perpetual encroachments. If the smoker has a difficult physical or mental task to perform, he seeks his cigar; if a burden weighs heavily, he takes to his cigar; and thus, as occasions multiply, his smoking is more frequent and prolonged, till at length it becomes an imperious necessity, against which, bitterly as he may regret it, he has no nerve to contend. Or, perhaps, under some crushing blow, he surrenders absolutely to the tyrant, and dies its victim.

Now, why should he venture at all on this enchanted ground? Besides, as the very atmosphere of the noxious weed is not only extremely offensive, but positively injurious to many, and moreover, since the example of the moderate user is an incentive to the young to follow in his steps, will not the broad law of divine charity lead him to sacrifice the small and doubtful good, thereby to save others from incalculable harm?

A beautiful illustration of this law of charity is the case of the well-known philanthropist, S. V. S. Wilder, who was a snuff-taker. When asked by a brandy-drinker, with whom he had been expostulating on his habit, whether he thought tobacco did him any good, Mr. Wilder explained that he took snuff by the prescription of his physician for feeble eyes. "Well, sir," responded the gentleman, "your case is exactly like mine. I have a feeble stomach, and have long been compelled to take an occasional drop of spirits for its relief and restoration." "Is it possible," Mr. Wilder asked himself, "that my taking snuff should serve as a pretext for drunkards to ruin both body and soul?" And the good man instantly abandoned his habit.

The following, from the *Boston Evening Journal*, bears on the assertion that tobacco lessens the power of endurance: "According to Lieut. Greely's account of the nineteen men who perished" (in the Lady Franklin Bay Expedition) "all but one were smokers, and that one was the last to die. The seven survivors were non-smoking men."

To make sure of the correctness of this report, a letter of inquiry was sent to Lieut. Greely. His reply substantially confirms it, except on a single point, which is that one of the seven rescued was an inveterate tobacco-chewer. Candor requires this correction, whatever inference the devotees of the weed may be inclined to draw from it. The lieutenant closes his letter by saying: "That no undue weight may be given to the facts, I add that the seven rescued were all temperate in eating and drinking."

PROMOTING SOCIABILITY.

Man is pronounced an unsocial being, and it is claimed that smoking is the antidote for this. In olden times, it was supposed that women were the great promoters of sociability. But this impression must have been a mistake. The fact seems to be that their presence is an incubus on the spirits of mankind, so that, after dinner, they are expected to withdraw, and allow gentlemen, through their cigars, to have a good, social time.

This is, certainly, an important advantage and worthy of cultivation in other directions. There is frequent complaint of the formal, unsocial prayer meetings in the church. We all are familiar with the long, painful silences when no one has anything to say. Strange that some one has not, at this juncture, introduced cigars to loosen the tongues of the silent brethren! The only awkward thing about it would be the presence of the sisters. One would hardly like to turn them out of the meeting, even for the sake of greater freedom among the brethren. Besides, on these occasions the spell of silence is on the sisters also. Why not set *them* to smoking likewise, thus securing a lively prayer meeting?

The great question as to the promotion of sociability by the tobacco habit is — Does it pay? Taking into account the trespassing on good manners which is inevitable to the most gentlemanly assemblege of smokers, and the tendency to a disintegration of society by the separation between man and woman that it necessitates, to say nothing of the physical, mental, and moral results of the habit, I emphasize the question — *Does it pay?*

SOCIAL AND ÆSTHETIC VIEW.

OLD-TIME VIEW OF TOBACCO.

In our search for the pedigree of smokers, we sail
up the stream of time till we cast anchor in 1499,
where,—as Columbus, lying off Cuba, sent two
men ashore, — we put our finger upon the record
of their right honorable ancestry,—to wit, — "*The
naked savages twist large leaves together, light one
end at the fire, and smoke like devils.*"

In 1535, Cartier writes of Canada, —"Where
grows a certain kind of herbe, whereof in summer
they make provision for all the yeere, and only
men use it, and first they cause it to be dried in
the sunne, then weare it on their necks wrapped
in a beaste's skinn, made like a little bagge, with
a hollow piece of stone or wood like a pipe ; then
when they please they make powder of it, and then
put it in one of the ends of said cornets or pipes,
laying a coal of fire upon it, and at the other end
smoke so long that they fill their bodies full of
smoke, till that it comes out at their mouth and
nostrils, even as out of the tonnele of a chimney."

In 1576 was born one Robert Burton, who, in his *Anatomy of Melancholy*, discriminatingly says of tobacco, " A good vomit, a virtuous herb, if it be well qualified, opportunely taken, and medicinally used ; but as it is commonly abused by most men, which take it as tinkers do ale, 't is a plague, a mischief, a violent purger of goods, lands, health ; hellish, devilish, and damned tobacco, the ruin of body and soul."

This arrogant pretender which in our advanced period of civilization and culture is admitted into the first society, was received, in the old days of comparative barbarism, with marked disfavor. Soon after its introduction into the Eastern Continent, it was prohibited in various countries. Physicians pronounced it injurious, priests denounced it as sinful, and princes enacted laws against it.

It was not, however, from mere æsthetic considerations that it was thus, in those olden times, put under the ban by physicians, priests, and potentates, but because of its effects in deteriorating and depleting the population.

Any Turk caught smoking was conducted through the streets with a pipe-stem transfixed through his nose, and later, the Sultan made the act a capital offence.

In Russia, the first offence was punished with the bastinado, the second with the loss of the nose, and the third, with the loss of life.

The Shah of Persia made the use of the drug a capital crime, and proclaimed that " every soldier in whose possession tobacco was found should have his nose and lips cut off, 'and afterwards be burned alive."

In Switzerland, children ran after the offenders, innkeepers were ordered to report those who smoked in their houses, and all transgressors were cited before the Council and punished.

In 1624 Pope Urban VIII. issued a bull excommunicating all who took snuff in church, while the Empress Elizabeth authorized the beadles to confiscate the snuff-boxes to their own use. In 1690 Pope Innocent renewed the bull of excommunication.

It is related that Frederic the Great, at the coronation of his mother as Queen of Prussia, observing that she watched her opportunity to take a pinch of snuff, sent a gentleman to remind her of what was due to her high position.

Queen Elizabeth of England published an edict against its use, " as a demoralizing vice, tending to reduce her subjects to the condition of those savages whose habits they imitated."

Her successor, King James, took still stronger ground. About five years after the Common Version of the Bible was made, appeared his *Counterblast to Tobacco*, in which the royal writer indignantly launches forth : " Moreover, which is a great iniquity and against all humanity, the husband shall not be ashamed to raise his delicate, wholesome, and clear-complexioned wife to that extremity that she must also corrupt her sweet breath therewith, or else resolve to live in a perpetual —— torment. Have you not reason, then, to be ashamed, and to forbear this filthy novelty, so basely grounded, so foolishly received, and so grossly mistaken in the right use thereof? — a custom loathsome to the eye, hateful to the nose, dangerous to the lungs, and in the black, stinking fume thereof, nearest resembling the Stygian smoke of the pit that is bottomless?"

"See the works of the most high and mighty Prince James, by the grace of God, King of Great Britain, 1616."

We find recorded four years after this *Counter-blast*, a remarkable fact, viz.: that in 1620, *The London Company* exported to the Colony at Jamestown ninety poor, but respectable women, who were sold to the planters at the rate, one to each, of a hundred and twenty pounds of tobacco worth sixty cents a pound, the value of a wife being thus estimated at seventy-two dollars. The following year, another batch of wives was sent over and sold at a slight advance.

The tobacco policy of the Bay State Colony was entirely different.

When the Puritans came to Boston in 1630, it was under the following instructions.

"We specially desire you to take care that no tobacco be planted by any of the planters under your government, unless it be some small quantity for mere necessity, and for physic, and that the same be taken privately by ancient men, and *none other*, and to make a general restraint thereof as much as in you is."

In *Prince's Annals of New England* we find that a similar public sentiment was embodied in the laws of this colony. In 1632 it was "Ordered, That no person shall take *any tobacco publicly*, and that every one shall pay a penny sterling for every time of taking tobacco in any place."

Two years later: "The General Court forbid any person to use tobacco publicly, on fine of 2*s*. 6*d*., or privately in his own dwelling, or dwelling of another, *before strangers*, and they also forbid *two or more to use it in any place together*."

Such was the æsthetic view in the olden time (the italics are modern.) Are we growing more or less civilized? When will the sentiment of this enlightened age require the affixing and the executing of suitable penalties on this practice, so far at least as it interferes with the rights, the comfort, or the health of others?

LIST OF BRANDS.

Considering this habit merely in its relation to *good-breeding*, a volume might be written. This will be easily believed by anyone who will glance over the long list that follows of tasteful and appetizing brands which I have sought to arrange artistically to suit my artistic subject. It will not be expected of one unpractised to discriminate between the smoking, chewing, and snuffing brands, as this involves nice points known only to the initiated. The list, however, is gathered from documents obtained at headquarters, and may therefore be relied on as accurate, *so far as it goes:* to wit, through a hundred and thirty-four brands.

Admiration.
Ambassador.
American Eagle.
American Gentleman.
Annot Lyle.
Atlantic.
Banner Brand.
Big Gun.
Black Diamond.
Blunt Heads.
Bright and Black.
Bright Navy.
Bright Smokers.
Bright Wrappers.
Brown Dick.
Caporal ¼.
Captive.
Cataract.
Cavendish.
Cheroots.
Chew Fast.
Chew Globe.
Clear the Way.
Clipper.
Club.
Colorado.
Concha.
Conqueror.
Corporal.
Common Lugs.
Dark and Light Grape.
De Soto.
Dew Drop.
Doctor's Prescription ("the finest and best cigar in the United States, for the money.")
Durham Smoking and Chewing.
Dutch Saucer.
Early Bird.
Eclipse.
Entre Nous.
Erie Cigar.
Fine Cut.
Fine-fibred Clarksville Wrappers.
Fig.
Flush.
Forest Rose.
French Rappee.
German Lancer.
Gold Corn.
Gold Drop.
Golden Crown.
Good Lugs.
Halves.
Happy Thought.
Head Light.
Heart of Gold.
Hold Fast Tobacco.
Honeysuckle.
Horse Head.
Indiana Kite-foot.
Ironsides.
Jockey Club.
Lighter.
Little Dutch.
Little Hatchet.
Little Joker.

Live Oak.
Long John Nines.
Londres.
Lone Fisherman.
Lugs.
Lundy Foot.
Maccaboy.
Magnet.
Magnolia.
Manilla.
Matinee.
Mexican Baler.
Mild.
Mille Fleurs.
Nabob.
Navy Clippings.
Negrohead.
Neptune.
Old Dominion.
Old Honesty.
Old Judge.
One Jack.
Onward.
Own.
Perique.
Pigtail.
Planet.
Plug.
Prince Albert Cigarettes.
Rag Tag.
Raleigh Plug Smoking.
Reina.
Richmond Gem.
Royal Palm.
Royal Puck.
Sailors Choice.
Sailors Solace.
Saint George.
Saint James.
Scotch.
Seal of North Carolina.
Semi.
Senator.
Shag.
Signal.
Smokers Fat Lugs.
Snuff Lugs.
Solid Comfort.
Sport.
Sweet Corporal.
Sweet Oronoke.
Sweetened Fine Cut.
Tidal Wave.
Tobacco Baggin.
Trade Dollar.
Turkish Patrol.
Twist.
Uncle Tom.
Union Club.
Union Jack.
Vanity Fair.
Veteran.
Virginia Yellow and Mahogany.
Virginia Dare.
White Burley Lugs.
Yellow Prior.
Zetland.

Sorry am I to say that a *Grant brand* must be added to this list.

In view of such a multitudinous array, we cease to wonder at the British imperial " tobacco pipe," kept always lighted, and holding, as we are informed, a large number of tons. This vast tobacco-shop, which is unequalled in the world for size, covering, as it does, an extent of five acres, and which is rented by the government for fourteen thousand pounds, or seventy thousand dollars, annually, has been christened—it would seem rather ungallantly — *The Queen's Warehouse.*

WHAT PROTECTION AGAINST SMOKERS?

What shall be said of puffing pipes or cigars along the streets and upon the sidewalks into the faces of men, women, and children? What right has any one to fill God's pure air, which is as much mine as his, with such loathsome fumes, so that I am compelled to keep my mouth tightly closed, and every few steps make futile attempts to blow away the noxious cloud?

"To be sure, it is a shocking thing," Dr. Johnson writes, "the blowing smoke out of our mouths into other people's mouths, eyes, and noses, and having the same thing done to us."

Says Neal Dow: "The forcibly taking away one's pure air by tobacco-smoke is as much stealing, in the moral sense, as picking one's pocket."

Must we go out and come in all our life long, making an everlasting but unheeded protest? Will deliverance *never* come? Even in places where it is forbidden, can we have no security? It is not simply disagreeable, it is oppressive, suffocating, I would say intolerable, except that we *have* to tolerate it.

" Cigar smoke puffed in a man's face by another man is assault and battery" is the declaration of a New York judge.   " If that is the case," says one, "cigarette-smoke puffed anywhere in one's neighborhood should be considered murder in the first degree."

Now, have gentlemen the smallest idea of the discomfort and annoyance occasioned by this habit? It is bad enough to encounter it in public, or sometimes in entering a room where the sickly fumes have been caught and imprisoned; but to have it sprung suddenly upon us in our most unsuspecting mood and with no possibility of escape !

You are a guest in a charming household, and at a late hour seek your room in the third story. As the weather is blustering, and your bed stands near the window, you dare not raise it ; but, instead, you open your door. Soon that unmistakable vapor ascends from away down-stairs. Beginning to cough, you get up and shut the door. Through the cracks and the keyhole it still creeps in, causing a sense of faintness and suffocation. There is nothing for it but to open your window. Between the cold air on the one side and the "choice Havana" whiffs on the other, so subtly telegraphed up to you from the polished gentleman and scholar, luxuriating in his paradise of smoke below, you both shiver and cough. Tired out, you fall, at length, into a disturbed slumber, till, becoming suddenly conscious of a strong wind blowing through the window, you quickly close it. Too late, however; for you awake in the morning with a sore throat and an aching head, followed, it may be, by a severe sickness.

Has your accomplished host the smallest idea of his own responsibility in the case? *Not he;* and you open not your mouth to accuse him. Indeed, if you once do this, can you ever shut it? For, alas, wherever you go, still that everlasting perfume! You encounter it on land and water, going out and coming in, walking and riding, in omnibuses, cabs, and cars. Even through the pretence of its banishment from the latter, the all-pervading breath of the inveterate smoker or chewer catches you before and behind, on your right hand and on your left, while from the smoking-cars comes floating in that indescribable tobacco-laden air.

You purchase a garment; but when it reaches home you perceive the same sickening smell, and, before you can wear it, are obliged to give it a thorough airing.

You lend a book. It comes back telling the same stale story. So that, too, must be ventilated.

You call at the post-office. You have not escaped it. Besides, you may receive a foreign epistle bearing an infectious breath, which even the passage of the broad Atlantic has not been able to sweeten.

You enter a lawyer's office. Behold, it is there.

You flee to the parsonage; but sometimes even

from the minister's sanctum you are forced to beat a hasty retreat.

You seek refuge in the church. *It* has got there before you; indeed, it may have seized the pulpit itself. Think of the incongruities to which this has led! For instance, a clergyman, giving out a portion of the Psalms, took occasion, while his hearers were opening their Bibles, to steal a hasty pinch of snuff, and then read, "My soul cleaveth unto the dust."

Hospitably inclined, you open your pew-door to a stranger. He no sooner enters than you repent of your good deed; for with him enters such an offensive odor that all your comfort in the service vanishes.

You come out of a concert or lecture-hall, and in the passage-ways are well-nigh choked with tobacco fumes; but you are wedged in among the crowd and must abide your time.

You visit your honored Alma Mater. After the grand Commencement dinner, and sometimes even before it is through, you find yourself enveloped in clouds of smoke, which enwreathe alike the youngest graduates, the oldest alumni, and the most respected professors.

Stopping transiently at some boarding-house, you go to your room, and have occasion to open a drawer. There rushes forth an offensive stench that almost knocks you down. It is as if the long-imprisoned ghosts of a thousand cigars were struggling to escape.

Even your pleasure excursions are half spoiled by this ever-following foe. If you venture to protest, you may be told that, if you don't like it, the world is wide, and you can go elsewhere.

Unfortunately, good sir, the world is *not* wide enough to afford us a hiding-place from smokers. To make sure of this, we must get into another and a totally different world.

Of the West someone writes: "Tobacco is here the ever-present deity. Circles into which whiskey gains no admittance are cursed with to-bacco. The judge on the bench and the lawyer at the bar, the witness in the box, and the jury in their seats, are, in three cases out of four, rumi-nating animals, and are all tributary to the tan-colored flood which deluges the court-room. The railroad car and the stage-coach, the steamboat cabin and the bar-room, the lyceum hall and, alas! the Christian conference-room, are all *splashed* with disgusting fluid. Chewing, smoking, spit-ting, are the low and vile enjoyments of animal-ized man."

Could not substantially the same picture be drawn of the East and the North and the South? And what a picture!

Writes Dr. Harris: "I have seen the floors of the lecture-rooms of the University of Pennsyl-vania as filthy as any stable before the groom has performed his morning cleansing. I have seen the passage between the seats of a railroad car in such a foul and *mucky* condition that no lady could walk with safety or comfort from her seat to the door."

"A proper description of the habit of chewing tobacco," says one, "would exhaust the filthy adjectives of the language, and spoil the adjectives themselves for further use."

The old-time English and French gentleman carried around with him his own private spittoon, silver or otherwise, thus gallantly securing a monopoly of that which many a modern gentleman dispenses freely to all.

In our legislative halls, the ancient snuff-boxes have been largely displaced by the modern spit-boxes, although these are far from sufficient to protect Congressional floors and furniture. This civilized custom of the nineteenth century prevails *par excellence* in our national capital, making it, according to Dickens, "the headquarters of tobacco-tinctured saliva."

Doctor Stanton writes in the *Independent*: "Enter the chamber of the House, the first thing that greets you is the smoking ' nuisance.' See the member of Congress from ——, a clergyman, and the son of a clergyman, sitting at his desk, or walking the aisle, smoking and puffing. And why should not he, a young member, smoke, when older members, and scores of them, indulge the habit while engaged in the business of the House?"

And the smoke poison borne upward into the faces of the assembled ladies in the galleries! Can anyone deny that this is barbarism?

Now, there are common civilities which it is not expected any true man will violate. To refrain from smoking or chewing in the presence of others is no special virtue, any more than to refrain from rude elbowing and crowding, and stepping on your neighbor's toes. To insist, however, on doing this, and in the very face of others — is it not an infraction of the commonest laws of courtesy?

"Is it offensive to you for a gentleman to smoke in your presence?" inquired a smoker of a lady. "No *gentleman* ever smokes in my presence," she made answer.

Another lady, in reply to the same question, honestly admitted that it *was* offensive. "It is so to some," responded the offender, and coolly continued smoking.

Suppose now, my gentlemanly friend, we ladies take our turn at this game, not indeed with cigars, but with tallow candles, successively lighting and extinguishing them till you have had a good taste of the smoke. Although compared with that which you bestow so abundantly upon us, it is quite innocent, yet I think you would speedily cry *Peccavi*, and sue for mercy.

A writer in the *Congregationalist*, referring to a sign in a steam-boat, — "*Out of consideration for the ladies, gentlemen* WILL NOT *smoke on this deck*," goes on to remark, — "The sign, 'No smoking,' is hung up in a gentleman's own mind whenever he is in the company of those who do not smoke. He *will not* sacrifice the comfort of

others for a needless indulgence. There are so
many well-dressed men who are not gentlemen,
but only hogs in disguise, that every transporta-
tion company has to say to them, ' must not,' by
frequent signs against smoking. They would
never know how to be courteous without these
perpetual suggestions."

Now, please take note that it is a *gentleman*
who makes these grievous charges. Had I ventured on such expressions, I should, doubtless, be
arraigned as guilty of "great exaggeration and in-
vective."

An eminent physician asks, " What should we
think of a person who *spit* in the water we were
about to drink? And what is the difference between such a person and one who spits a quantity
of tobacco-smoke into the air we are about to
breathe?"

It is frankly admitted that among the transgressors are some of our most refined and cultivated
men. But in what a predicament will they sometimes place a luckless woman! She is a visitor
in some house, and her agreeable host, being accustomed to smoke in the parlor, brings thither his
cigar, when suddenly he turns to her with the
question, " Is smoking disagreeable to you?"

Now, if it happens to be repulsive to both
her natural and moral sense, what is she to do?
What *can* she do but tell the truth? Does the
gentleman thereupon lay down his beloved cigar?
By no manner of means, but retreats to enjoy his

smoke elsewhere. And the woman almost feels that she has been guilty of some rudeness. Ought these things to be?

These refined gentlemen by no means regard smoking as an animal indulgence, but rather as an intellectual enjoyment. They will talk of the ethereal mood to which it lifts them, and it may be of the loftier essays and more eloquent sermons they can produce under its inspiration. This, however, is precisely the argument that some urge, and with equal reason, for the use of opium and hashish. Into what mental exaltation did the former raise De Quincey! Yet how terrible the retribution! The principle in all these narcotics is virtually the same, though tobacco is far more offensive than any, or than *all* the rest.

But whatever pleas may be urged, it remains an unalterable fact that the public highway is *not* a smoking room; and, if it would be regarded as an indictable offence for one to carry around with him assafœtida or any other vile compound, and fling it broadcast as he walks the streets or enters private dwellings, why should not the doers of the same with this noxious weed be also liable to indictment!

You don't *regard* it as an annoyance to others? Do you take others at all into the account?

Not an annoyance! How, then, do you interpret the conspicuous posters in various countries?

No smoking here!

Smoking positively forbidden!
No smoking abaft the shaft!
Nicht rauchen!
Hier wird nicht geraucht!
Niet rooken!
Ne fumez pas ici!
Il est defendu de fumer!
And what means the label, *Smoking-car?*

Think for a moment of the potency of a habit which makes the public parading of such rules necessary. It is bad enough as it is — indeed, it is often more than the innocent part of the travelling public knows how to bear; but were these very few and sometimes ill-kept regulations entirely done away with, such a dreadful tyrant is this TOBACCO, that a reign of terror would speedily ensue, when no uncontaminated man, woman, or child · would dare to venture forth. Is not this strange lack of consideration and courtesy due, in part, at least, to the benumbing, and may I not add *demoralizing*, influence of the habit?

Would that the regulations were far more stringent! that our railroad directors might label certain cars — *For the Unclean*, and then prohibit smoker or chewer from entering any other! As it is, the irrepressible smoker follows you wherever you go. You seat yourself in a car, and in utter disregard of the printed ordinance — *Smoking forbidden* — in some subtle, indescribable fashion, the dreaded odor assails you in front and in rear. You pay an extra dollar and retreat to a

Pullman. Vain effort! From regions unknown comes the same sickening vapor.

A great responsibility rests on railroad directors who encourage the tobacco-habit, not only by running special cars for the benefit of smokers, but by providing for luxurious offenders rooms in the palace cars, whence the fumes and sometimes the accompanying profanity find their way to many an innocent victim.

In order to make your travelling connections you are doomed to pass several long hours at a station. In the Ladies' Room is posted conspicuously — *Smoking positively forbidden.* All in vain! for through the telegraph window comes pouring in that same perennial stream.

TWENTY MINUTES IN A SMOKING-CAR.

Once, strange to say, I spent twenty minutes in a smoking-car. It was on approaching Hoosac Tunnel, and as this was the rear-car, it was our best point of observation. Over and above this, however, I admit that I made the most of the occasion, urging this singular visit, — greatly to the surprise and protest of my companion, — because I desired the enlightenment of my own sight and smell and hearing.

Yet it was with a half-guilty feeling that I stole in behind him, almost as if I were seeking entrance to some Tartarean abode. The sense of hearing was not offended, as an instant hush fell on the surprised-looking smokers at the unwonted presence of ladies. Their cigars, too, seemed to drop instinctively from their lips. But the senses of sight and of smell were abundantly filled, I will not say *satisfied*.

A card-table, evidently not a mere ornamental appendage, stood conveniently between every two seats, — an expensive indulgence not granted to any other class of passengers, — a seeming premium offered to smokers. After twenty minutes of forced endurance I withdrew, saddened and indignant, with profound pity for the women whose dear ones such places could attract. Most of all I wondered how any man of religious principle, or even ordinary sensibility, could bring himself to tolerate such a social and moral atmosphere; still more, how he could *seek* it. My one experience was enough for a lifetime.

" I was glad," said Thoreau when at Cape Cod, " to have got out of the towns where I am wont to feel unspeakably mean and disgraced, — to have left behind me for a season the bars of Massachusetts, where the full-grown are not weaned from savage habits, — still sucking a cigar. My spirits rose in proportion to the outward dreariness. The towns need to be ventilated. The gods would be pleased to see some pure flames from their altars. They are not to be appeased with cigar-smoke."

PRESENT OUTLOOK.

The outlook has not improved since Thoreau's day. On a hot summer's night you invite your guests to sit by the windows and enjoy the cool air. No sooner are you all fairly seated than strolling smokers begin to pass, compelling you to shut out the air which they have poisoned.

On a Sunday evening, you wander forth to an out-door meeting on the hill-side. Once, twice, and yet again, the near presence of some smoker drives you from your seat.

You engage a room at some fashionable seaside hotel, — Nantasket, Coney Island, Atlantic City, or any of the popular resorts. Through the open windows, with the fresh breath of Ocean, enters a totally different breath. It pervades the verandah crowded with ladies, filling the wide atmosphere; "and sometimes," writes a sojourner who had vainly sought an escape, "the finer sex seem to like to have it so."

You enter a city ferry-boat. If you are a gentleman and not a smoker, and the ladies' cabin is full, whither shall you betake yourself? According to the best of testimony the so-called gentlemen's cabin is not a fit place for a decent man. Says one who had been obliged to occupy it several times, "I have invariably suffered headache or dizziness or nausea after standing in the filth, and breathing the abominable smoke from hundreds of vile cigars and viler pipes." How long will our ferry companies be more considerate in their arrangements for tobacco-votaries than for all their other passengers combined?

You go on board a steamer for a pleasant sail, and seat yourself on the deck. Presently you are haunted by that unmistakable odor. Turning your head, you find a person near by, puffing away in serenest complacency. You change your seat. This only brings you into the range of another equally serene offender. Verily, there is no escape. The smokers plant themselves before you and behind you and beside you, and no one says them nay.

A traveller writes: "If I were an artist, and desired to picture absolute selfishness, I would paint a smoker seated on the forward deck of a steamer, his face radiant with that familiar expression of complacency, while his fellow travellers, sickened and disgusted, are trying to shield themselves from the fumes of his pipe.

"We spent one of the loveliest days of the past summer in 'shooting the rapids' of the St. Lawrence. Three persons, dressed like gentlemen, seated themselves on the forward part of the boat, and from after breakfast till we reached the dock in Montreal in the evening, they rivalled the furnace fires in polluting the balmy atmosphere."

A lady on a journey fell in with a recently married couple. When the bridegroom saw that the smoke from his cigar annoyed his bride, so that she tried to brush it away, he brought himself squarely in front, and then smoked straight into her face !

You betake yourself to a rural retreat. But no matter how secluded it may be, there will be some way of getting to it, whether by car, coach, or cart. And whatever the vehicle, somebody will be in it, and that somebody will be sure to smoke or chew, or both.

Even the broad ocean offers no asylum. In spite of printed enactments, the lawless wind bears the dreadful odors " abaft the helm," directly into your face. Can the moral atmosphere engendered by this habit be any more securely locked in? A traveller says : " One of the foulest places I ever saw for blackguards, profanity, and indecent language, was the smoking-room of an ocean steamer." And this testimony is abundantly repeated. Let me give that of Dr. Charles S. Robinson : —

" It is deemed to be a prime advantage on the part of steamer companies to publish that their vessels are provided with ' smoking-rooms, beautiful and clean, quiet and comfortable, in the steadiest part of the deck.' Oh, the sarcasm of those sweet words of recommendation ! Whoever enters one of these reserved saloons after the first twenty-four hours from the start, will find it a noisy, stenchful pandemonium of smoking, drinking, betting, and gambling, into which no decent person can enter, and in which no peace-loving person can stay without exasperation.

" It has been my lot to cross the ocean many

times during the last fifteen years; I have chosen my passage on the vessels of nearly every line which plies between New York and Liverpool, and on a number of vessels of some of them; and I distinctly aver that the smoking-rooms are the centre of demoralization and offensiveness, and this is on the increase, summer after summer, as the travel increases."

The very literature of the day is tinged and flavored, and sometimes saturated, with tobacco. Many a hero in our most popular novels is made to luxuriate in the elegant accomplishment of smoking. "He gracefully knocks the ashes from his cigar." "With gentlemanly ease he enjoys at once his smoking and her conversation."

In a serial by a favorite, and, in the main, high-toned, young novelist, issued in one of our first-class magazines, we find the following: "The discussions, it was observed, were always more enjoyable when the Professor, having his easy-chair placed in exactly the right position with regard to light and fire, found himself with his cigar in hand carefully smoking it and making the most of its aroma. His tranquil enjoyment of and respect for the rite were agreeable things to see. 'It soothes me,' he would say. 'It even inspires and elevates me. I feel as if I had discovered a new sense. I am really quite grateful.'"

Another of our charming writers, in connection with one of his characters, speaks of the " fragrance of admirable cigars, that active and passive perfume, which comes from smoking and being smoked in the best company."

And the heroines of these tales are blandly resigned, even if they do not actually smile upon the deed. Now, for variety's sake, why can't we have a hero who will none of this, — who always and everywhere eschews the weed?

Just look back to the degradation to which this luxury of being smoked had brought the Aztec civilization at the time of Spanish discovery and conquest. It may be found in Herbert Bancroft's History of the Native Races, vol. I., page 776, a quotation from Wafer's New Voyage: "Laying two or three leaves upon one another, they roll up all together sideways into a long Roll, yet leaving a little hollow. Round this they roll other Leaves one after another, in the same manner, but close and hard, till the Roll be as big as one's Wrist, and two or three feet in length. Their way of Smoaking when they were in Company together is thus: A Boy lights one end of a Roll and burns it to a Coal, wetting the part next to it to keep it from wasting too fast. The end so lighted he puts into his mouth and blows the Smoak through the whole length of the Roll into the Face of everyone of the Company or Council, tho' there be 2 or 300 of them. Then they, sitting in their usual Posture upon Forms, make with their Hands held hollow together, a kind of Funnel round their Mouths and Noses. Into this they receive the Smoak as 't is blown upon them, Snuffing it up greedily and strongly, as long as ever they are able to hold their Breath, and seeming to bless them·selves, as it were, with the Refreshment it gives them."

In a letter bearing on this point, John G. Whittier writes : "The vile practice is increasing — the blessed air of heaven is foul with it. Our novel-writers, women especially, on both sides of the water, make their heroes announce their coming to their fair ones by the smell of tobacco-smoke, and take their cigars from their mouths only when they stop puffing to kiss! It is a shameful and filthy habit, indecent and *unmanly*."

Now I have faith enough in my own sex to be-lieve that anything of this on the part of a true woman must be from ignorance or inconsideration. How otherwise, dear sister, would it be possible for you or for me to speak lightly of such a prac-tice? How could we give our seeming approval to it by accepting an invitation to walk or to ride with a gentleman who has a cigar in his mouth; or by voluntarily putting ourselves in the way of inhaling cigar-smoke, no matter how delicately scented it may be? Is a poisoned chalice any the less fatal for being wreathed with roses? How can we dare to countenance that which not only has been proved perilous, but which our Quaker-poet pronounces "a shameful and filthy habit, indecent and *unmanly*?" Could we ask a higher æsthetic authority?

Let me introduce other testimony from a

wholly opposite direction. When the trainer of Barnum's clown-elephant, proposed to add to his many wonderful performances that of smoking a tobacco-pipe, Barnum replied that "his army of employees were men of exemplary character, and his clown-elephant should not be permitted to demoralize them by setting them a bad example."

Is there, then, I repeat, absolutely no refuge, no quarantine, by which these noxious, ever-poisoning, ever-persecuting spirits of the air can be effectually shut out from the innocent?

"Chewers," writes one, "ejaculate their saliva upon the sidewalk, in the store, in spittoons which become incorporate stenches, in dark corners of railroad cars to stain the white skirts of unsuspecting women, in lecture-rooms and churches, upon fences, and into stoves that hiss with anger at the insult. And the quids after they are ejaculated — ! "

Some smoke till their bedrooms and shops can scarcely be breathed in, and until their breath is as rank as the breath of a foul beast, and their clothes have the odor of the sewer.

And this loathsome *without* is only a fit exponent of the equally loathsome *within*. Says Dr. Alcott : " If the interior of the tobacco-user could be fairly exposed to the public gaze, I am not sure but it would do more to deter the rising generation from falling into this habit than all our lectures, and essays, and homilies."

Did no one suffer except the willing victim, the

case would be different. But the dreadful penalty falls heaviest on the nearest and dearest: on those who cannot escape the sickening atmosphere, no, not for a moment.

A writer of experience tells us that there are professional men, lawyers, physicians, clergymen, college professors, and not a few prominent literary men, who carry with them into society, as well as into the street and the railway car, not the odor of a fresh cigar, which, in comparison, would be endurable, but the "vile, vulgar scent of a cigar long since burned to ashes."

Who, indeed, has not seen a gentleman (?) enter a car, and leaving his satchel or overcoat in possession of a seat, retire to the smoking-car, lose himself in the dense clouds of some half a hundred cigars, have his smoke out, and then return saturated from hat to boots with the sickening fumes? And, alas! peradventure, this may be a Reverend, a Professor, or a Doctor of Divinity, and a man of refinement too.

If an Arab regards spitting in his presence as an insult, even outside his tent, can one conceive of the just indignation of American women when travelling in the cars? There's little use in carefully holding up one's dress, and looking warily from place to place. One may as well make a covenant with her eyes, and take the first seat that comes. The men chew and spit, they read and spit, they talk and spit, they laugh and spit, they breathe and spit, and some swear and spit.

Windows may be open at right and left; but, apparently, they consider it a sin to spit out of them. Well, it *would* be a pity to sully the fair face of Nature; indeed, one might well compassionate a country drenched in such narcotic showers.

By lamplight, as by daylight, the process goes on. And what scenes do the flickering lights disclose! Men, shaken out of their dignity, tumbling and rolling every way; while some, from their horizontal positions, now spit more directly upon their neighbors! Women, huddled up on the seats, starting, even in their slumbers, at these ever-threatening showers!

Will any one deny that this fashion is an outrage against all propriety? Ought passengers who have paid honestly for their tickets to be thus doomed to perpetual terror?

Daniel Webster said: "If gentlemen *must* smoke" (or chew, he might well have added) "let them take the horse-shed." This seems to have been the prevailing sentiment in that staunch temperance town, Oberlin, Ohio. Years ago, a doctor-of-divinity smoker, who was passing a few days there, found himself out of cigars. After a long hunt in search of them, he was directed to a hostler who might, perhaps, supply him. He sought him out, and obtained a cigar; but when told that he must go behind the stable to smoke, such a sense of shame came over him that from that time he foreswore the indulgence.

Not so apt disciples were two New England ministers who, being at the same place, at a convention, some years later, walked down the railway-track for their daily smoke.

It is not uncommon to find among temperance lecturers ardent devotees of the weed. A total abstainer, yet a tobacco-sot!

We have suffered quite enough from these demi-semi-reformers. Our parlors and our chambers, our halls and our sanctuaries are often desecrated by their performances. "Why don't you use the church for your temperance addresses, and devote to the cause the money you expend in hiring a hall?" "Oh, it would never do, the church is so fearfully defiled by these lecturers." When such men come out from a smoke-room, pallid, trembling, and bearing the nauseous signs of the indulgence, instead of mounting the platform to exhort others to temperance, would it not be more fitting that they should take the back seats, and listen in silence and humiliation? Thou that sayest another shall not drink, dost thou smoke or chew?

CIVIL RIGHTS *vs.* TOBACCO.

Why cannot the civil-trespass law be brought to bear on this matter? Our statutes forbid that any man shall, from greed of gain, or to gratify any unnatural appetite, cause a nuisance in any public place where all have equal rights and a common interest. Is not the wide-spread use of the weed a nuisance so offensive, so unwholesome, that, if suddenly sprung upon the community, there would be a spontaneous uprising, an indignant mass-meeting, which should demand its immediate expulsion? No pipe or cigar ought to be smoked within a thousand yards of a church or place of public gathering. Cannot the early New England statute be revived, at least so far as to impose a fine on any person using the weed publicly?

In point here is the opinion of Dr. John H. Griscom, president of the New York Society for the Advancement of Science and Art, and for twenty-three years attending physician of the New York Hospital: "If every human being should understand and appreciate the value of pure air when inhaled, and the injurious influence of any foreign substance when absorbed into the blood through the lungs, the writer hereof cannot doubt that tobacco-smoking would be totally discarded voluntarily and, perhaps, legally."

Joseph Cook says: "I believe that the natural instinct of man concerning tobacco, if he has not inherited a taste for it, is repulsive. When I was in Harvard University, Dr. Shattuck, of the Medical School, gave a lecture on Health to the freshman class; and he told its members that he, as a physician, could not deny that tobacco was a sedative; but that if they must take it, he would advise them to put it in a bowl on the mantelpiece, and take it as a decoction; for then it would have all its sedative effect, and not injure anyone else besides the taker of it. That was the coolest advice I ever heard concerning the use of tobacco."

Yet five-sixths of the Harvard students are addicted to this habit! Would that the old order issued by the overseers of the University in the time of President Dunster could be revived! —

"No scholar shall take tobacco, unless permitted by the President, with the consent of parents or guardians, and on good reasons first given by a physician; *and then in a sober and private manner*."

Speaking of another of our leading New England colleges, a writer recalls the past, when " no student could have maintained his character for scholarly instincts who should have smoked on the public streets, or at an Alumni dinner or supper." "Now, however," he adds, " the modern student, with no more sense of propriety than the Irishman, puffs in public places, and forces his foulness into the presence of the older graduates at Commencement-dinner and other college festive occasions. Such rudeness is bad enough anywhere, but it is simply unpardonable in men who claim the refinements of good learning and of gentle manners."

An alumnus of one of our highest New England colleges, in speaking through the press of a recent Commencement, tells us that at the business-meeting of his class a great many smoked, the cigars being furnished and distributed by one of the professors: and that, at the Alumni dinner, presided over by the college president, many began smoking, while a large number were still eating !

TOBACCO-PICTURES.

Among the various methods of using this æsthetic weed, a few of those less familiar may be mentioned.

The Indians were accustomed to insert the forked ends of a hollow cane into the nostrils and then apply the other end to the burning leaves or to the dried and powdered tobacco, thus inhaling smoke or snuff as the case might be.

In Micronesia, as the missionary, Mr. Rand, tells us, all smoke, men, women, and children, though the habit of sitting down alone to enjoy a smoke is never practised. On the assembling of a crowd, a chief calls for his pipe! This is brought, filled, and lighted by a little boy or girl, who, in the process, takes early lessons in the fine art. When the lighted pipe is handed to the chief, he passes it to a chief higher in rank, and he again to one still higher, till the topmost man is reached. This man takes a few whiffs, then hands it to the next one, and so on, till all the company are served.

Dr. Titus Coan, the late venerated missionary of Hawaii, says of the Patagonians : "They would inhale the smoke of tobacco, hold it for a time in their mouths, then blow it out through the nostrils, or swallow it into the lungs, and become deadly drunk. I have been aroused at midnight by the most fearful groans of savages in the wigwams near by, and on entering them have been struck with the ghastly and cadaverous look, and chilled with the agonizing groans of Indians drunk with tobacco fumes. The same was true of the Marquesas group, of the Hawaiian Islanders, of the Polynesians generally, and of all savage tribes, so far as I can learn."

Of the snuff-taking habits among the Zulus, Rev. Josiah Tyler, who has been a missionary in Africa over thirty years, gives the following account : —

"The Zulus make their snuff of tobacco, dry aloes, and ashes, grinding it very fine. It is exceedingly pungent, causing tears to flow profusely down their cheeks, which they wipe off with a snuff-spoon made of bone or horn; this being their only handkerchief. Old and young of both sexes carry snuff-boxes made of small calabashes tied to a girdle around the waist. Sometimes diminutive reeds full of snuff are inserted in holes in their ears. When they meet — after the usual salutation, 'I see you, friend' — the snuff is passed round, each one taking a good pinch. It is a nasty habit; their nostrils, after this operation, being covered with filth; and it is also injurious to health.

"Zulu men, especially young men, are becoming fearfully addicted to smoking; and I perceive, after thirty-two years' observation, that it makes serious inroads on their constitutions. This is one of the unpleasant results of *European civilization!* I am glad to say that, so far as my knowledge extends, no American missionary in South Africa uses tobacco in any form. We shall, ere long, have anti-tobacco societies in all our missionary stations ; and shall fight against this vile habit till we lay our armor down."

What pictures may be seen in Mexico ! — the schoolmaster with a cigar in his mouth, and his scholars smoking around him, either at their recitations or studying in their seats, as *a reward of merit!*

In the law-courts, judges, jury, and prisoner all smoking ; the latter, if his cigarette happens to go out in the excitement of the charges against him, coolly lights it by that of the officer who is his guard ! No wonder that an inveterate smoker is said to have become Mexicanized.

Mr. Pixley, another missionary in Africa, writes : " It has sometimes been said, and very truly, that Africa is a land where the people eat with their fingers and take snuff with a spoon. The first request on meeting, after the salutation, invariably is, ' Give me some snuff, my friend.' Down they sit ; each takes his snuff-spoon, and the one who consents to treat shakes his box and pours some snuff into his open hand. From this each one dips a portion with his spoon, and all begin to snuff; often continuing snuffing and chatting till the tears roll down their cheeks.

" Everywhere men and women who do not take the weed as snuff delight to smoke the pipe ; some have learned from Christians the degrading habit of chewing; and a few women and girls have become adepts in the art of ' dipping ' as adroitly as any Southern lady.

" This tobacco habit blunts the sensibilities of Zulu Christians so that missionaries feel that it is almost as much of a hindrance to the progress of the Gospel, and to the elevation of the people as intemperance."

Dr. Lizars relates that he once travelled with a South American, " who first filled his nostrils with snuff, which he prevented from falling out by stuffing shag tobacco after it, and this he termed ' plugging; ' then put in each check a coil of pig-tail tobacco, which he named ' quidding; ' lastly, he lit a Havana, which he put into his mouth. This *gentleman* was as thin as a razor, and frightfully nervous."

What a body of living death !

TOBACCO MANUFACTURE ; CIGARETTE MAKING.

The following is a description by Lillie E. Barr, of the preparation of tobacco as she saw the process in Richmond, Virginia : —

" After a certain amount of drying and dipping into various solutions, it goes through the supreme process which makes it palatable to the chewer. The leaves are laid on the floor, not necessarily a clean floor, and then a negro man, with pants rolled up to the knees, walks backward and forward upon it. As he does so, he pours upon it a solution of loaf sugar, licorice, delicate essences, etc., which, to use a darkey's expression, 'are well stomped in by dese two foots.' If, while performing this 'stomping' business, he desires to spit, the leaves get the benefit of that juice, also; while with his bare feet he kicks them over and over, and 'stomps' both sides well. The mess is then swept up into a pile, and afterward strung on poles and dried.

"Do the men wash their feet before going on the tobacco?" I inquired.

"'Well-l—they wash them when they come off,' was the smiling answer."

Truly an appetizing process!

A writer in the New York *Times* furnishes additional pleasant information : —

"A prominent physician told me lately that from the practice of cigar-makers wetting the wrapper with their saliva, and biting the end of the cigar into shape, a spread of syphilitic disease was taking place; and that he knew of several cases. Somewhat alarmed, I managed to visit a number of factories. Two thirds of the cigar-makers, I found, daub the whole end of the cigar with their saliva. Thinking that Cuban workmen might not do it, I visited places where they were employed, and found not only did they use their saliva to make the wrapper stick, but that most of them before wrapping bit the end of the cigar into shape with their teeth. As the physician informed me that many of the cigar-makers have sore mouths from disease, it is a dangerous as well as a beastly habit."

A Detroit paper gives an account of a squalid old man whom a reporter saw picking up cigar-stubs. In his collection, he also had "ends of villainous five-centers-stubs picked out of office-spittoons, and swept from the floors of saloons."

After replying to the reporter's questions, a policeman took him to a little tenement, in the front room of which were a man, a woman, and two girls. Passing through to a back room, they found five dirty boys sprinkling cigar-stubs from a rusty old pot, then cutting them into shreds and spreading them out to dry, after which the whole mass was taken to the front room. Here, with shreds of this stale tobacco scattered all over the floor and around their bare feet, the slatternly woman and girls were rolling out the repulsive material. Wetting the wrappers with their lips, they would poke the hair out of their eyes, and then, moistening the finger tips of the same hand with their tongue, would smooth out the edges till a dainty cigarette was the result. The man's business was to do up these cigarettes into bunches, and then put fancy labels on them.

"Are there many who smoke this second-hand tobacco?" asked the reporter. The policeman's reply was: "Thousands upon thousands. Not such as this old scavenger, but nobby young bloods who never did an hour's manual labor in their lives, and never will; young fellows who wear the latest fashions, and carry little canes. They 're the ones who smoke those old stubs."

There is a kind of tobacco — I cannot give the brand — whose fumes are exceedingly offensive even to the smoker,—I mean to the *refined* smoker; nor is he a model of patience when it is inflicted on him. Strange he cannot realize that to most of the uninitiated, *all* tobacco is obnoxious; that they instinctively repel the whole genus.

The pervasiveness of the weed has been more than once spoken of. There is in fact no such thing possible as absolutely cleansing a home afflicted with chronic smoking. Even a few whiffs leave their mark. What was my consternation one day on opening a closet-door, to perceive the unmistakable fumes! Had one of my male members turned traitor? I summoned them both. They emphatically declared their innocence. On close examination, the offender proved to be a garment just brought from an establishment where smoking was in vogue.

WIVES OF TOBACCO-USERS.

What shall we say as to those women whom these inveterate smokers call wives? I have seen a man whom I loved and respected, who showed by many a sad token the effects of his cruel bondage. I have heard his wife, who had borne the trial patiently, though with suffering health, speak with feeling of the clean and sweet atmosphere of houses untainted with tobacco.

Think of a delicate woman who is unpleasantly affected by the least breath of the vile weed yoked to one who makes use of it perpetually. The health of many a wife has been sacrificed by such a union. But has not the husband sufficient love, or even common gallantry, to abandon the habit he formed before marriage? *Not he!* In the scales are placed on the one hand his wife, and on the other his ugly idol; and the latter outweighs the former!

I should fail in justice, however, if I did not affirm that I know of two or three men who, loving the wife more than the cigar, did actually, once and forever, trample it under their feet.

I have heard of a few others who from a similar motive broke their fetters. The wife of a certain smoker was affected with palpitation of the heart, deathly faintness, and hysterical symptoms. Her physician was at first puzzled, but concluded that she was a victim of tobacco-poisoning. The unconscious husband, on learning the views of the doctor, instantly abandoned smoking, and was rewarded by the speedy recovery of his wife.

I know a gentleman in Philadelphia, who did more than that. In his young days, cherishing a high respect for womanhood, though he had not then found his ideal, he fell into reflections, as young men sometimes will, on the subject of matrimony. Believing that the habit of smoking rendered him less worthy the love of any true woman, with a high chivalric feeling, he abandoned it. This was genuine æsthetics. When, in our civil war, he entered the army, many prophesied a fall. But his wife knew him better. While multitudes succumbed to the subtle tempter, he never wavered.

Another striking case is that of a physician who thus graphically describes his conflict. When his wife, soon after their marriage, asked the sacrifice, he readily replied, —

"'Nothing will afford me greater delight than to yield to your request.' So I entered upon my renunciation," he says, "and in twenty-four hours was thoroughly conscious of my enslavement. Oh! how my nervous system suffered from the want of its daily draught of poison! The most violent headache and blindness, equal to that which was induced when I first indulged in the use of tobacco, came upon me; and such complete prostration of my physical powers and depression of mind, with perturbation of spirits, I hope never during my mortal life to be called upon again to endure. My blood played through my veins as if it were a sea-surge. I saw all invisible things that were ugly and demon-like; devils in the shape of old women, haggish and witch-like, danced around me. For the first time in my life I became sensible of the enslaving powers of appetite. No force of will, or vigor of conscience was competent to my deliverance. My love for my wife, which usually absorbed all my self, faded away into nothingness. I saw nothing, thought of nothing, felt nothing but the overpowering desire for my tobacco,"

For three months this process of resolving and falling went on, every successive fall being deeper than the preceding. He continued, —

" I was about to leave home on a journey. Beseeching the Saviour to help me, I went out into the darkness. From that hour to this the poison has not passed my lips. For four months, however, I was in a wild, dreamy haze, staggering through mist and darkness, a dozen times a day tempted and well-nigh overborne, but conquering for the hour and struggling on."

Is it strange that a woman should be unwilling to share a man's heart with so base a rival, getting the smaller share at that? Nay, is it not the wonder of wonders that any woman should feel otherwise?

In the fact that not a few wives, sisters, and mothers, from lack of information on the subject, and a loving readiness to sacrifice their own comfort to the gratification of their dear ones, submit quietly to this ever-encroaching tyrant, — in this fact, may we not find some slight explanation of its almost universal sway?

But the case, I fear, is sometimes worse than this. The perpetual strain that comes upon some men from the ambitious craving and promptings of their wives and daughters for a more elegant style of dress and of living, is doubtless irritating as well as wearing. I pity the man who, feeling that he ought not to be thus taxed, and who, failing, in spite of all his toil to satisfy these cravings, is driven to a cigar for consolation. But I pity far more the woman who has any share in driving him to this. Better that she and her daughters should live in an Irish shealing and wear tow-cloth all the days of their life than thus to be a drag upon their best friend, ruthlessly turning the sweet sentiment of life into bitterness and gall.

FEMALE DEVOTEES.

Can any picture be more revolting than that of the miserable, snuff-dipping women of the south? Their life is not life, — hardly existence, — but one continuous stupor — faculties, feelings, conscience, everything dead, except the single sense of snuff — snuff.

But this dipping is not confined to the poor whites. In other classes, circles of young ladies and married ladies meet expressly to practise it. Each snuff-dipper carries her bottle or box, and also a swab, by which she conveys the filthy stuff to her mouth, afterwards, perhaps, passing it to her neighbor.

The ladies prepare this swab by taking a little stick of green wood about an eighth of an inch in diameter, and chewing one end of it till the fibres are separated, giving it the appearance of a small broom. Saturating this with saliva, they dip it in their box of snuff, and then place it as far back in the mouth as possible, leaving the other end sticking out. Many walk along the streets with the dip in their mouth.

Nor does this loathsome custom stop at the South. Careful investigation has proved that for a number of years it has prevailed to a considerable extent in the city of New York, the tobacconists, who call it " digging," admitting that a large part of the demand comes from fashionable circles. These diggers, however, conceal their performances, seeking the privacy of their own rooms when giving themselves up to their disgusting debauch. With a horn or a spoon the abominable stuff is deposited inside the lower lip, and thence, when sufficiently moistened, passed round the mouth.

Says the journal from which most of the above facts are taken : " That our readers may form some idea of the enormous prevalence of this habit in their midst, we may state that one tobacconist, having a small store on Broadway, retails one hundred pounds per week, to his ' digging ' customers alone. Another firm, which keeps a store on Broadway, and also one down town, makes and sells three barrels — seven hundred pounds — in three days, all of which is consumed by women of New York city. The amount used by each ' digger,' varies from one quarter of a pound to a pound a week."

A victim of this terrible mania, finding when she had started on a journey, that she had forgotten her snuff-box, gave a black stewardess five dollars for a little of the baneful dust which she had in her possession,

Alas for the woman who has surrendered to this vilest habit! The costliest gifts and the most earnest rebukes are alike unavailing. Neither conscience nor reason, neither ruined health, nor pleading friends can move her.

But this unspeakably dreadful custom is by no means confined to grown-up women. Indeed it would seem to be, in the South, a part of common-school education; while the boys spit tobacco-juice all over the floor, the girls hold their snuff-swab, or *dip*, between the teeth, except indeed, when they share it with some less-favored schoolmate.

Many have supposed that the snuff taking, formerly so common among women and girls in the North, and which frequently was an understood part of the social gatherings, had long ago died out. But it would seem that the habit has only changed its form, and that from bad to very much worse. Indeed the use of snuff among factory-girls, "to lie as a sweet morsel between the cheek and gums, is growing alarmingly prevalent. In response to inquiries, a druggist in a large manfacturing town affirms that "there is no limit to its use by these girls."

The outlook as to feminine *smokers* is equally disheartening. A tobacco-dealer affirms that "nearly half his trade in cigarettes is directly or indirectly among women and girls."

A graduate of one of our best ladies' seminaries has so fearfully retrograded that she indulges in a daily after-dinner cigarette.

On a crowded boat, between New York and Boston, a lady (?) passenger, unable to sleep, rose at three, virtuously mended her gloves, and then, O shade of Minerva! leaning back in her arm-chair, gave herself up to a cigarette; while, stretched on mattresses around her, many looked on with undisguised amazement and disgust.

Riding in an omnibus in the New England metropolis, I heard one young girl in a loud voice ask another, "Did you forget the cigarettes?" "I was afraid I had left them, but I find they are in my pocket." I could scarcely credit my senses. I had another shock, however, at what, after this, ought not to have surprised me, — the hearing of profane words from those same youthful lips.

But there is a still darker view. The smoking father's darling, who climbs into his arms, and clings around his neck, and whom he kisses fondly with lips redolent of a Havana, is made familiar with its flavor. A drop of its poison on the tongue of her pet kitten would be fatal. But she becomes gradually accustomed to it, and, associating it with her papa, will sometimes "play smoke." And now her little brother appears with a dainty cigarette in his mouth, seemingly a bit of white, fragrant paper, so delicate that with a puff or two it disappears. "How nice!" she exclaims, "please give me one." He complies, for there is no protesting voice. Why should there be? Her father, now and then, smokes these cigarettes as "baby cigars." Her brother, too, smokes them; why,

pray should should n't she?　Alas! what is to be
the end of all this?

A writer in the Washington *Post* gives an account of a well-dressed lady who entered a drug-
store, and, coolly asking for a couple of cigars,
paid for them as unconcernedly as she would for a
bottle of cologne.　In answer to his questions, the
druggist informed him that he sold as many cigars
either to ladies or on their order by messengers as
he did to gentlemen, remarking that at first the
ladies were quite shy as to their purchases, and
that he managed matters so as to save their blushes.
"But after a while," he added significantly, "they
don't mind."

And what shall be said of ladies' smoking-clubs?
From the *Retailer*, of New York city, we learn
that a cigar-dealer of Louisville, Ky., pronounces
the members of such a club his most profitable
customers.　By his account, it seems that they are
from the aristocracy of the city; that they insist
on the very finest of tobacco, flavored with the
most delicate perfumes; that they meet at one
another's houses, and, with locked doors, *have out
their smoke;* that they seek to remove all traces of
the habit, or, if any tell-tale scent betrays them,
charge it to the account of their smoking gentlemen friends.　One of these young ladies is reported as saying that, although she would prefer
not to have her smoking habit known, yet that, if
the secret got out, and was unfavorably commented
on, "she would snap her fingers in the objector's
face."

Since writing the above, I have met with a Kentucky young woman who confirms the above account, but begs that it may not be taken for granted that all the Kentucky girls are of this sort, as some of them are strongly opposed to tobacco.

On the other hand, I have learned from authentic sources that in Philadelphia, the city of William Penn, there is also a ladies' smoking-club, and composed, like the former, of the *crême de la crême* of society.

How many other of our cities are thus desecrated?

There is, if possible, a still lower deep to which the fair sex has fallen, — the chewing of tobacco. I learn from accredited witnesses that this degrading habit is quite common among Western and Southern women; and a picture was given of one of these chewers too revolting to repeat. Yet these women, say the narrators, are sometimes from the so-called respectable class.

In heaven-wide contrast to such women and to the clubs above named is an association of young women, in a certain town, who passed resolutions that they would not have intercourse with any young man who used tobacco, or who was not strictly temperate. At first, the young men made themselves merry over this, declaring that they could stand out as long as the girls. But these girls quietly held to their resolves; and gradually one young man after another broke from his obnoxious habits, till tobacco and the wine-cup were banished from the circle.

DEMANDS OF MODERN TRAVEL.

A keen observer writes : " Your genuine smoker comes to feel that he has a right to all the air, in doors and out of doors, and feels himself wronged when a man or woman puts in a claim to breathe it without the tobacco admixture."

Let me give a recent experience bearing directly on this point. After various inquiries as to the different routes from St. Louis to Chicago, the glowing representations as to " *The Palace Reclining-Chair Cars*," on the Chicago & Alton Road, led my companion and myself to make choice of that. So, on a bright morning, we entered the car, anticipating a delightful journey. As we stopped at the various stations, passengers came in through the door in front. They were mostly of the male sex, and now and then one of them had a cigar in his mouth. I cannot assert positively that these cigars were lighted, but I noticed that they were laid aside with seeming reluctance, or held tenderly in the hand; and in one or two cases, that they were still burning. The seats near the door, and facing the chairs, were occupied by persons whom it needed no diviner's rod to pronounce smokers, while the same might be said of several who sat in the chairs.

The atmosphere soon became thoroughly impregnated with tobacco-fumes. It did not take long to discover that the smoking-room was close by, between the inner and the outer doors. As a matter of course, the little hall, or vestibule, was filled with unmistakable odors, which made their way through every cranny and crevice; while each time the door was opened — which I should say occurred about every other minute, — thick clouds of smoke were borne directly into our faces, bringing with them headache, nausea, sore throat, and a sense of suffocation.

I ventured to ask the porter to open the ventilators. As he hesitated, I urged that the smoke sickened me, begging for a *little* fresh air, if only for a few minutes. He replied courteously, but to the effect that people couldn't expect to have the cars like a private parlor; yet he *did* slightly open one or two of them. I have no fault to find with him, knowing how many are opposed to ventilation; indeed, it was a hard alternative, for even strong and perpetual currents could only partially have purified the atmosphere, while they might have cost some of the passengers a severe cold.

As it was, the faint breath that stole in was no match for the ever-increasing fumes. For, in addition to the poisoned air so freely bestowed on us from the smoke-room, we were forced to endure the presence of the smokers themselves, as one after another returned to the cars. Gentlemen, as some of them evidently were, — with a good number of honorable legislators, — they surely could not have realized how saturated were their whole persons with offensive odors. Over and over again I asked myself, "Am I, verily, in one of 'THE FINEST PALACE RECLINING-CHAIR CARS IN THE WORLD?'"

After a time one of the aforesaid gentlemen carefully closed the ventilator. Feeling too miserable for resistance, I said not a word; indeed, I had entirely succumbed to the inevitable. For twelve long hours were we thus imprisoned,—our much-anticipated trip being turned into disappointment, discomfort, and positive suffering.

Yet we were pilgrims all the way from the old Bay State, and never again expected—I might, on that day, have added, never again *desired*—to be in the Mississippi valley. Need I say that I was thankful when the last mile was ended; when sick, weary, and *disgusted*, I was free to leave this much-lauded "luxurious" car.

To show that my statements are not exaggerated, let me say that neither a long waiting in the ladies' room, nor a ride of a mile and a half, proved a sufficient quarantine. We carried with us a strong tobacco-flavor, which our friends instantly noticed. If they had inferred that we were just from a smoking car, would they have been far out of the way? For several days the dreadful tobacco-odor clung to my garments, and the tobacco-poison lingered in my system.

Now, I am a peaceable woman, not given to complaints; and were I the only victim, I would keep silence. But I speak in behalf of hundreds

of fellow-sufferers, who are beguiled, like ourselves, by alluring advertisements. The common
smoking-car is quite bad enough in the penalties it
inflicts, sometimes, on a whole train. But to have
one's expectations of something super-excellent *end
in smoke* — this is a cruel imposition.

Is there no remedy for all this? Have not the
lovers of God's pure air certain rights as well as
the ever-increasing — may I not add, ever-*en-
croaching* — army of smokers? And will not you,
mighty men of the railroads, help us in securing
and preserving these rights?

In justice to at least one of these autocrats, I
ought to state that, on venturing to send an account
of my unfortunate journey to the general manager
of the road, he returned the following courteous reply : " I very much regret that you were annoyed
in the manner indicated. The demands of modern
travel have compelled us to place these smoking
rooms in many of our chair-cars, and in our sleep-
ing-cars; but it is the intention to have them so
constructed that they will not in the least way
interfere with the other part of the car. We will
look into the matter of which you complain, and
see that a remedy is applied."

While fully appreciating these assurances, I
could not help pondering the expression, "the
demands of modern travel." What, then, *is* this
modern travel? And who are these *demanders*,
to whom must be sacrificed women, children, and
non-smoking men?

One of this latter class, a sick banker, in making an extended pleasure trip through the country, represents that at the stations he usually found the *Gentlemen's* Room "a smoking pen;" that on the boats, whenever he took his seat, "a smoke factory" would be planted in his face; that when on the cars, with the stopping of every train, gentlemen were sure to be at the open door filling the car with smoke, while along the route the stock was frequently replenished by the passage through it of a lighted cigar; that he came to shun the palace-cars, as he there had to pay higher prices for less comfortable seats, and for staler smoke, which, from the close vicinity of the smoking-room, was distributed without stint. This banker's experience quickened his inventive powers to the extent of making some adequate return, in the form of a thousand trumpets imitating cigars. Armed with these, boys were commissioned to go forth, and, like another Gideon's host, to blow their trumpets in the ears of all offenders; and thus avenge on their sense of hearing the torment they inflicted on others.

This tobacco habit is making fearful strides, and sometimes under an illusive guise. A friend tells me of a journey he took on *The Limited Express of the Pittsburg, Fort Wayne & Chicago Road.* Attracted by the proclamation of a fine library in the cars, he sought it out to find all the books locked up, and the room so dense with smoke that he could scarcely see from one end of it to the other; could not easily have read the books, had they been open before him.

Another friend has given me her experience. It seems that a number of the passengers had taken through tickets from Philadelphia to Cleveland, and with the understanding that there was no change of cars. At Harrisburg, where the train stopped for a few minutes, a gentleman and his wife stepped out to get refreshments, leaving their little ones with the nurse. While they were absent, a brakeman came along, calling on the passengers to go at once into another car. So, with only the nurse to attend to it, the children, with their many scattered wraps, and bags, and parcels, must be quickly gathered up and hustled out. A lady in the same car, to whom this move was as annoying as it was unexpected, in an aggrieved tone asked the brakeman, "Why is such a change necessary?" "Because," replied the brakeman, "*we have to make this up for a smoking car!*"

"THE DEMANDS OF MODERN TRAVEL!"

And where will these demands end?

TOBACCO-BARBARISM.

There is a close if hidden connection between the minor and the major moralities.

No one can violate the former without blunting his finer feelings and becoming far more likely to infringe the latter.

In the *Art Journal*, Jackson Jarves, in treating

of " the manners of the Latin and Ango-Saxon
races, considered as a fine art," attributes much of
the decline of good manners to the increasing use
of tobacco.   He says : —

" I refer to the anti-æsthetic influence.   The
supreme test of the virtue of the knight in the days
of chivalry, which was the highest ideal of fine
manners, was his self-denial and desire to succor
the oppressed.   The severest test of the modern
gentleman is his willingness to forego his pipe for
the comfort and health of another.   It takes a
thoroughly well-bred man to withstand this form
of self-indulgence, when it can only be practised
to the annoyance of another.   Whatever the benefit or harm the use of tobacco may do the consumer's body, its common tendency is to render
the mind indifferent to the well-being of his
neighbors.   Smokers crowd into rooms or seats
reserved for those who would escape their presence,
and claim the right to fumigate, sicken, and half
strangle those, be they delicate women and children, whose physicial organizations are more
sensitive than their own, and sometimes add insult
to the contemptuous indifference with which they
inflict positive distress on their victims."

Mr. Jarves concludes with an illustration showing the tendency of this tobacco habit to develop
boorish manners : —

" I have known a German of rank, with his
daughter, get into a ladies' compartment in a railway carriage, and insist on using his pipe, despite

the expostulations of the lady occupants, who finally were compelled to apply to the guard for protection, when he was made to go into the smoking carriage. As he reluctantly went, his daughter turned angrily to the ladies, exclaiming, ' See what you have done to my poor papa! You make him leave his place to smoke away from me.'"

A writer describes a scene he witnessed at a hotel in the vicinity of one of the most popular New England colleges. Around a coarse, illiterate man, enwreathed in clouds of smoke, gathered a circle of young loafers, to whom he passed cigars. As they joined him in smoking, they talked slang and profanity. It was difficult for the beholder to credit the fact, which incidentally became known to him, that these same smoking, swearing loafers were veritable college students.

I believe it will not be denied that, as tobacco comes, good manners are apt to go, yet if you express concern that a young friend is in this bondage, one sometimes breaks out on you with the remark, " Be thankful he does n't drink. Let him smoke as much as he will, and in your parlor, too, that you may thus save him from the saloon." And it is said without a suspicion that this habit often leads to that very place.

All honor to the brave young woman, who, in uttering her protest against tobacco, declares that " there is one girl firmly resolved never to marry a man who uses tobacco, and to do what she can

by prayer and works to break up this growing
evil." In her own family she had so learned this
evil by heart that she could not help lifting up her
voice. Are there not many other girls who will
join her ranks, and thus present a fair, solid front
to the invading foe?

"Tobacco is the worst natural curse of modern
civilization." Such is the declaration of our æsthetic seer.

That the general tendency of this weed is to bring
men down to a lower plane will not be denied.
The effect on the lower classes themselves is to
degrade them still lower, to deaden the sense of
their own pitiful condition, and stifle any flickering
sparks of ambition. Smoking is called the poor
man's solace, because " it makes him contented
with his lot." That is one of its very mischiefs.
He has no business to be contented. He is living
in a miserable tenement, and in the most meagre
fashion, when he might be owning a home and
educating his children. But there, day in and day
out, he sits, selfishly and stupidly smoking his
pipe, while his pinched and joyless wife patiently
waits on him, and does her best to keep the wolf
from the door.

As for the refined and scholarly, what but the
strange charms of this narcotic could reconcile
them to the companionship and the habits to which
it not unfrequently degrades them?

Says Elizur Wright : "A man calling himself a
gentleman, with all the outward appointments of

a gentleman, and everything *but* the smell of a gentleman, will do in your house, in your parlor, in the very presence of ladies, things which, if not under the spell of tobacco, no money would have tempted him to do."

No spot is too sacred for the encroachment of the tobacco-tyrant. The neat ingrained carpet of your guest-chamber and the elegant tapestry of your drawing-room alike bear his defiling marks; and with all your painstaking you can never efface them.

Writes Horace Greeley: "I have intimated that the tobacco-consumer is not, indeed, necessarily and inevitably, but naturally and usually, a blackguard; that chewing or smoking obviously tends to blackguardism. Can any one doubt it? . . Go into a public gathering where a speaker of delicate lungs and an invincible repugnance to tobacco is trying to discuss some important topic so that a thousand men can hear and understand him, yet whereinto ten or twenty smokers have introduced themselves, — a long-nine projecting horizontally from beneath the nose of each, a fire at one end and a fool at the other, — and mark how the puff, puffing gradually transforms the atmosphere (none too pure at the best) into that of some foul and pestilential cavern, choking the utterance of the speaker and distracting the attention of the hearers, until the argument is arrested or its effect utterly destroyed. If he who will selfishly, recklessly, impudently, inflict so much discomfort or annoyance on many, in order that he may enjoy in a particular place an indulgence which could as well be enjoyed where no one else would be affected by it, be not a blackguard, who *can* be? What conduct would indicate bad breeding and a bad heart, if such conduct does not?"

Something, however, should be said in behalf of the smoker. In the universal practice of what is the joy of his heart, and in the ready tolerance, if not actual encouragement, of some of our own sex, it is not altogether strange that he becomes incredulous as to the offensiveness of his deed. More than this, it is one of the tendencies of tobacco to blunt the sensibilities. In a recent lecture on this narcotic, R. L. Carpenter, of England, dwells emphatically on its peculiar influence in rendering its devotees indifferent to the discomfort of others. "The high-bred nobleman who is the slave of tobacco is, in that respect," he says, "not above the smoker who blacks his boots."

From an article in the London *Times*, in September, 1879, the following pertinent remarks are taken: "There is a reason against public smoking, — perhaps, in effect, against all smoking, — which has scarcely received sufficient recognition. It is the absolute indifference to the comfort and convenience of society at large that it is certain to produce. The smoker does not care whether you are happy or miserable. . . . Smokers monopolize far more than their share of our railway accommodation. Their exigency knows no limits. A smoker must have a compartment in which he enjoys the free exercise of his privilege, even if he have it all to himself and a dozen people are rushing about the platform, looking in vain for room, the guard's whistle already sounding. Tobacco is a powerful drug, administered through the respiratory organs, that is, through the atmosphere ; and as we breathe one another's atmosphere, as it were, in common stock, the smoker administers his drug to all about him, whether they wish it or not. The indifference or apathy with regard to the comfort of others is one of the most remarkable effects of tobacco. No other drug will produce anything like it. The opium-eater does not compel you to eat opium with him ; the drunkard does not compel you to drink. The smoker compels you to smoke, — nay, more, to breathe the smoke he has just discharged from his own mouth."

"Tobacco *demoralizes*," says Dr. Parker. "It makes a man careless about his hair ; he lets his nails go uncleaned ; his clothes are soiled ; in a word, he is dirty."

A writer in *Blackwood* asserts "that tobacco is the favorite filth of every savage life within the circumference of the globe ; that it fills the atmosphere of the continent with a perpetual stench ; . . . that it is in its own nature the filthiest, most foolish, dullest, and most disgusting practice on the face of the earth."

TOBACCO *vs.* WOMAN.

Tobacco is the relentless foe of woman. It withdraws man from her society, and makes him glory in his isolation, thus greatly marring, if not positively undermining, the relation between the sexes.

In the words of Cowper, —

> "Thy worst effect is banishing for hours
> The sex whose presence civilizes ours.
> They dare not wait the riotous abuse
> Thy thirst-creating streams, at length, produce,
> When wine has given indecent language birth,
> And forced the flood-gates of licentious mirth."

In an account of "The Founding of the *Atlantic Monthly*" which appeared in the *Golden Rule*, it is stated that it was for a long time the custom for the editor and chief contributors to dine together once a month. After giving a constellation of illustrious names by which the festival was usually honored, it is said: "Whittier came rarely. His health was always delicate . . . and he was evidently troubled by the clouds of smoke that succeeded the dinner. Once, only, the women-contributors were invited. The experiment was not repeated."

The tendency of this habit will be more and more to separate woman from man, unless, in self-defence, she, too, forms the habit, and learns to revel in tobacco-smoke.

Gentlemen, would you hail the advent of such a day?

Bulwer writes : " Woman in this scale, the weed in that. Jupiter, hang out thy balance and weigh them both ; and if thou give the preference to woman, all I can say is, the next time Juno ruffles thee, O Jupiter, try the weed."

"The fact is," says Thackeray, "the cigar is a rival to the ladies, and their conqueror, too."

"What is the real attraction of these gorgeous establishments?" inquired some one of a gentleman, entering a new club-house on Fifth Avenue, New York. And what was the graceful and gallant reply? "No woman can enter them. Once within these sacred walls, we are safe from everything that wears a petticoat." "Are we getting to be Turks?" the narrator adds. "The Turks shut women in, we shut them out." No wonder that Parton writes, " There is something in the practice of smoking that allies a man with barbarians, and constantly tends to make him think and talk like a barbarian."

Is such a disintegration and degradation of society in this nineteenth century of the world a thing to glory in?

Sure I am that, were the tobacco-problem fully comprehended, every true woman would cease to condone so grave an offence, — an offence which puts in jeopardy the health, not only of the wrong-doer, but, in a greater or less degree, that of his whole family ; which tends to lower its æsthetic and social tone, and involves a lengthening train of discomforts and miseries.

Very dark is this cloud in our horizon. In true gallantry American mankind is ahead of all the world. Could we only secure this earnestly coveted, much-prayed-for reform, it would add the one finishing touch. It would exalt this same American into the ideal gentleman. But where will the present current land him?

Wrote Mary Clemmer in the *Independent:* "Gazing on the average American who crowds the corridors of the capitol on the last day of the session, it is impossible to believe him the fraction of a civilized nation. Nothing in their way could be more exquisite than the staircases of tinted marble leading to the galleries of both Senate and House. Yet had they been tottering staircases leading to dens of dissipation instead of to the highest legislative chambers of the nation, they could not be more defiled. From base to summit they reek with tobacco. It drips from their edges and is piled in 'quids' in their corners, while the spittoons that line the way would disgrace a pot-house. With tobacco reeking under your feet; tobacco spurting diagonally on your clothes; tobacco making the air blue with smoke and foul with smell, over acres of marble that should be stainless as your conscience, altogether it is quite sufficient to make you doubt the civilization of the people who claim to be the mightiest on the earth."

MORAL AND SPIRITUAL VIEW.

DETERIORATING INFLUENCE.

According to a New York doctor, "The universal experience of all mankind will attest, and the intelligent observation of every individual will confirm, the statement that, precisely in the ratio that persons indulge in narcotic stimulants, the mental powers are unbalanced, the lower propensities acquire undue and inordinate activity at the expense, not only of the vital stamina, but also of the moral and intellectual nature. The whole being is not only perverted, but introverted and retroverted. Tobacco-using, even more than liquor-drinking disqualifies the mind for exercising its intuitions concerning the right and wrong : it degrades the moral sense below the intellectual recognitions."

It is the testimony of Dr. Lizars that "in some instances the starting-point of a criminal career dates from the first indulgence of the tobacco-vice, — producing by slow degrees, when acting upon a constitution still extremely flexible, a complete moral and intellectual transformation as well as physical degeneracy."

The professors in the University and High School at Ann Arbor, Michigan, who have had a long experience among thousands of young men, regard this weed as having a worse effect than even liquor, affirming that more young men break down in body and mind, and finally go astray as a result of smoking, than of drinking, while the former often leads to the latter.

Prof. Moses Stuart, of Andover, who at one time was himself a user of the weed, writes: "That it undermines the health of thousands; that it creates a nervous irritability, and thus operates on the temper and moral character of men; that it often creates a thirst for spirituous liquors; that it allures to clubs and grog-shops and taverns; and finally, that it is a very serious and needless expense, are things that cannot be denied."

Prof. Mead, of Oberlin: "The tobacco habit tends to deaden the sense of honor, as well as of decency; and none are more likely to practise deception unscrupulously than those who use the weed."

In the same spirit, President Bascom, of the Wisconsin State University, affirms that "every man who uses tobacco is in one degree or another enslaved by it. The habit is vulgar and low in all its associations. It uniformly degenerates into that which can only be fittingly characterized as filthy. No one who uses tobacco can fully escape the taint. His breath is impregnated with it; his clothes are full of it; his presence is a constant reminder of it to delicate organs. The use of tobacco is an unclean habit and belongs to unclean persons. There are few spectacles giving a more disgraceful impression of our civilization than that of a mere lad sporting a pipe or a cigar in self-congratulatory imitation of the bad habits of those older in years than himself, but alike immature in wisdom."

A physician who has well considered the matter, writes: "I believe that the habit of using tobacco in various forms is not only laying the foundation for many diseases of serious character, and not easily removed, but that it is damaging the moral fibre of many of our students."

The superintendent of the Reform School at Westboro, Mass., reports that all the boys sent there have been users of tobacco; and that it is the one thing that occasions him the most trouble, and that he is working hardest to extirpate."

Chancellor Sims, of the Syracuse University: "The tobacco-habit is expensive, offensive to others, and deteriorating to the one indulging in it."

Dr. Harris: "There is not another practice in civilized society that will so directly introduce a young man to vicious associates and to all the haunts of wickedness, as do the unrebuked, fashionable habits of tobacco-using; nor is there another article of luxury that so secretly and yet so surely saps all the foundations of manliness and virtue. It paves the way to every vice, and tends directly and powerfully to habits of the grossest immorality."

CLERICAL TOBACCO.

" But good men smoke and chew ! "

The more 's the pity. There 's no use in blinking the fact that many Christians, ministers among them, are not guiltless in this matter. The very utmost that can be made of the plea, however, is that some good men are not free from the dominion of very bad habits. This, unfortunately is no new thing.

Years ago the use of intoxicating liquors was practised and approved by the majority of clergymen, one or more of them being now and then taken home drunk from some association or convention dinner, where wines abounded; but precisely because drinking was in such good repute was there the more pressing need of bold leaders to raise the banner of reform.

Let us not use the goodness of a man as a garment to cover his sins, little or great. This very goodness brings upon him a tenfold responsibility.

A rich man, in acknowledging the receipt of one of George Trask's tobacco books, sensibly remarks, —

" The best proofs of its utility should be its effects upon the clergy. We can hardly expect youth to refrain from tobacco when their moral teachers set them so bad an example; when you have reformed those of your profession, if you will apply to me, I will give fifty dollars to reform the rest of mankind."

The London *Christian World*, after commenting on the Spurgeon case, thus closes : " To ourselves this tobacco pest is a daily martyrdom, and we could earnestly wish that every Christian teacher, at all events, felt no desire to indulge in a habit . . . which is unquestionably most fearfully destructive, both to the bodies and souls of tens of thousands of our young men."

Neal Dow, who was in England at the time of the Spurgeon-Pentecost affair, relates that he was soon after a guest in a family where the matter came up. The father told him that by long and painful labor he had obtained a promise from his son, who was a great smoker, to abandon the habit, and that he had kept his pledge till the great preacher's declaration, " I shall go home and smoke the best cigar I have got to the glory of God." After this he returned to his cigar, saying that Spurgeon's example was good enough for him. Even a clergyman pleads, in excuse for his habit, that " Mr. Spurgeon, the greatest preacher in the world, smokes."

Since then, if report speaks true, this " greatest preacher " has abandoned his cigar, not, as we wish he had done years ago, from religious principle, but because he was driven to it by its injurious influence upon his health. A similar report prevails as to some of our great American preachers.

A clergyman's son overheard his father telling another clergyman that he could never write well without his cigar. Arguing analogically, the boy naturally inferred the same thing would improve the working of his own brains, and thus better enable him to reach the head of his class. So, stating his reasons, he begged for a cigar. What could that father do?

Another clergyman walking with his boy of six, and meeting a group of young smokers, with cigar-stubs and broken pipes in their mouths, pointed them out warningly to his son, declaring that the city authorities ought to break up such practices. "Is n't it worse for a man to smoke, father?" "Do you think it is, my son?" "Please father, boys would n't want to smoke if men did n't do it." The arrow, so innocently aimed, hit the mark. "I threw away my cigar," relates the father, "and have never touched tobacco since."

That a clergyman's influence is greatly impaired by the use of the drug is painfully evident. A young man was deeply moved by the eloquence of a preacher, and lingered after the services to speak with him as he came out, but when he saw him spitting tobacco-juice, he retired in disgust.

A lady of the Episcopal church, who had come up to the communion altar, on seeing the rector take a quid from his mouth and deposit it carefully on a chair, was impelled to withdraw, shrinking at the very thought of receiving the sacramental cup from such hands.

An eminent divine relates that at one time when walking the streets of the city where he resided, with a cigar in his mouth, he met an infidel acquaintance who burst into laughter. On being challenged as to the cause of his merriment, he replied; — "Oh, I was thinking how you would look going up to meet the Lord amid wreaths of tobacco-smoke, and with that cigar in your mouth." Neither the infidel nor anyone else ever again saw a cigar in that man's mouth. It was a case of instant conversion.

To show to what grievous indecorums even a minister who is in bondage to tobacco may be driven, one or two instances are related.

At the close of a revival meeting in some town in Illinois, the preacher who was conducting it made the following appeal : " As I am a great lover of tobacco, I would be very thankful if some kind friend in this audience would present me with twenty-five cents or a half dollar that I may supply my wants in this direction." Had tobacco killed his religion, and his common sense as well?

A negro preacher in Richmond, Va., thus sets forth his view of heaven : " My brethern and my sistern, you ain't a gwine to have to pay no ten cents a plug for tobacco there, you kin get jist as much pure Golden Leaf as you wants, and a little more ; and you kin chaw and chaw and chaw all day long, and it won't cost you a cent." " Not a cent ! " came exultantly from all parts of the little church.

What an idea of future blessedness!

As an offset to this may be given the following, which was delivered on the stage at St. Louis : —

The circus preacher told the crowd that "there are some professors of the pure principles of Christ, so filthy from the use of tobacco, that if the Lord put him on sentinel duty, when they arrived at the haven Moody tells of, he would keep them quarantined outside the pearly gates until they were aired, and the cleansing angel had had time to perfume them, in order that they might be fitted to enter into the presence of a pure and holy God."

It is a relief to indicate the better side of ministerial influence.

A well-known preacher, who had renounced the weed on assuming the charge of a metropolitan church, found that a large number of his members were enslaved to the appetite. His efforts against it were so earnest, that, when he left the church, out of nine hundred members only one remained its victim. With his smoking successor, however, the people lapsed again into the old bondage.

Some years ago, an eminent divine from the Old World was invited to deliver a course of lectures in the virtuous old-fashioned town of Oberlin. Before the course was completed, his supply of chewing-tobacco was exhausted. Making his extremity known to the professor in whose family he was a guest, he requested that a supply might be procured for him.

As no use of the weed by professor or student is

tolerated in that institution, his host was in a predicament. Should he, in defiance of law himself purchase the forbidden article? Or, not venturing on this, should he delegate the commission to one of the students? He decided on the only right step. Seeking the room of his distinguished guest, he frankly explained that he could not supply his wants without breaking the rule which, from the beginning, had been observed by all the teachers and twenty thousand pupils.

The good doctor made answer that he should not bring dishonor upon the rule while he was in that pure atmosphere.

It can hardly be pleasant to a D.D., and perhaps LL.D. to boot, to have it bruited abroad: "He is an extraordinary man; but he is also an extraordinary smoker, his study being sometimes perfectly black with smoke. He is a great and a good man; but he *will* smoke a pipe. He is a fine preacher; but then he goes through the streets puffing a cigar."

Eloquence and tobacco flowing from the same lips — the eloquence, perchance, born of the narcotic! To many a hearer the edge of the sermon is blunted by his knowledge that the preacher has a quid adroitly hidden in his mouth. The more devout the man, the more deplorable the conjunction.

During the sessions of a religious body, it is not uncommon to see ministers smoking in the vestibule, while the committee-rooms are saturated with tobacco-fumes.

Says James Parton : " Clergymen hurry out of church to find momentary relief for their tired throats in an ecstatic smoke, and carry into the apartment of fair invalids the odor of ex-cigars. . . A parishioner who wishes to confer upon his minister — if a smoker — a real pleasure, can hardly do a safer thing than send him a thousand cigars of a good clerical brand. It is particularly agreeable to a clergyman to receive a present which supplies him with a luxury he loves, but in which he knows in his inmost soul he ought not to indulge."

I cannot forbear to quote here one or two passages from the satirical remonstrance of "A Smoking Minister." In writing to *The Advance*, he says, —

" I had hoped, it seemed vainly, that, after the death of Mr. Trask, no more unjust and exaggerated statements and no innuendos and covert reflections upon us who puff and chew would be admitted into the newspapers, or prayer-meetings, or the pulpit. I write while smarting under some spoken and some implied criticisms that have touched my sensitiveness."

After enumerating at length the manifold benefits he has derived from tobacco, he sums up, —

" If I am deprived of my usual smoke, my nerves are so unstrung that I am unfitted for any utterance demanding consecutive thought, accurate expression, and deep religious feeling. It only aggravates my difficulty to have it referred to in the Sabbath-School, or prayer-meeting, or the pulpit.

"I do not, however, object to a quiet discussion of the subject in ministers' meetings, if the majority are smokers and are very witty. I am a Congregationalist, from conviction and early training: but I have seriously thought of joining the Presbyterians, as I have heard that, while they are strict in doctrine, they are more liberal than we are in the non-essentials of practice. If *The Advance* would use its influence to have all the public or printed allusions to this trivial and entirely personal matter abated, it would be a great relief to me and many brethren, in the ministry and out. Indeed it might save us to the denomination."

It is stated on good authority that a well-known divine, on arranging to give a lecture to the young ladies of a certain academy, agreed to take in payment for his service a box of the best Spanish cigars. The lecture was delivered; the cigars were made over and the debt was thus squared.

I am tempted to give a few humorous but very pertinent passages from a letter purporting to be written by a zealous deacon to his offending pastor: — "I don't know the Hebrew for terbakker, but I know what terbakker is, to my sorror; and I'm agin it . . . In the space of six years grandfather took over three hundred cuds out of Parson Hawker's pulpit. He thought he would collect 'em as a sort of ecclesyasticle curiosity. Sometimes he found 'em on the floor, sometimes on the seat or cushion, sometimes on the Bible, and now and then,

as a mark in the him book. . . . And now, sir,
I'll say a few words about them spittoons that the
young ladies were agoin' to present you on New
Year's day. I went to three of the gentlemen
whose darters was most perminent in the bisness,
and asked 'em if they would be so good as to meet
me on Monday mornin' at the meeting-house, and
bring their darters. So they said they would. I
told 'em it seemed to come nat'ral to you to spit
off broadcast, and no spittoon smaller than the
pulpit would be of any use. I them told 'em I
had n't yet cleaned the pulpit, but left it for them
to examine, just as it was arter you had operated.
I asked 'em to step up and look at it. On Monday
they came. They all looked in, and agreed they
would n't have believed that one minister could
have done it without assistance. Old Col. Pickets
was the last to go up; and when he came down, he
shook his head, and said it did n't smell Orthodox.
It's been proposed by some, instead of a pulpit,
to have a raised platform, with nothin' round it,
so that every secret thing shall be brought to light.
Father Cleverly, who's amazin' quick for a text,
said, in such case you might well preach from the
latter part of Isaiah, 1: 6. 'I hid not my face
from shame and spitting.'"

If such things are possible with clergymen, what
better can we look for in church-officers and Sunday-school teachers? One writes of a certain deacon that he has many a time seen him, in church,
fill his pipe and take out a match, waiting with

evident impatience till the meeting was dismissed, when the pipe was instantly lighted, and everybody assailed with its odors.

When the news was sprung upon a little village in Ohio, that an old and respected deacon was attacked with delirium tremens, no wonder that consternation seized the residents. Nevertheless, the report was true, and after several attacks the good man died, a victim of tobacco.

A Sunday-School scholar begged to be removed to another class, but declined to give his reasons till, being urged, he confessed that he could n't endure the tobacco-breath of his teacher.

A student who went from Yale College to Union Theological Seminary there learned to smoke, — when he expressed his regret that he had n't learned sooner, " thus securing years of delight." In all fairness, however, it should be added that his habit was formed in intercourse with fellow-students fresh from college, and, with a single exception, from Yale.

While it is true that a number of young men have given up tobacco during their course in Union Seminary, it must be admitted that at least one of the students, a man of abilities and earnest piety, and who offered himself to the foreign field, was unfortunately both a smoker and a chewer. In speaking of this case, a young theologue pertinently remarks: " It has been my feeling that it would be much better if, while he lays down his life at his Master's feet, he would also give up this indulgence for his Master's sake. I cannot get rid of the notion of incongruity between a pure heart and a foul mouth; a breath now laden with the utterance of inspired truth, and now with fumes of tobacco."

Think of a smoking clergyman standing at the communion table, on which are spread the emblems of that self-sacrificing Love that surpasses mortal conception! Think of him as ministering to suffering and disease; — as approaching the bedside of a sick member of his flock, and being feebly waved away because of the offensive odor radiating from his whole person! A dying woman was so affected by the tobacco-breath of her pastor as he leaned down and talked with her, that she begged her friends to employ at her funeral a minister who would breathe no poison over her coffin.

A gentleman who had listened with deep interest to a powerful sermon from a distinguished theological professor, was greatly surprised the next day to see him smoking a cigar, and confessed that the sight destroyed the impression of the sermon. He adds, — "A young man trying to reform from this habit remarked to me, — 'Never say anything against it again, when a man who can preach such a sermon as that was yesterday indulges in it.'"

Says a well-known clergyman in addressing his brethren, — "Do you say, — 'I am not going, because there are weak men in this world, to deny myself any lawful and proper pleasure.' Then you are not fit to be a preacher and a disciple of the Lord Jesus Christ."

In a discourse to the graduating class at Williams College, President Hopkins, after some preliminary remarks on the use of tobacco, thus sums up: "I may express to you my conviction that habitual narcotic stimulation of the brain is not compatible with the fullest consecration of the body as a temple of God. Good men may do this in ignorance, as other things prevalent at times have been done, and not offend their consciences; but I believe that greater earnestness, more self-scrutiny, fuller light, would reveal its incompatibility with full consecration and sweep it entirely away. The present position on this point of the Christian Church as a whole, and largely of the Christian ministry, I regard as obstructive of the highest manhood and of the spread of spiritual religion. I know that strong men have in this connection been bound as in fetters of brass, and cast down from high places, and have found premature prostration and a premature grave, and that this process is going on now. Let me say, therefore, to those of you who expect to be ministers, that I believe that sermons, even those called great sermons, which are the product of alcoholic or narcotic stimulation, are a service of God by ' strange fire;' and that for men to be scrupulous about their attire as clerical, and yet to enter upon religious services with narcotized bodies and a breath that 'smells to heaven' of anything but incense, is an incongruity and an offence, a cropping out of the old Phariseeism that made clean 'the outside of the cup and the platter.' Not that abstinence has merit or secures consecration; it is only its best condition."

Consider what an almost insuperable obstacle the tobacco-example of clergymen opposes to the efforts of Christian parents and teachers against this evil in their children and pupils!

Dr. Higginbottom, an English physician, testifies: "After fifty years of most extensive and varied practice in my profession, I have come to the decision that smoking is a main cause of ruining our young men, pauperizing the working-men, and rendering comparatively useless the best efforts of the ministers of religion."

In the session of a district Congregational convention held in Wisconsin, a layman made an address on the subject, "What the pews want from the pulpit." Towards the close he said, "The example set by some of the pulpits in the use of tobacco is strongly objected to by many of the occupants of the pews. The Wisconsin State Congregational Convention, at its annual session in 1869, declared, —

"The common use of tobacco is an offensive practice to persons of neatness and refinement, hindering the influence of those who use it; it is a wasteful practice, using money that is needed for other purposes; it is a practice injurious to health of body and mind; it is a practice of injurious moral tendency; and it is setting a mischievous example to our youth.

"If what the State Convention said in 1869 is true, then the pews say, without any hesitation or mental reservation, that no man who is in the habit of using tobacco ought to enter the pulpit to preach the Gospel as a minister of the Lord Jesus Christ until he renounces the habit.

"It may seem hard to say it, dear Christian Lrother, but it is none the less true that the knowledge that you were in the habit of using tobacco would completely destroy your influence, and render it impossible for you to do any good to a large portion of many of the Christian congregations of the land, should you stand in their presence to speak as a Christian minister."

Bishop Huntington, of Syracuse, writes: "I could give you many reasons why the use of this narcotic seems to me especially incongruous with the calling of the ministry, which it is a large part of my duty to guard. Among them are a waste of money, an injury to health, the offence sometimes given physically to sick or sensitive persons, the moral harm done to tender consciences, the lowering of the sacred office in their estimation, and a check put upon ministerial usefulness."

MISSIONARY-TOBACCO.

"What reception may we suppose the apostles would have met with," inquires Dr. Rush, "had they carried into the houses where they were sent snuff-boxes, pipes, cigars, and bundles of cut, or rolls of pigtail, tobacco?"

The missionaries in some of our stations are greatly embarrassed in their efforts against tobacco by the influence in its favor of so many Christians in this country. When the native converts quote the honored American Reverends, Professors, and Doctors of Divinity whom they have heard named as addicted to the weed, the missionaries are struck dumb with sorrow and shame.

But what shall be said — what *can* be said — concerning any such missionaries as are themselves in bondage to this habit? Let them learn a lesson from a young colored missionary, once a slave. During the examination in reference to his going to Africa, some one inquired as to his use of the drug. He made answer that he was free from this habit, — " that a *gentleman* would not use tobacco and that a Christian gentleman would not *wish* to use it."

Mr. Rand, of the Micronesian Mission, writes; " Much as we need help in the Caroline Islands, we had rather work there alone than to have the best of men come to our aid, *if he uses tobacco.*"

TEMPERANCE AND TOBACCO.

With what conscience can a temperance man who is unwilling to give up his tobacco urge drunkards to give up their drink, especially when it is the prevailing testimony of medical authorities that tobacco-using leads naturally to liquor-drinking, that it is the "*facilis descensus Averni,*" and that multitudes of reformed inebriates have fallen again by its use? In point here is the wish of the poor, doubly-wronged Indian: "I want three things, — all the rum in the world, all the tobacco in the world, and then more rum. I smoke, because it makes me love to drink."

A reformed inebriate, in relating how he first signed the pledge, says: "I soon found that in renouncing one stimulant I used a double quantity of another; or, in the words of Theodore Weld, I had 'swapped brandy for tobacco.' Then, impelled by the feeling, 'drink I must, and drink I will,' I went back to the gutter." Two years later, hearing a lecturer affirm that the Washingtonians who apostatized were tobacco-sots almost to a man, and that the pledge, to be safe, must interdict both drug and drink, he took the double pledge, and had remained firm, but with an increasing conviction that "*you can't cure a drunkard while a slave to his pipe.*"

To the same effect, Dr. Justin Edwards declared: "Not much more can be done in behalf of the temperance cause till there is an anti-narcotic movement, particularly against tobacco, the handmaid and ally of intemperance."

Says the well-known temperance-worker, E. C. Delavan: "I have had my fears for the safety of the temperance cause through the insidious influence of tobacco. It is my opinion that while its use continues, intemperance will continue to curse the world."

It is the testimony of Jerry McAuley, who has rescued multitudes from drunkenness, that it is extremely rare to find a reformed man that continues a slave to tobacco who does not fall back into the gutter. This fact is so patent that it is coming more and more to be taken for granted that the converts in his mission, when giving up drink, will also give up the weed. The case is related of one who, being persuaded to smoke a single cigar, relapsed into drunkenness.

Says Dr. Stephenson: " The use of tobacco is one great leading-step towards intemperance. But it is a lamentable fact that very many who stand the most prominent in the temperance reform are grossly intemperate in the use of tobacco."

A noted temperance-worker in Illinois, who was a votary of the weed, was induced by a Methodist clergyman to sign a pledge of total abstinence. But the man who waxed so eloquent in urging inebriates to forswear the demon of drink found himself enslaved to as remorseless a tyrant, and broke his pledge again and again.

George Trask writes: "I have known a temperance lecturer of great distinction positively refuse to lecture till he had been furnished with a pipe of tobacco to screw his nerves up to the point of eloquence."

So enslaved do these victims become that, in spite of all remonstrance, of all propriety, they will smoke, not only in parlors and in halls, but, strangest of all, in temperance meetings. Indeed, a certain lodge of the Sons of Temperance passed a resolution that they would not lay aside their tobacco even during the hour they were gathered for temperance purposes!! God be praised that woman's crusade against intemperance has never been set back by any such marvellous inconsistency!

The author of *Temperance Tales* tells a story of the accredited agent of a temperance society. He was one day soliciting contributions with tobacco in his mouth, when he was accosted by a gentleman,—"You, sir, are not a proper person to be an agent in the cause of temperance, for you are not a temperance man yourself; you are enslaved to tobacco." No answer was made; but some one present afterwards told the rebuker that the lecturer was one of the very best men in the country. He was surprised to hear this, and would have sent an apology, had he known the agent's address. Some time after, meeting this same agent, looking like a different man, he was beginning to apologize, when he was interrupted,—"No apology is needed. Your reproof led to much reflection and to new resolutions. As the consequence, you behold me to-day a free man; and you are my deliverer."

Gough, who became a temperance-lecturer while still a smoker, relates that on his way to an outdoor meeting a friend offered him cigars. "No, I thank you; I have nowhere to put them." "You can put half a dozen in your cap." This he did, and so, soon ascending the platform, addressed two thousand children. To avoid taking cold, he kept on his cap, forgetting what it contained. At the close he exclaimed, "Now, boys, let us give three rousing cheers for temperance." Lifting his hat, he waved it vigorously, flinging the cigars right and left at his audience!! And it is not strange that this occurrence set him thinking.

At a later period, being a guest at an English house, he sought the river-bank for a quiet smoke. Finding it difficult to light his cigar, he got down on his knees by a rock, sheltering a match with his hat, while he puffed. Suddenly the thought flashed on him that, if people should see him, they would conclude that he had sought this spot for private devotion. "And what am I doing? What would the audience say who heard me last night?" The conviction of his inconsistency struck him so forcibly that he exclaimed, "I 'll have no more of it ; " and away into the river went both matches and cigars.

TOBACCO BONDAGE.

It is seldom that we find one who entirely justifies himself in the tobacco habit, while many and many a good man groans under his self-imposed bondage —a bondage not one whit less degrading because of the high standing and excellent Christian character of the victim. The wonder is how anyone can forbear groaning, and repenting, and forsaking.

A clergyman, enslaved to snuff, labored with a

drunkard. "If you will give up your snuff, I will give up my rum." The minister assented; but within two days was in agonies for his idol. Setting a watch over the drunkard, the moment he learned that the cup had passed his lips, he seized his snuff-box, and shortly after died in idiocy.

"Why did you send me that pamphlet on smoking?" said a pastor to a friend. "Because I thought you needed it." "Who told you that I smoked?" "You told me as you go about." "I will confess that I know it is wrong, and that I once gave it up; but, fool as I am, I took to it again, and I have been in bondage ever since."

An eminent minister exclaimed: "I would gladly lay down a hundred pounds if I could give up smoking."

"Oh," exclaimed a sufferer, "I need tobacco to give me resolution to give up tobacco."

"I would give half my farm to get rid of this master," declared another.

"I have given up my pipe a dozen times, and then returned to it," said a third victim. "I will try no more."

So imperious is the appetite, that during our civil war men were sometimes shot by the enemy simply because they *would* strike a light and smoke. And many risked capture in their perilous search after what smokers call "a little fire."

"I know my pipe is injuring me," a young man confessed, "but were I certain that it would curtail my life fifteen years, I could not give it up."

A prominent physician, who himself both smokes and chews, is honest enough to admit that "tobacco is too deadly a poison to be used even as a medicine;" and declares that he "would give five hundred dollars to be free from the habit." Yet he chews and smokes on.

A Christian professor, in her dying agonies, repeatedly entreated her friends, "Give me snuff, give me snuff." They were her last words.

Earnestly implored to give up the filthy weed, a clergyman made answer, "Not I! I will smoke if it shortens my life seven years. I will live while I do live."

A lip-cancer, which had been occasioned through smoking, was removed by a physician. "Twenty-four hours after the operation," says the doctor, "I found the patient propped up in bed, with his face bound up on one side and a pipe on the other side of his mouth."

George Trask writes: "I have known men to dream and rage about tobacco like madmen when deprived of it. I know an excellent clergyman, who assured me that he had sometimes wept like a child when putting a quid into his mouth, under a sense of his degradation and bondage. I know a man who confessed that tobacco was the dearest thing on earth, dearer than wife, child, church, or state."

Pitiable thraldom! Bound hand and foot!

It takes the very manhood out of one. Dr. Henderson relates the case of a member of Congress, who, from having been a man of force and fearlessness, became, to use his own words, "Sick all over, and timid as a girl." Though he had long been a practising lawyer, he had not nerve enough to present a petition to Congress, and still less to say a word concerning it. Indeed, he grew to be such a coward that he was afraid to be alone at night.

Tobacco-fetters! oh, it makes one's heart ache to witness the vain struggles to break them! I have known a young man of fine natural instincts, under a strong pressure, resolve over and over again to burst his chains. It was pitiful to note his struggles and his falls, with his keen self-abasement at his repeated failures, till finally, in a sort of moody despair, he gave up the attempt.

A deacon, on his death-bed, exclaimed: "I thank God that, as my last sickness has come, I shall be rid of this hankering for tobacco."

"You are wasting away under it," pleaded one minister with another. "Alas! my brother, it is true; but I cannot help it." "Would you take that excuse from a sinner?" "I cannot answer you. I cannot leave it off. It is out of the question; I *cannot*. I feel what you say; but—" The poor slave to this appalling appetite died soon after.

THE YOKE BROKEN.

In contrast with this melancholy instance it is cheering to read the experience of Dr. S. H. Cox:—

"From about fifteen to thirty," he wrote, "I am ashamed to say I smoked; my conscience often upbraiding me, as well as my best earthly friend. Still I made excuses, and my physician, a smoker, helped me to some. So I continued, till once, on board a steamer, a drunken gentleman staggered up to me, exclaiming, 'Give me a-a l-ight, Dr. Cox.' I handed him my cigar. He returned it. I threw it overboard; and since have never ceased to thank God that I have been enabled to keep myself from so foul and odious a sin."

In replying to a letter from Dr. Cox, John Quincy Adams writes: "In my early youth I was addicted to tobacco, in two of its mysteries, — smoking and chewing. I was warned by a medical friend of the pernicious operation of this habit upon the stomach and the nerves; and the advice of the physician was fortified by my own experience. More than thirty years have passed away since I deliberately renounced the use of tobacco in all its forms; and although the resolution was not carried into execution without a struggle of vitiated nature, I never yielded to its impulses.

"I have often wished that every individual of the human race afflicted with this artificial passion, could prevail on himself to try the experiment which I made; sure that it would turn every acre of tobacco land into a wheat field, and add five years to the average of human life."

Prof. Dascomb, of Oberlin, learned to smoke when a boy. His physician, though himself a smoker, said to him, "You will live only a few years if you continue this habit. *I* cannot break it off, but you are young and may be able to do so." The boy undertook it, and succeeded; although to the end of his life he suffered from the effects of his early indulgence.

A well-known doctor relates that, after smoking for twenty years, he took a vow of abstinence for one month. "Never," he says, "did boy long more eagerly for election day than I longed for the end of the month." Such was the good doctor's passion for the drug, that if cigars failed, he would resort to snuff. Thus he went on till the indulgence had so injured the nerves and softened the coats of the stomach that he could retain no food. Then he gathered his forces for the conflict, and broke forever from his bondage.

A slave to the weed in Macomb, Illinois, finding his family at one time out of flour and meat, and himself out of tobacco, but who was possessor of only a dollar and seventy-five cents, went to market. He returned with fifty cents' worth of meat and a dollar and twenty-five cents' worth of tobacco, telling his wife that they must trust the Lord for flour. At the age of seventy-six he became a Christian, when, without hesitation, he instantly renounced his idol.

A theological student, in breaking off smoking, gives three reasons for so doing: —

"1. No *gentleman* would like to smoke in the presence of ladies.

"2. There is possible harm, and no possible benefit.

"3. As there is no possible benefit, it is an unlawful expenditure of time and money."

A professor in one of our colleges who had smoked for many years, and had then been led to abandon the habit, also gives his three reasons : —

"1. I did n't like to indulge in a habit that I was compelled to apologize for.

"2. I knew that, however little I might smoke, I should be quoted as a smoker.

"3. MY BOYS!"

In *The Congregationalist* was found the following incident : "Two clergymen, than whom few are better known all through the State, happened to meet in our office. Both have been inveterate smokers ; but both stopped short more than a year ago, and have not blown a whiff since. They came to the conclusion that the only way to stop was to *stop*. And neither of them is likely to repent of his repenting. Who will go and do likewise ? "

A member of the Massachusetts legislature, who was a smoker, was led, by someone's inquiries as to statute laws on the subject, to reflect on his habit, and to see that he had come into a bondage which was holding him closer and closer. Although he had not been conscious of injury from the habit, he instantly broke from it.

A distinguished pastor in one of our city churches was induced to abandon smoking by the innocent remark of a young convert whom he was examining, that he " had given up all bad habits, including smoking." The shepherd felt that he must not fall behind the sheep.

The venerable Rev. Job Washburn, widely known in Maine, had formed in boyhood the habit of chewing. He made several efforts to give it up, but without success. In his later years, when he would again have attempted it, his friends discouraged him, fearing the effect of such a change at his years. He could not rest, however; and at the advanced age of ninety-two, he went to God in earnest prayer, and soon, to the surprise of all, was able to announce his victory over his lifelong habit.

Mr. Washburn's daughter, to whom I am indebted for these particulars, writes that after this conquest his health improved, and he seemed to her a fairer and better man. About two years later, a few days before his death, he expressed his joy and gratitude that he had been enabled to free himself from his galling yoke.

Another striking case is that of Mr. Joseph Harper, father of the publisher. He was an excellent man, *but* a great chewer; and nobody dreamed he could be induced to give up the habit. Mr. Harper had a neighbor who was a notorious drunkard. A friend was one day laboring with the man and entreating him to quit drinking. "Why, I could no more stop drinking," he replied, "than old Joe Harper could give up tobacco." When this remark was repeated to Mr. Harper, he exclaimed,— "Does that old drunkard say so? He shall not get behind me with his rum. I will show him that old Joe Harper *can* give up tobacco." And from that moment he never touched it.

I knew a man in Marblehead, Massachusetts, who was a great smoker from his youth till he was about fifty, when his health was so undermined that he saw he "must quit tobacco or die." He did quit it and from an abject slave became at once a freeman. At the age of ninety he declared himself stronger in body and mind, and better fitted for work than at fifty.

Dr. Titus Coan, of the Sandwich Islands, to whom reference has already been made, relates that when a boy, suffering from toothache, his father crowded a piece of tobacco no larger than the head of a pin into the defective tooth, which soon put him to sleep. "But in a little while I awoke, and felt my bedstead whirling round and round like a top. I thought the whole house was revolving and that my end was near. Retching and in distress, I cried for help ; and my parents came to comfort me and to assure me that this state would soon pass off."

It did pass, but for many years the boy could n't bear the smell of the poison. At last, however, resolving to be manly and brave like other young men, "I began moderately, so that in time all went well, and I felt that I had mastered the situation, little dreaming that the seduction was about to master me. At this time I did not look upon the use of tobacco from a moral standpoint. At length I went into a store with an elder brother. Here I found the choicest of tobaccos, and assisted in selling, still feeling that the business was legitimate. My brother smoked freely, but suddenly, fearing injury to health, and restive under the sense of slavery to that habit, he resolved to abandon the use of the narcotic poison. For about a month he struggled with the entrenched foe, under such a pressure of languor and depression as to unfit him for business. The fight was for life. He consulted physicians, he used substitutes, but all in vain. He had harbored an enemy which had poisoned his blood, coursed over his nerves, disturbed the action of the heart, and chained him like a galley slave to an unworthy and unmanly habit.

"In despair of victory he returned to the pipe, and died in middle life. Without a word with any one, I then resolved to conquer the foe. On the second day the call for indulgence was strong, but resolution held the fort. Day after day pleaded for indulgence, but will prevailed over appetite and habit. As the mornings succeeded one another, my motto was What the Lord helped me to do yesterday, I can do to-day with His help.

"The battle lasted two weeks, when appetite surrendered at discretion. Since that happy day, I have had no more taste or desire for that deceitful poison than for an adder; and I give the foregoing testimony as a kind legacy to encourage all who feel the fangs and the tightening toils of that enchanting serpent, tobacco! No earthly gift could bribe me to return to the use of the weed; and I am sure that unyielding resolution, and a patient looking for divine help, will enable all who honestly desire to break the slavish chains of that unnatural and degrading appetite, to become free from its toils."

A good deacon gives me his experience: "I commenced the use of tobacco when under ten, became a habitual consumer at about fifteen, and when thirty began to realize that it was injuring me. Then came the struggle. I would leave it off for a week, for a month, and then for a year. The moment my pledge was up I would commence with renewed energy. This continued till I was about forty, when I became satisfied that I must either die or break from my bondage. I attempted the latter. For more than two years I wrestled with the appetite, at the end of which time my craving was, if possible, stronger than ever. I felt that I must have relief from this craving, or succumb to it. In my despair, I took the matter to the Lord with strong crying. He soon delivered me from the dreadful appetite, and it has never returned, praised be the name of the Lord."

Dr. Talmage tells us that he was once an excessive smoker, and that in writing his sermons he was accustomed to take a fresh cigar with every new head. On one occasion, after an experience of this kind, he found himself in the highest state of nervous excitement. The falling of a book startled him like the firing of a pistol, and the creaking of his own boots made his hair stand on end. Alarmed by these symptoms, he instantly broke from the habit, and found himself born into a new physical, mental, and spiritual life.

Thurlow Weed, according to his own account, smoked cigars during fifty-four years, giving away in that time eighty thousand. Being in Saratoga for his health, Dr. Freeman, an old friend, called on him. When some reference was made to the cause of his being there, the doctor, pointing to the cigar still burning in Mr. Weed's hand, remarked,—"I see the time has come when *that* luxury must be foregone." "Do you mean it?" "I do." "Then *that* is the end." And with true Spartan heroism he threw away his cigar and never touched tobacco again.

CHEERING TOKENS.

It is a cheering fact that many German, French, English, and American physicians of the highest standing are waging war upon this drug. A meeting of Sunday-school and week-day teachers in England has been held for the purpose of considering measures to check its use. It was presided over by an eminent physician of a royal eye-infirmary, who affirmed that paralysis of the optic nerve and other diseases of the eyes were directly caused by tobacco.

It is encouraging, in the almost overwhelming current of public sentiment that sets the wrong way, to note any straws floating in the right direction ; among such, we reckon the following : —

A minister of talent and piety, a good preacher, and of acceptable manners, who had supplied three different churches, received no call from any of them, and, as was plainly stated, simply because he was known to be an immoderate user of tobacco !

Two New England churches recently refused to call two Andover theological students because they used the unclerical weed.

If all the churches were of the same mind, we should soon witness a wonderful advance in this much-needed, ardently-prayed-for reform.

At a monthly collection in a church, a ten-dollar bill was put in the box, with a paper affixed, on which was written : " To be given to a missionary who does not use tobacco."

Writes " a mother " : " I would as soon help a saloon-keeper furnish his bar as to help tobacco-using students ; or contribute toward a ' Brewers' Union ' as to a society which aids such young men in getting into the ministry."

An itinerary preacher, being refused entertainment by an old woman, where he asked for it, quoted to her the passage, " Be not forgetful to entertain strangers, for thereby some have entertained angels unawares ; " when she promptly made answer : " You need n't say that. No angel would come down here with a big quid of tobacco in his mouth."

The Iowa Central Railroad has published an order forbidding its employees to drink any intoxicants and also to smoke while they are on duty.

San Diego, California, has passed an ordinance prohibiting cigarettes to boys.

At a Universalist convention the following resolution was offered : —

" *Resolved*, That this convention memorialize the General Convention, at its next session, asking it to refuse beneficiary aid to all students in our theological schools who make use of tobacco ; believing such practice to be incompatible with the highest Christian service."

This resolution was adopted by an almost unanimous vote.

In " The Doctrines and Discipline of the Methodist Episcopal Church " is found the following : —

"*Resolved*, 1. That we advise all our ministers and members to abstain from the use of tobacco, as injurious to both soul and body.

" *Resolved*, 2. That we recommend to the Annual Conferences to require candidates for admission to be free from the habit, as hurtful to their acceptability and usefulness among our people."

To cut off any possible loophole, the General Conference of this church advises that no man who uses tobacco be received into an Annual Conference. For years, the Central Illinois Conference has refused to admit any votary of the weed.

Says Bishop Simpson : " In some places congregations are unwilling to receive ministers who indulge in tobacco. Many families almost dread the visits of such ministers, lest their growing sons may be led to adopt a practice which they so earnestly discountenance and oppose."

A presiding elder in the Methodist Church, in answer to inquiries on this subject, writes: " Our Conferences have been growing more exact from year to year. In the New England Conference, we never receive any man as a preacher without questioning him on this point."

Rev. Mr. Evans, presiding elder in the Central Illinois Conference, writes: " I am glad to say that for about twenty years, the Conference, at nearly every session, has adopted radical anti-tobacco resolutions; while the use of the weed has been uniformly denounced as expensive, filthy, injurious, and unchristian. The Conference refuses to admit any one addicted to the tobacco-habit, unless a pledge of abstinence be given; and it has also requested the Bishop not to transfer to the Conference, nor appoint to the office of presiding elder, any tobacco-user. The discussions of every year have served to make it more unaminous and radical in its action."

With the Free Methodists no one is allowed to become a church-member who uses tobacco in any form, —a rule strictly enforced upon the ministers.

Of the Primitive Methodist Church, the " Canadian Discipline " declares: " No preacher on probation shall be received into full connection unless it be stated on his Station's Report that he has not used tobacco during the previous year." A similar rule obtains in the English body.

John Wesley refused to admit to the ministry any man addicted to the use of the noxious weed. Both English and American Wesleyans follow his practice in this respect, and Bishop Janes cheers us by his avowed belief that the time will come when congregations will not accept a pastor who uses it. The New York State Congregational Association a few years since adopted, without dissent, the following resolutions : —

" 1. That the tobacco-habit is an enormous evil; and, on account of its waste of money, positive injuries to health, and pernicious example to the young, Christians ought to abandon it.

" 2. That this Association earnestly recommend to all our churches thorough measures for instructing the people as to the manifold mischiefs flowing from the use of narcotic drugs, as well as drinks ; and that special efforts be made to guard children and youth from any and every use of tobacco."

At the Synod of the Reformed Presbyterian church in Pittsburg, Penn., a report was adopted, declaring that " members using tobacco ought to strive earnestly to give up the habit, as offensive to good manners and cleanliness, and inconsistent with self-denial."

If one may be allowed to comment on a declaration emanating from so respectable a body, the suggestion is ventured that the omission of the clause "to strive earnestly" would render the report more terse and effective. We must remember, however, that the various Presbyterian bodies are more conservative than some other denominations, — a fact borne out in the Cumberland General Assembly at Austin, Texas, where a resolution condemning all ministerial use of tobacco was fully discussed, but unfortunately was finally laid on the table.

At a Baptist General Convention, in a Western city, the subject of tobacco was ably presented, and a resolution passed deprecating its use.

Professor Hovey, of the Newton Theological Seminary, writes: "For many years past there have been very few of our students who have used tobacco. The Northern Baptist Educational Society has adopted a rule which prevents it from furnishing pecuniary assistance to any student who uses the weed; and, so far as I am informed, there is no fault found with the Society for taking this stand."

Great reason as we have for deploring the general low public sentiment on this subject, we would not ignore the fact that, in certain respects, there is a manifest improvement. A well-known gentleman, son of one of our excellent New England pastors, writes of the custom that prevailed in his boyhood: "When the Berkshire Association of thirty ministers was to meet at my father's, I was sent to the store for two quarts of Jamaica, four quarts of Santa Cruz rum, two dozen pipes, and two large papers of tobacco!"

In view of such usages, the ecclesiastical good tokens that have been named are truly encouraging. A few in the secular line are no less cheering.

The enterprising firm of Jordan, Marsh, & Co., of the New England metropolis, occasionally furnish brief, practical lectures to their employees in the large hall connected with their establishment. In one of these lectures the tobacco-subject was discussed; and, as a result, every one of the clerks, with a single exception, voted to abandon it.

After the women of Massachusetts had been admitted to vote on the education question, the Commonwealth, in 1881, passed an act to aid in preserving order at elections, of which the following is the substance : —

" During any town-meeting, held for the election of national, state, county, or town officers, no person shall smoke, or have in his possession any lighted pipe, cigarette, or cigar, in any town-hall where such meeting is being held. Any persons violating any of the provisions of this act shall be deemed guilty of disorderly conduct, and the moderator shall order the person to remove any such pipe, cigarette, or cigar, or withdraw himself from said place of meeting ; and, on his declining to obey, shall order any police officer, or other person, to take him from the meeting, and confine him in some convenient place until the meeting adjourns. The person so refusing shall forfeit a sum not exceeding twenty dollars."

In the Jewish *Messenger* is an account of a club of young ladies who are pledged to kiss no man whose lips are tainted with tobacco. May its membership rapidly increase!

A Western gazette tells us of the suspense for ten days of an engineer on the C. B. & Q. Railroad by the superintendent, because, when on his engine, ready to pull out the passenger-train, he held in his mouth part of an unlighted cigar. Thanks to the superintendent, and a speedy reform to all engineers!

The city corporation, Manchester, England, fines a cabman if he smokes while conveying a passenger.

A Philadelphia smoker, on entering a horse-car, insisted on retaining his cigar in his hand. Its smoke being offensive to the ladies, the conductor warned him to throw it away, and, as he refused, put him out by force. The smoker sued the company for damages; but the verdict was against him, the court charging the jury that he was "a nuisance which the conductor had a right to abate." Later, a smoker in New York city was fined fifty dollars, because in a street-car he insisted on retaining his cigar.

A New York editor remarks with regard to the Treasury at Washington: "It is no secret that that fine building has been for several years past, as to many of its departments, a cross between a bar-room and a smoking-car." It is cheering to know that Secretary Folger issued an order forbidding smoking in the halls or rooms of the Treasury. This is understood to be, in part, an act of consideration toward the lady clerks, who, he saw, were greatly annoyed by the universal cigar.

Concerning this example, so worthy of imitation, the New York *Evening Post* remarks : "The order is not acceptable to the male clerks, the great majority of whom are accustomed to smoke at all times during business hours. The abuse of smoking has been very great. Since Secretary Bristow's time, the secretaries themselves, not only have not forbidden smoking, but have smoked at their desks. Even in the file-rooms, where valuable papers are stored in lofts of pine-wood partitions, the custodians have often been seen with cigars. Secretary Folger's order forbidding this is strictly a revival of the order which has been in disuse since Secretary Bristow's time."

In view of the alarming increase of the use of tobacco among children, the Boston *Woman's Christian Temperance Union* sent a circular with several tracts on the subject to all the teachers and officers of the public schools of Boston and the suburbs.

In November, 1882, a statement appeared in the Boston *Journal* to the effect that seventy-five per cent of school-boys over twelve or thirteen smoke cigarettes. A Cambridgeport teacher places the age between eight and fifteen, and gives the results of his efforts against the evil. Out of three hundred and fifty boys, he induced all but thirty to sign a total-abstinence pledge for the year; and of these, fifty per cent kept their pledge.

In the Latin School, one half of the upper classes are smokers, many of them with the concurrence of their parents. While a number of teachers do all they can to banish tobacco from the schools, the ignorance and indifference on the part of parents, with the smoking example of some of them and also of a portion of the teachers, are almost insuperable hindrances to a thorough reform.

In Barnard's *Journal of Education*, ten cities are named, among which are Chicago, New Orleans, San Francisco, and Washington, in which the use of tobacco during school-hours or in school-rooms is forbidden to both teachers and pupils.

In Germany, the Minister of Public Instruction has addressed a circular to the directors of all the Gymnasia (higher classical schools), in which he condemns in the strongest terms the practice of smoking; and students of these institutions have been officially forbidden smoking in the streets. And this in the very land of smokers!

The principal of Phillips Academy, at Exeter, N. H., issued a circular to the parents of his students, desiring their view as to the prohibition of the weed, and received answers in favor of this from quite a number of them.

The trustees of Williston Seminary, Easthampton, Mass., have passed the following vote : " No member of the school shall be allowed to use tobacco, unless he bring a statement in writing from his parent or guardian that he does it with his approval." In a letter, speaking of this circular, Principal Fairbanks says : "Many young men connected with this institution have been injured physically, mentally, and morally by the use of tobacco. At present, very few use it, and only those who have the written consent of parents or guardians. We shall enforce the prohibition more strictly from year to year."

Principal Bancroft, of Phillips Academy, Andover, Mass., writes that in reply to a similar circular sent to parents, guardians, school-officers, and physicians, he received "a hundred and forty-seven replies, not one of them approving the use of tobacco by boys." He goes on to say : "Tobacco is the bane of our schools and colleges, and increasingly so. Teachers who have given any attention to the subject agree that boys go down under its use in scholarship, in self-respect, in self-control. It takes off the fine edge of the mind, injures the manners, and dulls the moral senses. School disorders are always rank with the fumes of tobacco. We can select the boys who smoke heavily by a certain hesitation in answering questions, by a peculiar huskiness of voice, by a dulness of complexion, by a tremor of the hand.

"Boys learn to smoke because it is a habit of our times; because it is sanctioned by the practice of many eminent men in all the walks of life, — some of them intellectual leaders of the age; because literature, art, and song have been saturated with the fragrance of the choicest tobacco, till it affects the taste, as well as appetite. Gen. Grant's smoking is the boy's answer to many an appeal in this country, as the Prince of Wales's smoking is in England. I have had under my charge a boy who could reply to my argument on the ground of health, 'My physician smokes;' on the ground of morals, 'My minister smokes;' on the ground of high-breeding, 'My father smokes.'

"Parents are surprisingly ignorant of the habits of their boys in this regard, surprisingly helpless when they find their sons using tobacco, or surprisingly timid, and criminally indifferent.

"The tobacco-reform must begin in the enlightened conscience. A habit which destroys or enfeebles the physical powers, which affects the whole nervous system, and thus reaches the will and the moral character, is a *sin*.

"It is specially important that parents, preachers, and all others whom boys propose to themselves as *models* of deportment, honor, and usefulness, should themselves be exemplary. I would not have a teacher here who used tobacco, or sympathized with those who do."

Prof. William Stephens, of Philadelphia, has caused to be pasted on the inside of every textbook used in his school a brief printed statement of the physical and mental diseases produced in the young by tobacco. That it is high time for such information to be diffused, we learn, from his alarming statement that of the fifty thousand pupils of the city a large majority use tobacco, the habit having rapidly increased since the introduction of the cigarette.

"A Williams student reports that the greater part of his class, on entering college, did not smoke, but that, on graduating, the larger majority had become smokers. They had in tutors and professors the example; why not follow it?"

In Oberlin, in marked contrast with this toleration, no professor or teacher is employed who uses tobacco, and it is strictly prohibited in the college.

If a student uses it surreptitiously he is expelled; if he frankly states to the Faculty that he cannot give it up, he receives what is called an honorable dismission, accompanied with a statement of the reason for this dismission, — which, being interpreted, is, that he is in bondage to tobacco. The sentiment of the town is in accordance with this course, and at one time, when the tobacco-habit seemed on the increase, an enthusiastic meeting was held to take measures against it. After dwelling on the injurious influences, physical, mental, and moral, a resolution was adopted that pastors be requested to preach on the subject from time to time, and that a committee be appointed to visit those engaged in its sale, urging them to desist, and to devise means for putting an end to the use and the traffic.

Among the terms of admission to the Training-School for Boys, at Oxford, Ohio, is found printed in Italics : —

"*No pupil will be received into the boarding hall who uses tobacco in any form.*"

This condition was made in the face of public sentiment, and with the probability of its diminishing the numbers; but it is winning its way, as right, in the long run, must ever do.

In the advertising columns of the *Washington Star* appears the following : " The prayers of God's people are most earnestly requested for the thorough purification of a young church, whose pastor and officers are inveterate tobacco-users, much against the wishes of its members."

In New York and Brooklyn the evil is felt to be so great that petitions have been circulated, asking for a statute law prohibiting the sale of tobacco to minors.

As we have already seen, tobacco is forbidden in the Naval School at Annapolis. There is the same prohibition at Girard College, while at Cornell many of the students have voluntarily signed a pledge of abstinence. At West Point, the prohibition which had been recommended by the trustees is carried into effect by the order of Lincoln, Secretary of War.

At one of the annual meetings of an English anti-tobacco society the chairman stated that they had met, in the name of science, humanity, and Christianity, to enter their most solemn protest against the growing use of tobacco. The following resolution was moved by Dr. Edmunds, of London : —

"That this meeting, impressed with a deep conviction of the physical, mental, and moral evils resulting from the use of tobacco, and regarding with a profound alarm and apprehension the rapidly extending habit of smoking amongst the youth of our country, calls upon parents, Sunday-School teachers, members and ministers of Christian churches, and all true patriots and philanthropists to discountenance the practice to the utmost, both by precept and example."

At Exeter Hall, London, a National Society for the Suppression of Juvenile Smoking has been founded; Dr. B. W. Richardson being elected honorary president, and the Hon. Arthur Kinnaird treasurer.

HEATHEN EXAMPLES.

Now, how do we find it when the heathen come under the power of the Gospel? Do their native preachers and teachers and deacons continue this indulgence? So far from this, the Christian sentiment is strongly against tobacco.

As an evidence of the sincerity of Indian converts in Idaho, it is said that, though devoted to the pipe, growing up with it in their mouths, yet on being converted, with the laying aside of paint, they also lay aside their pipe.

At Ponape, in the Caroline Islands, more than half the church members, who had smoked all their lives, had given it up. In other islands of Micronesia, where, a few years ago, every one used tobacco, at the present time, of eight hundred and thirty Christians not a single one now makes use of it.

Dr. Coan states that on his arrival at the Hawaiian Islands in 1835, the missionaries were debating the tobacco question. Some argued for strong decisive measures, and others for a moderate course, while a small number advised silence, saying, — " Preach the Gospel and convert the people, and let these little matters alone." But unfortunately it was discovered that some of this class were secret devotees of the weed, while others did not scruple to take puffs from the pipes of the native smokers.

Dr. Coan continues : " During one of my visits as delegate to the Marquesas Islands, one of our Hawaiian missionaries there told me that a former delegate of our mission had made them trouble in this way. He chewed tobacco secretly, but a keen-scented Marquesan smelled his breath, and on a certain occasion, when the delegate walked out, this savage followed him, and watched for his spitting. At length it came, and fell on a rock. The savage waited a little for the delegate to pass on, then knelt down and smelt the rock. The secret was out, and it spread like wildfire among the natives. They accused our Hawaiian teacher of guile and inconsistency in teaching them to abandon tobacco while our own ministers used it. And the missionaries in those islands begged of me to see that no more tobacco-consumers be sent them as delegates."

This honored missionary, now gone up to his reward, relates that in his labors among the people of Hilo and Puna, he "was careful, in illustrating the commands and prohibitions of the law and Gospel, to be specific, and so to illustrate as to make their untutored minds understand what was right and wrong in heart and act. Our people must be told how to catch the little foxes." The result on the tobacco question was that hundreds of little patches of the weed were rooted up and destroyed; thousands of pipes were smashed or burned. And it is probable that ten thousand natives of this parish have promised to let the poison alone. Some played the hypocrite, of course; others forsook it for a season, and, like many of our educated clergymen and other professed Christians, returned to it when appetite overpowered resolution. But many thousands of our church members held out to the last, and were faithful to their vows until death. Numbers are still living, and they are our most reliable men in all that is good.

" But the great increase of example on the part of smoking and chewing clergymen and lay professors from other countries is demoralizing this generation of Hawaiians, rendering church discipline difficult, our labors hard, and the simple practical truths of the gospel of little effect among the lovers of pleasure."

A Baptist missionary in India, writing of the interest in the mission work by the native helpers, states that they have resolved to abandon tobacco and the betel nut, which has a similar effect, and to give the money thus saved to the good cause. Why not send some of these converted, sin-renouncing Indians and South Sea Islanders as missionaries to this country, that they may exhort alike all tobacco-sinners and all tobacco-Christians to cast their detestable idols to the moles and the bats, and to consecrate the gold and silver thus redeemed to the service of the one living and true God?

CLAIMS OF THE TRADE.

In addition to the clamorous appetite which sets itself squarely against reform, is another formidable obstacle, — the greed of grain, or, as some put it, and it may be honestly, the claims of a family dependent for their daily bread on the culture, the manufacture, or the sale of tobacco. The extent to which moneyed interests have become involved in this wretched business appears in the vast amount expended for the drug throughout the world, with the immense revenue it brings to the various governments. The arguments thus resulting for the continuance of the traffic are only too familiar to those who have fought in our anti-slavery and our temperance battles.

Dr. Johnson was once remonstrating with a man engaged in some occupation which he confessed to be wrong. The man excused himself by the common plea: "But I must live, sir," when the sturdy doctor rejoined, "I don't know that that is necessary."

"Fear to endanger your craft," the wholesale and retail distribution of poison! If those medical and scientific men who assert that "*Indulgence in narcotic luxuries is the great highway to the grave*," have uttered the truth, then let all such crafts sink to the bottom of the sea! If your plea of necessity is a true one, then, better live and die in poverty, or trust to God's ravens, than to thrive by poisoning your fellow men. Besides you cannot wrong your neighbor without reaping, sooner or later, a bitter harvest. To commit a doubtful act injures the doer as really as the receiver; to sanction an admitted wrong will in• some way bring you incalculable harm.

Put your commercial interests, as you call them, into one scale, and the welfare of the community into the other. How is it with your end of the balance? Do not reason and conscience make your path plain? What if you should resolve that not for another day will you curse the ground with the growth of the rank poison; that you will never manufacture, that you will never sell, another ounce of it?

HELPFUL SUGGESTIONS.

A miserable tobacco-slave, who had tried again and again to break his fetters, but in vain, exclaimed in his despair, "Tobacco is killing me by inches, and yet I cannot help using it." And it did kill him.

For such persons, with energies so sapped by the narcotic that they have neither grit nor grace for the breaking of their yoke, the best plan would seem to be a retreat where this insidious foe could be effectually excluded. Said a Boston man : "The tobacco-disease is the great disease of our times, and the most difficult to cure. I will give land worth a thousand dollars towards an institution for the cure of tobacco-victims."

I have recently heard of the bondage being broken by animal magnetism. Dr. Dodge, the well-known magnetic healer at Riverside Institution, Hamilton, Ill. tells me that he has produced with some inveterate users of the weed, an utter *loathing* of it, and that this loathing is not a mere transient mood, but an abiding condition, so that the result is total abstinence, unless the enfranchised slave *chooses*, by the same process as in the beginning, once more to come under the tyrant's yoke.

For one who has no magnetic opportunities, but is willing to enter on a warfare against this appetite, there is a right physical as well as mental and moral treatment. The dreadful poison has wrought itself into the system, and induced a diseased condition. And to meet this condition, common-sense dictates hygienic treatment. To overcome the tobacco-habit, plain and easily digested food is strongly recommended, with abstinence from all spices and condiments and every stimulating article. In addition frequent packs or baths are helpful. The baths may be Russian or Turkish, or, if these cannot be secured, an old-fashioned vapor-bath. But in all this, one must keep the will at the helm; he must not for a single moment let go the *resolve to conquer*, or the effort will result in a miserable failure.

There are some who maintain that all which is needful in order to break from this bondage is the *determination* and *backbone* to carry it out.

In reference to this, Dr. Ringland, of the Riverside Institute, to which allusion has been made, writes : " While it is true that will-power — '*backbone*' — is the essential quality in overcoming the habit, we cannot overlook the fact that the giving up tobacco causes a disturbance of the vital forces which may properly be treated with remedial measures.

" The *use* of tobacco induces *many* chronic affections; the *disuse* of it, *one* acute affection, The former may be for life, the latter for a few days only. There are none who cannot overcome the habit if they will recognize the condition induced by the giving it up as one of disease, and submit to treatment accordingly.

"If the will is stronger than the appetite, the man, unaided by any treatment, can overcome it; but if the will has become so weakened that appetite is the more powerful, the subject yields his will and appetite prevails.

"By the long use of tobacco we have, in the smoker or chewer, a system saturated with the poison; and when he ceases to use it, the nerves become excited, because they are deprived of their accustomed stimulus. To meet this want, the system is drawn upon to give forth the latent tobacco that has become deposited in the tissues throughout the body. In this effort, it is aroused to intense action. The supply failing to satisfy the demand, a fever ensues, and a nervous craving that dominates the whole being.

"What we wish to do is to allay the feverish condition by eliminating the poison, and, by building up the nervous system, to render its action normal, and quiet its cravings.

"To accomplish the first, packing in wet sheets, or warm bathing that will induce perspiration are speedy and effective methods. To prove that poison can be eliminated from the body, we may experiment upon one who has for some weeks been using the tincture of iron. Let him be packed several times in a wet sheet, and this tincture will be drawn through the pores, so that the sheet will actually begin to rot away.

"A warm bath at bedtime, for a few days, followed by a brisk rubbing and the drinking of hot lemonade, will make the battle with the habit comparatively easy. During the day, whenever the craving becomes intense, two or three swallows of strong, cold lemonade will allay it. If the man be going from home, let him carry a supply with him for the time of need. The acid of lemons is one of the best antidotes for this and many other poisons."

Medical men who have had large experience in this matter, declare that *instant emancipation is entirely safe*. Says Dr. Kirkbride: " I have never seen the slightest injury result from the immediate and total breaking off the habit of using tobacco, and the experience of this hospital is a large one in this particular."

Another physician writes: " The struggle of the sufferer may be terrible — he may even feel like death. But there is no danger of dying; such a result has never yet happened. Though the pain and misery are intense, their duration is short, and, when once over the bridge that spans the great chasm of reaction, the smoker or chewer can raise his voice and shout : — ' *I am purged of the vile weed; I am free; I am clean; and as long as I live, I will continue to be so.*' "

But the world is not yet without men who have had " backbone " enough to conquer the habit by sheer will. The head of the eminent house which has electrotyped this work was thirty-five years ago a chewer of tobacco. He left that off at the advice of John Quincy Adams, but still smoked.

Twenty-five years ago he lighted his last cigar, and, at the dictate of his own conscience, threw it away unsmoked. The hope of humanity is in such men, who, victorious over their own vices, lead the young safely into paths where all temptations to slow suicide cease to be attractive. No men more than the ex-slaves are destined to prize liberty, and especially if they have won it for themselves.

I cannot better close this chapter than in the following earnest words by that untiring soldier in this warfare, President John Bascom, D.D., L.L.D. :

"Many sages in various forms of philosophy, many saints in diverse phases of faith, have insisted on the conflict between lower and higher impulses in man, between the flesh and the spirit. We have some additional wisdom as to the best method of stilling this strife, as to the way in which the two sets of powers are to find their union in higher forms of work; but the strife itself remains an early and unavoidable fact in moral and spiritual life. The trio of evil influences in Christianity is still the world, the flesh, and the devil. Certainly the use of tobacco belongs on the wrong side of this enduring struggle into which we all enter singly and collectively. It belongs to the flesh, and smacks, at times, of both the other two. This habit gains ground at the expense of emotional refinement and spiritual force.

"There is scarcely a smoker to be found that does not, at some time, in a careless way, put upon others the discomfort of his habit.   How can it be otherwise?   He is driven by an exacting demand, whose disagreeable effects are very much hidden from him.   The smoker loses the power to see himself as others see him.   If those who use tobacco were decidedly in the minority, the habit would be thought to be a strange, outlandish, outrageous perversion of the decorum of life, and, in its open indulgence, a surprising trespass on good taste and delicate consideration.   I think we shall see this to be so if we consider the effect the habit of chewing, or smoking even, would have on our estimate of a refined woman.   The union is almost an impossibility.   Yet there is nothing but the nature of the habit that renders the use of tobacco unfit in a woman.   It is superior purity and refinement only that banish it from such a presence.

" We have something of this feeling, though unfortunately in a much less degree, in connection with the most noble-minded and venerable men. Veneration is weakened by this indulgence.   The very mildest word we can apply to it is that of indulgence, and the earthly appetite carries an earthly odor with it wherever it extends.   Old age casts no glamour over habits, but leaves them to stand on their own merits.   The infirm old man who must needs have his snuff-box, or tobacco-box, or pipe, is a less agreeable inmate of any home than he otherwise would be.   His better nature does not ascend heavenward in and by this smoke of sacrifice, but out of it, and in spite of it, if it ascends at all. Age should purge away the grossness of the flesh, should stand on tiptoe in the physical world, and, like a bursting chrysalis, hold the wings of faith astir. The best that can be said for tobacco under such conditions is, that it is the expiring appetite of an expiring body; one not held in subjection by the spirit, but one that has subjected the spirit to itself. The only fortune that remains to such a one is the fortune of escaping from himself. We can conceive of no refining process, that fits one as pure gold for a New Jerusalem, that would not quickly, at the very outset, refine away this habit. The River of Life does not flow through a tobacco field."

TOBACCO INDICTED AND TRIED.

INDICTMENT.

It is a formidable indictment that has been brought against tobacco, but I have sought to sustain every point by evidence from trustworthy witnesses, many of them entirely outside of any reform movement.

It has been shown what a fearful expenditure of time and money is involved in the use of this narcotic; what an interminable train of physical and intellectual evils follows in its path; how it sometimes destroys the finer sentiments and lowers the whole tone of a man's character, rendering him inconsiderate, selfish, and discourteous; how it tends to unman and animalize, if not to brutalize.

But worse than this is the deep injury it inflicts on the moral and spiritual nature, planting in the system an appetite which not only renders its victim obtuse in his nicer perceptions, but which deadens his conscience, cuts the sinews of his will, and bears him irresistibly onward in a course of vicious indulgence, over-riding reason, charity, love for wife and children, and whatever else would stay its progress, and, more dreadful still, transmitting a heritage of physical and mental disease even to the third and fourth generation.

Certain I am that in all the light which science and medicine, experience and observation, have cast upon its character, the cases are exceedingly rare in which an intelligent tobacco-victim is not sometimes disturbed by doubts as to the rightfulness of the indulgence. Think, then, of the injury to his moral nature from persistence in it!

The shutting one's eyes against overwhelming evidence, the poor attempts at justification — who has not witnessed all this? And even where the admission of wrong is clear and abundant, how many fail in their endeavors to reform! "There is probably no tobacco-user in the world," writes Beecher, "who would advise a young man to commence this habit. Yet against all advice, against nausea and disgust, against cleanliness, against every consideration of health and comfort, thousands every year bow the neck to this drug, and consent to wear its repulsive yoke."

The question presses: How shall we stem, if we cannot turn the mighty current? Shall we petition Congress to pass laws for abating this nuisance?

But are not many of our wise men and our honorables in both houses in complicity with it? Are they not themselves helping to swell the current? Seeing that tobacco-users form the great majority of voters in both parties in this republic, and that non-smoking men are hardly ever found in political conventions, of what avail would be petitions to Congress?

A writer in the *Independent* remarks : "Those whom we esteem and love share in the indulgence. Our theological seminaries are scarcely cleaner than our colleges . . . and as for the lawyers and politicians, one is under suspicion of being ascetic, mean, or somehow unfinished, if he does not smoke. We know of some districts where a man could not be elected to Congress if it were thoroughly known that he disapproved of the use of tobacco in any form."

A strong indication of the prevalent feeling is contained in the Report, December 1884, of Hugh McCulloch, Secretary of the Treasury. Here is a passage :—

"An article which is so generally used as tobacco, and which adds so much to the comfort of the large numbers of our population who earn their living by manual labor, cannot properly be considered a luxury, and as the collection of the tax is expensive and troublesome to the Government, and is especially obnoxious and irritative to small manufacturers, the tax upon tobacco should, in my judgment, be removed."

In view of such a proposal from so high a source —a proposal that entirely ignores moral considerations —we might well despair, did we not know that, in the days of our fathers, whiskey was not regarded as a luxury, but as a necessary of life, especially for laboring men. And now, as the Secretary of the Treasury goes on to say, "The tax upon whiskey could not be repealed without a disregard of public sentiment."

But how shall we bring about a similar change in public sentiment concerning this poisonous drug?

Shall we implore the pulpit and the press to cry aloud and spare not? Thank God for all that has been done and is now doing! ·Thanks for that fearless champion, George Trask, who fought single-handed till he went up to take his crown!

The pulpit and the press! The authorized re-bukers of wrong, the creators of public sentiment! Sorry am I to be obliged to admit that so many of the moral and religious leaders in the land, — the *should-be* besiegers in this warfare, — are them-selves among the besieged, that it is considered too delicate a subject to be dealt with uncompro-misingly. One is permitted to walk softly round about it, and to touch it very carefully; but no sword must be lifted, lest blood be drawn; no gun fired, lest somebody chance to get hurt. And all this trembling solicitude lest, forsooth, it might possibly reflect on many excellent Christians, in-cluding not a few ministers, elders, and deacons. and thus injure their influence! But does our Book of books set an example in favor of such delicate approaches? Does it hesitate to make unsparing comments on the most saintly sinners? Not so do we read it.

OBJECTORS SUMMONED.

" But the appetite is so imperious."

No one can deny this. Its clamorings are more urgent than those even of hunger and thirst. Neal Dow relates that when Pumpelly, in his tour round the world, found himself and others in a great desert without food or water, they sent off men after supplies. And for what did these famishing sufferers beg, as they hastened to meet the returning messengers? " Food? We were almost starving. Drink? We were almost perishing with thirst. No, we asked for no food, for no drink, but for *tobacco.*"

While on the Pacific, the vessel went down. Pumpelly relates that as the life-boat, his last chance for preservation, was getting off, he bethought him of his cigars, and rushed below to seize them, adding coolly, " *People who smoke will understand why I was ready and willing to risk my life for a few cigars.*"

Yea, verily, the appetite *is* "imperious." It is a tyrant whose dominion is absolute. All the more reason, then, why it should be trampled under foot. Unless you set upon the tempter your iron heel, it may strike its fangs through body and soul.

" With all your assertions and facts as to the injurious influence of tobacco, smokers sometimes attain a great age."

Simply quoting the adage that " one swallow

does n't make a summer," I will refer to George Trask's disposal of this same plea, when the case was brought up of a great smoker who lived till he was a hundred and four. After making several inquiries, he summed them up : "In a word, did he love anybody, or hate anybody, dead or alive, in this world or in any world?" "I think not." "Well, well, your old man died fifty years ago, and your only mistake was that you did n't bury him."

An eminent physician remarks that although, owing to the wonderful power of toleration in the system, there are occasional instances of long life among tobacco-users, as among drinking men and opium-eaters, yet it is, with rare exceptions, only a dragging, half-and-half life, the natural and moral forces being greatly diminished.

There are good men, and men wise in most matters, who say : "Tobacco belongs to the same category as tea and coffee, sweetmeats and confectionery, which are to be taken with discretion. When thus used, and in a manner gentlemanly and Christian, its use is fitting and proper."

Now let the examples of this discreet, gentlemanly, and Christian use be given, and that so plainly that there shall be no mistake, — examples by which no religious principle is violated, no fellow-mortal harmed or annoyed, least of all, one's neighbor, or friend, or bosom-companion.

But, for argument's sake, granting this immaculate method, how about those abundant testimonies of medical and scientific men to its injurious effects on body and mind? Can it be doubted that every candid man, however inveterate his habit, would be led by a thorough examination to the one conclusion? Benjamin Franklin affirms that "he never knew a person who used tobacco habitually that would recommend another to do the same."

A young man tells me that when a boy he was made so sick by his first and second cigars that he desisted from farther attempts; and that, some years later, on expressing to his smoking companions his regret that he did not persevere till he had conquered his repugnance, they replied, "Don't talk so; for, on our part, we thoroughly regret that we *did* persevere."

Does the victim plead, "I smoke but little, not enough to harm me any, and I can break off at any time?"

My friend, you have little idea how completely tobacco is robbing you of your power. You can break off at any time? Then, if you are a wise man, you will do it *instantly*, else the sly enchantress may bring you into a bondage where you *can't* break off.

"I, surely, cannot be called a smoker; for I indulge in a cigar only on rare occasions, such as in vacations or on Christmas and other red-letter days."

Just enough to temporize with conscience, and utterly to nullify any good influence on the subject which you might otherwise exert. An eminent

and popular divine, who entirely repudiates all
narcotic stimulants while engaged in his ministerial duties, frankly admits that when off duty he
now and then smokes a cigar. It may seem pre-
sumption in me to comment on this apparent
inconsistency in so devoted a pastor and so excellent a man, especially as it is claimed that such an
example illustrates the power of self-government.
But would not the entire subjugation of this habit
show a far higher degree of self-government? So
conscientious is this divine, that I verily believe,
if he would look on all sides of the question, he
would no longer stand on dubious ground, but
would place himself in the sight of all men in the
most uncompromising attitude towards the tobacco
habit.

"But the poverty-stricken in our almshouses,
and the criminals in our jails, prisons, and penitentiaries, ought not to be deprived of this comfort.
Even some of their overseers approve its use,
believing, under the circumstances, that it is a
preventive to a worse demoralization."

Is tobacco, then, to be regarded as an indispensable in such institutions, not a few of whose
inmates it has been, more or less directly, the
means of bringing there? And is this deteriorating
luxury to be furnished them at the expense of the
industrious and the law-abiding? The inmates
need every possible reformatory influence that can
be brought to bear upon them. Is this such an
influence?

"We plead for the poor sailor in his isolation from the world. By all means, let *him* retain his tobacco."

The surroundings of sailors are sufficiently unfavorable to mental and moral growth without unnecessary additions. There is a tendency to sluggishness in the monotony of sea-life, which needs to be resisted rather than strengthened. Shall the sailor, then, be encouraged to use a narcotic which aggravates the difficulty he constantly encounters? Though he has the broad ocean for a quarantine, and can use tobacco with less annoyance to others and less peril to himself than any other class, shall we not make every effort to free him from the bondage of this appetite, and to devise some resource which, instead of benumbing the faculties and killing all ambition, shall arouse and stimulate?

In some of our boarding-schools for boys, we no sooner enter the hall door than we are startled by the sickening fumes which rush forth. So surprised are we that we can scarcely gather voice to speak. The boys are evidently learning some things on which we little reckoned, and from a most unexpected quarter. And you, a gentleman, a Christian, perhaps, to whose care a confiding mother has trusted, it may be, her only boy; you, whom he is accustomed to look up to as his model, are giving him, by your example, his first lesson in this vice! You surely have not considered how harmful it has proved to the young, so much so that by decree of certain governments, not over apt to magnify moral issues, tobacco in every form has been forbidden in their national institutions.

" But my pupils are girls or young women, and my smoking cannot injure them."

So be it, if to lessen their respect, and to make your presence an offence to them — yes, and a positive harm, — if in this there is no injury. And what of the example to their brothers? Let us not deceive ourselves in such matters. The young folks are better logicians than we fancy. What is right for the elder people, they argue, cannot be wrong for the younger.

One of the most-needed lessons for the children of this free and easy generation is that of unswerving loyalty to principle. If we would have men and women of character and stability, we must have children and youth who can say No, and say it emphatically and persistently. They must learn that every violation of law, whether physical, intellectual, or moral, is sure to be followed, sooner or later, by its inevitable penalty. To all the enervating self-indulgences, the doubtful practices to which they are continually tempted, they should form the habit of giving an instant and imperative denial. Let us have an army of young people thus trained, and the tobacco-warfare will be successfully waged.

PLEA WITH WOMAN.

Writes Rev. Dr. Brand of Oberlin: "When young ladies fully commit themselves against any social and degrading custom, especially among young men, that custom will begin to disappear. Woman certainly has the right, among many other things, to noble companionship and pure air, and it would be a very encouraging sign to see her assert it."

A woman's crusade would be a more hopeful movement than anything which could possibly be devised. Mention has been made of the Massachusetts ordinance prohibiting the use of tobacco at the polls. One of the law-makers who worked for this bill writes: "The inspiration for the act came from *woman*. And, as in all other matters when woman speaks, she does it on the side of the refining and elevating influences of life."

All admit that woman has much to do in fixing the moral tone of society. By every consideration, then, financial, hygienic, æsthetic, mental, and moral, all which are ignored, and, to a greater or less extent, violated by the habit, — women, who, on account of it, suffer as but few imagine, are called upon to give the whole weight of their influence, singly and collectively, against it. If they raise their banner, and in the name of God undertake the war, they cannot fail to batter down this grim Moloch past all resurrection.

TOBACCO BATTLES.

Desperate as may seem the undertaking, there is room for hope, — sometimes, even, when the case seems darkest. Many years ago there was a graduate of Andover Theological Seminary who was unusually popular and successful in his ministry for two or three years, and then broke down. He soon became a violent maniac, and was sent to an insane asylum. No one divined that the cause of this wreck was tobacco, or, if this was suspected, strangely enough, he was still allowed to use it. There, in his prison-house, champing tobacco day and night, he paced up and down for twenty years, cursing himself, his wife, and his children, and dealing " damnation round the land." One day, while thus walking back and forth, he stopped abruptly and asked himself, " What brought me here? Tobacco," he exclaimed indignantly. Then, breaking into tears, he flung through the grating his vile plug, and, looking up to heaven, cried, " O God, help, help! I will use no more."

God listened to his agonized entreaty, and out of the heavens reached down to him a delivering hand. With the dropping of his poison his reason and health gradually returned, and he re-entered the ministry, in which he labored earnestly for ten years, when, with the respect and affection of all, he went into the better world.

It may not be out of place to quote the substance

of a letter I once received from a clergyman who has passed into the other life, simply explaining that the subject had often been urged upon him while he was a theological student : —

" I have left off smoking. I indulged in it till I was thoroughly convinced that it was not only opposed to the fine socialities of life, but that it was detrimental to health, befogging to the intellect, and stupefying to the sensibilities. I will give you a few details of its moral bearings : —

" ' If meat make my brother to offend, I will eat no flesh while the world standeth.' A very practical text ; but I was a smoker, and that habit was opposed to the best Christian sense of my brethren, and even by many who were not Christians was regarded as a vice. I must waive that subject, lest my people say, ' Physician, heal thyself.'

" I wanted to preach upon the duty of self-denial — a duty which needs often to be urged ; but the idea of a *smoker* preaching such a sermon was simply ridiculous. That must be delayed, then.

"The subject of temperance came up. I felt that I ought to preach upon it ; but I could find no sound premise from which to reason that was not destructive to my peace as a smoker.

" I wished to preach on benevolence — saving the littles for Christ ; but my cigar bill faced me.

" It was my daily prayer that God would cleanse my heart from sin. Conscience would whisper : *Smoking is sin.*

" I wanted to visit my people. Both my clothes

and my breath indicated that I had been smoking. I had a little rather they would not know it; besides, it might be offensive to them. I must stay at home.

"I needed two or three hours of vigorous exercise; but I smoked after each meal, and an hour and a half or two hours were gone. A good smoke requires an hour. I had no time for exercise, and I soon got so it was irksome; in fine, I grew lazy.

"But I forbear. I don't know how others get along with these daily experiences; but I could endure them no longer, and I am no longer a smoker. I relate these experiences because I know you have a disposition to trouble people's consciences about this sin; but a sinner knows best how a sinner feels, and the above items may help you. Besides, I owe you this confession as an evidence of approval of your efforts and arguments for my reform in this matter."

Dr. Henson's experience, as related by himself, is most encouraging as well as instructive. He had long been in trouble on account of his tobacco-habit, having a sense of personal defilement, and realizing the possibility of coming to "such a pass of palpable filthiness" as some others whom he had observed. And along with this, he says, " came the conviction that tobacco-using was *against nature;* and seeing that God is the God of nature as well as grace, I could not help feeling that in running against nature, I was running against not *it* only,

but *Him;* and this, I was persuaded, was not a
thing to be safely done ; for, however slowly God's
mills grind, 'they grind exceeding small,' and
sooner or later, as sure as we live, they will grind
exactly all. . . I could not urge my people to ' lay
apart all filthiness and superfluity of naughti-
ness,' while the traces of such superfluity were dis-
coverable in my breath and on my body. I could
not insist that they should ' keep the body under,'
if *my* body kept *me* under.

" More and more imperious grew the demands
of an appetite that finally became impatient of
almost any intermission in its accustomed gratification. . . . I endeavored to persuade myself that the
Lord did not concern himself about such a trivial
matter, and said to myself, ' Is it not a little one,
and my soul shall live ?' But I had preached from
that text too often, and to too many just such sinners as myself, to extract much comfort out of it.
I remembered that Scripture, ' He that eateth is
damned if he doubt ; ' and I more than doubted,
and so was involved in danger.

" Then I deliberately, solemnly, prayerfully determined, God helping me, to have done with
tobacco at once and forever.

" It was just a question, and one of exceeding gravity, as to the possible consequences of so sudden and
complete a revolution in the whole habits of my life.
But having decided that it was the Christian thing
for me to do, there was nothing left but to do it,
trusting Him for whose sake I did it to take care

of all the consequences. And He did, in the most surprising and beautiful way.

"I could no more have made a sermon than I could have built a locomotive. And this continued for five weeks, in which I was wrapped in ' an horror of great darkness, and the very hair of my flesh stood up.'

" At length my mind, long eclipsed, came out like the moon when it has swept past the shadow . . . and if my whole life-work is not being better done and upon a higher plane, as I hope it is, I have a ' comfort in my conscience' which is to me of in-calculable value."

FINAL APPEAL.

The Levites were required to be thoroughly clean and pure. And even among the lamas, or priests, the rules of Buddha strictly interdicted the use of tobacco. Shall the Christian priesthood be behind the Levitical or the Buddhist? Shall that be allowed in our churches which would not for one moment have been tolerated in Jewish, Chinese, or Indian temples?

It were blasphemous to imagine the Master and his disciples chewing or smoking, as they sat to-gether on the mountain's side or sailed over Lake Gennesaret, or passed from the Supper to the Garden. Who does not shudder at the bare thought, inveterate chewer or smoker though he be !

And must we have tobacco-chewers in the Lord's house ! Spittoons in the pews and in the pulpit —

a dreadful need-be, or else what is far worse? Oh for some Divine purifying hand that with its scourge of small cords shall drive from the sanctuary all these incongruous, uncleanly sights and smells! Oh for a breath from the heavenly heights that shall lead every Christian, whether minister or layman, to wash his hands and cleanse his garments in innocency of this habit!

"It would be a sweet and blessed thing," writes one, "if, in addition to all a man's positive works of good in life, he could say, when he comes to die, 'I have not consciously done a single thing, in eating or drinking or pleasure, that I thought had a tendency to mislead or stumble to their destruction, any of those around me!'"

This tobacco problem is truly appalling. From the rapid increase of the evil; from its prevalence among all classes; above all, from the sanction of men high in position, it is threatening us with national degeneracy and degradation.

Is it, then, an impertinence for me to make a respectful, but most urgent appeal to every editor, philanthropist, and Christian, to every minister and teacher, to every college and every theological professor, to every member of a Young Men's Christian Association, and above all, to every wife and mother and daughter and sister in the land, not only that you rid yourselves of all complicity with this terrible evil, but that, with downright earnestness and persistence, you make common cause against it.

APPENDIX.

The "Easy Chair" of *Harper*, February, 1885, replies to the complaints of "Clarissa" against gentlemen-smokers. From this reply a passage is given : —

"And has Clarissa done all her duty? Has she plainly apprised those gilded satellites of hers, 'who wear the garb of gentlemen, and verily believe themselves to be such,' that they must choose between her and a cigarette, and that they cannot simultanously enjoy smoking and her society? Has she taken occasion to intimate that, in her opinion, no gentleman, truly so called, smokes in the street? . . . The problem that Clarissa propounds can best be solved by her and her friends. There are classes of offenders, indeed, whose smoke can be stayed only by stringent laws, vigorously enforced. These may be described as 'persons in the form of man.' But that other large company ' who wear the garb of gentlemen ' are amenable to the influences of Clarissa, and *such smoke she and her sister sylphs can suppress.*" (The Italics are mine.)

This is *an absolute certainty*. If woman only *will*, she can effectually solve the problem. Will she disregard her responsibilities?

WHY SHALL NOT YOUNG LADIES SMOKE?

The following is from "The Christian Union" : —
"I wish you would tell me if it is 'the thing' for a young lady to smoke? My brother Will is a great smoker, and he has taught me to be very fond of the aroma of his cigarettes. I think it is just delicious, and I envy him, oh, so much! when, after tea, he sits out on the piazza and smokes his cigar, and watches the smoke curl away from it in those beautiful little clouds. I have often wished I was a man, so that I could smoke. But Will has always laughed at me. Once he just let me try one whiff of his cigar, and it was, oh, so nice! — nobody was looking, you know. The other day my cousin Ned was at our house, and he says it is quite 'the thing' for a young lady to smoke; that there are cigarettes made just for them, and that it is all the rage; and I want to know if it is so, for if it is 'the thing' I am going to smoke too, I don't care what Will says; for it is just as nice for a lady as for a gentleman to smoke, and I don't see any reason why the gentlemen should have all the nice things; do you?"

Young gentlemen, shall your sister, or sweetheart, or wife offer up her daily incense with yours on the altar of your idol? Why not?

A SALUTARY GIFT.

In 1868 Mr. James Sugden of New York city, gave to the Trustees of Rutgers College, New Brunswick, the sum of two thousand dollars, the interest to be used for the purchase of books, which were to be divided among the senior class in the Theological Seminary of the Reformed Church, who would sign a pledge to abstain forever from the use of tobacco in any form. The professor to whom this charge was entrusted, writes : — "I have secured from six to ten pledges annually, and in many cases from students who had been in the habit of smoking or chewing, or both. This fund has the influence to call attention to the subject, and it has done much to create a public sentiment against the habit. It may not be entirely owing to this fund, but it is a fact that the use of tobacco grows less year by year among our theological students, so that whereas formerly nearly all used it, now nearly all abstain from it."

A NEW VOTARY.

A correspondent of the London *Telegraph* writes from Egypt : —

" I have just discovered that my camel is an inveterate lover of the weed. Let any one smoke a pipe, cigar, or cigarette in the compound called stables, and the camel will follow the smoker about, place his nose close to the burning tobacco, inhale the fumes with a prolonged sniff, swallowing the smoke, and then, throwing his head up, with mouth agape and eyes upturned, showing the blood-shot whites, will grunt a sigh of ecstasy that would make the fortune of a low comedian in a love scene. This is the plain, unvarnished fact, easy of corroboration. What have the Anti-Tobacco League to say about it?"

I think they would say that the gradual deterioration of camels is of far less consequence than that of mankind, and would therefore propose that all the tobacco the world produces should be sent for their use, that by their vicarious endurance of its penalties man might be spared.

ANOTHER ÆSTHETIC FACT.

In our large cities much of the cut tobacco is manufactured in mills erected for the purpose. A good part of the material is gathered from the sweepings of bar-rooms, streets, and sewers, consisting mainly of cigar stumps and old cuds of tobacco which have been chewed and cast away. Conceive the loathsome diseases thus generated!

REPLY TO MATTHEW ARNOLD.

Matthew Arnold's remark about wine-drinking, that it "adds to the agreeableness of life, and therefore to its resources and powers," has by some been applied to tobacco.

It has been the object of this book to show that so far as others besides the user are concerned, tobacco adds to the *dis*agreeableness of life, and in its results, later on, to that of the user also, so that, instead of *adding to*, it *subtracts from*, the " resources and powers " of life, as well as from its " agreeableness."

SMOKERS IN THE PEW.

A lady writes : —

" I am hospitably inclined towards strangers in church, but not long since my hospitality was severely taxed. We received into our pew a well-dressed lady and gentleman. I was so sickened by the tobacco-breath of the latter that I was obliged to turn my face entirely away from him, and so from the minister. ' Oh,' thought I, ' if he only knew how disgusting he is, would he continue this ? ' "

Unfortunately, excluding smokers from one's pew does not always exclude the tobacco-fumes, for they bear a free pass and travel where they list. Nor is the presence of the smoker always necessary, as garments worn in his home often bring their accusation against him.

Will not those who think they " cannot " break from this iron bondage be willing to hold up their experience as a warning, and thus, perhaps, do more to deter our youth from this slavery than the most eloquent anti-tobacco apostle.

If *ever* there was good and sufficient cause for woman's righteous indignation, is it not just here? In the lecture-room, in the concert-hall, in the opera-house, in the small, plain chapel, in the elegant church, in the grand cathedral, she is alike greeted with that insufferable tobacco-atmosphere. Sickened thus for a whole evening in some secular or sacred assembly, she is glad at last to hasten out as fast as the odor-pervaded crowd will allow. But even on the street it confronts her, it surrounds her, it pursues her.

One may well be alarmed, not merely at our social and æsthetic prospects, but for our religion, nay, for our very civilization.

Think, dear friends, what we have come to !

Tobacco-Christians at a prayer-meeting talking about self-sacrifice and entire consecration !

Ministers of the pure Gospel spitting tobacco-juice under the pulpit, and then dispensing the Word of Life !

Delicate, refined, yea, *Christian* physicians, skilful, genial, tender-hearted, yet persistent transgressors against common courtesy, — knowing that to sensitive patients this tobacco-odor is highly offensive, yet clinging to their idol !

One may talk about his choice, delicately-perfumed cigars, but to many the smoke, however disguised, is *poison*. Besides, staleness inevitably follows hard after freshness, and STALE TOBACCO — what words can describe it?

Oh, if gentlemen, whether saints or sinners, — *if* gentlemen only *knew*, *would they* not forbear, though it should be cutting off the right hand, or plucking out the right eye?

TYRANNY SUPERIOR TO THE RUSSIAN.

As an instance of the tyranny of the despot, may be related the case of the Russian envoy, after a court dinner given in Bulgaria in the latter part of 1884, by Prince Alexander. The rest of the company having withdrawn, the envoy lingered in the dining-room to enjoy his cigarette, while chatting with a Russian staff-officer who was in the Bulgarian service. The court chamberlain courteously took the officer aside, and delicately reminded him that there was a smoking apartment, and that to smoke in the dining-room was contrary to etiquette. When the officer made this known to the envoy, he instantly left the palace in high dudgeon. The next morning, the prince learning what had happened, hastened to the envoy to express his regret, and forthwith dismissed the chamberlain. Verily, tobacco is king.

The narrator of this event remarks: "I have heard of various immunities attached to the post of envoy, but I never heard that they were exempt from the rules of common politeness." If he had paused to think, he would have remembered that tobacco tramples on all such rules without let or hindrance.

AN ENCOURAGING TOKEN.

The following appeal from the *New Orleans Picayune* is an encouraging token : —

"If New Orleans proposes properly to care for

and treat the thousands of visitors now here at the Exposition or soon to come, it must abolish, at least for the period of the great World's Fair, an abuse which has grown unbearable here during the past few years — the smoking cars. In the name of visiting thousands, in the name of health, of common politeness and common decency, we ask for a suspension of smoking in the street cars of this city, at least during the Exposition, and we confidently ask the support of the ladies and gentlemen of New Orleans in this much-needed reform."

FROM DR. W. WALLACE NIMS, OF SYRACUSE.

"To say nothing of the scent of tobacco, so offensive to many, the habit of using it depraves the appetite, impairs the digestion, and tends to produce emaciation. Tobacco is a powerful sedative and acts directly on the nerves, prostrating the nervous system and laying the foundation for a long train of difficulties. And through the nerves it affects the heart and the circulation.

"For these and other reasons I consider the tobacco-habit one of the very worst, next, indeed, to the drinking-habit, to which it often leads."

SMOKING IN HIGH PLACES.

An Episcopal clergyman, who suffered from ill-health, was induced by the urgent advice of his physician to give up smoking. Happening some

days after to call upon the bishop of his diocese, —
not Bishop Huntington, you may be sure, — he
was invited to take a cigar. He declined on the
ground that his physician had forbidden tobacco.
"Oh, come in and have a good smoke with me,"
replied the bishop, "there are plenty of physicians
who approve of smoking."

TOBACCO-MANNERS.

A gentleman, who with several ladies was waiting his turn at a money-order office, ventured to
suggest to one in the act of smoking, who was also
waiting, that tobacco-fumes were unpleasant for
the ladies. "This is a free country," was his reply. To some other remark on the subject from
the gentleman, he made answer: "If you don't
like tobacco-smoke, *you can stick your head the
other way!*"

"I have reason to think," writes one, "that a
great many persons who smoke choice brands, and
who are told by ladies that the fragrance is agreeable to them, *fail to know that old tobacco-smoke is
everywhere and always a nuisance.*"

Says Dr. Drysdale: "The use of tobacco turns
the smoking rooms of most clubs into dens, which
remind the non-smoker of the lairs of wild animals,
so foul and pestiferous are they."

ADDITIONAL MEDICAL TESTIMONY.

A prominent dentist recently said that the use of tobacco gave his profession more than half of their business.

Dr. Zulinski has published, in a Warsaw medical journal, a paper giving the results of the investigations of years upon the effect of tobacco smoke in the case of men and animals. He declares it to be, even in small doses, a distinct poison. He finds such smoke, over and above its *nicotine*, to have a second toxical principle called *colidine*, with also oxide of carbon, and hydrocyanic acid.

Dr. Maxon, of Syracuse, known for his emphatic opposition to tobacco in every form, writes: "Whether operating through the nervous system, or by entering the circulation, tobacco directly diminishes vitality. And there can be no doubt that the physical prostration it produces may account for the fact that nearly every drunkard first used tobacco." Dr. Maxon also states that delirium tremens sometimes results from its use, the cases of two clergymen thus affected having fallen under his observation.

Dr. O. S. Sanders, an eminent Boston physician: "I am fully convinced, from clinical observation of forty years' practice, that tobacco produces blood-poison, and that its effect on the nervous system is appalling.

"Its pathological action is through the spinal cord and pneumogastric nerve, affecting the stomach and lungs, and relaxing and paralyzing the muscular system.

"Its toxical effect is to bring on nausea, vertigo, and an enfeebling action of the heart.

" The constant use of tobacco, either in smoking or chewing, predisposes one to epilepsy, and to symptoms resembling cholera morbus. It weakens the memory and sours the disposition. It acts upon the liver, making one hypochondriac, peevish, stupid, and morose, and producing oppressive apprehensiveness, restlessness, and melancholy.

" It not only vitiates the appetite for proper food, but impairs nutrition, and sooner or later engenders a desire for intoxicating stimulants. It cannot be otherwise expected, for tobacco not only causes general apathy of nerve-force, but produces great weariness, languor, and general debility ; hence, to meet such an extremity, the system naturally craves something more exciting than air, water, and wholesome food. While not all tobacco-consumers are drunkards, there are very few drunkards who do not use tobacco in some form.

" One argument is offered as an apology for the tobacco-habit, and that is that *it prevents many types of disease*. This is an error. Tobacco is not an antidote ; on the other hand, when a man, whose blood has been poisoned, and whose nerve-fluid has become abnormal from the use of tobacco, is attacked by any malignant disease, his chances for recovery are lessened fifty per cent."

Dr. Kostral, in the Austrian state tobacco manufactory, says that the workers are subjected to many diseases, especially in the case of young women and boys.

From Prof. Henry Mills, of Fairview Electropathic Institute, Binghamton, N. Y. : —

"For about twenty years I was in the habit of using tobacco in all its forms. My whole system became deranged, and there was every prospect of my being an invalid for life. I resolved on emancipation, and quit its *use at once and forever*. My health was restored, and for forty years I have hardly known a week's sickness."

In the preceding pages, extracts were given from the Reports of Drs. Gorgas and Gihon of the United States Navy. The following passages are from the sanitary column in "The Independent" for Jan. 22, 1885 : —

"Surgeon A. C. Gorgas, Medical Inspector, United States Navy, in his article on the 'Effects of Tobacco on Youth,' gives us, in full, the facts which led to its prohibition from cadets in the Naval Academy at Annapolis, as it has since also been prohibited at the Military Academy at West Point. When the order went into effect at Annapolis, the class of diseases, such as headache, disordered digestion, malaise, diminished at least one half in the next three months. The sympathies of the professors were in favor of its use, and Dr. Gorgas is himself a smoker, yet he bears testimony that the rescinding of the order, and the return to smoking for a year, had such unmistakable results, as that all the officers who had favored the plan of unrestricted permission to smoke confessed that the experiment had proved a failure.

"The use of tobacco by youths can never be regarded as moderate. It is generally excessive in the literal sense of the term; but its effects, even when but little indulged in, are those which characterize excess in adults. The depressing effect of tobacco upon growth, by diminishing the forces concerned in tissue change, its effect upon the heart and pulsation, the disturbance of muscular co-ordinative power, of ability to concentrate the mind upon study, the dyspeptic troubles, impairment of vision, headaches, and the retardation of sexual development and disturbance of that function, are conceded by most observers and clearly demonstrated by many. . . . At this academy instances of almost all the evil effects of tobacco have been brought to the notice of the medical officers. Many of the cases of irritable heart supposed to be induced by gymnastic exercises I believe to be caused by tobacco. . . . If, to-day, a census could be taken of all the boys who smoke, it would surprise, and ought to distress, our American people. For it is one of the facts that has to do with social, moral, and political degeneracy.

"We believe that all licensed tobacco sellers

should enter into obligations not to sell to those below a certain age, and that any person should have a right to enter complaint against children found to be indulging this habit. Besides the direct effect on impaired physical vigor, there is another view not enough considered, — the power of choice, self-control, self-restraint. Will-power, in its best sense, is the greatest power beneath the sky. The freedom of the will is far more than a theological doctrine. It is the reserve hope of manhood, and not only decides individual character and destiny, but social and national destiny also. Our most outspoken quarrel with tobacco, as with other stimulants and narcotics, is this : that, indulged in so early, they so affect the brain and nervous system that habits become dominant and uncontrollable, which lead to a general loss of self-restraint. We hear much discussion as to whether intemperance is a disease. The real disease that is gaining ground is debility in self-restraint ; it is producing that debility among the young. Tobacco is the most threatening power. It leads often to intemperance, to a general yielding of self-control, and so to many an evil greater than that of physical infirmity."

The following is from the widely known Nathan Allen, M.D., LL.D., of Lowell, Mass., who has written ably on *Hereditary Diseases, Laws of Inheritance,* and on various subjects connected with physiology : —

"I am glad to learn that you are soon to publish a work on Tobacco. Having made, for many years a specialty of the study of the laws of health and disease, I consider this one of the greatest evils of the present day. Language cannot describe the terrible effects which tobacco produces upon both body and mind. It perverts the taste, impairs mental capacity, corrupts the moral sense, and stimulates the animal nature.

" But its pernicious effects are not confined to the present generation, nor to this life. Its dreadful evils, through the laws of inheritance, extend to offspring, even to the second, third, and fourth generation.

"In view of such facts, that smoking should increase, especially among young men, is alarming, yes, shocking ! I pray that your book may prove a powerful auxiliary in this much-needed reform."

From Pres. Edward Hitchcock, D.D., L.L.D., for many years the honored president of Amherst College :

"I believe that tobacco is a cursed evil to our boys and young men, seriously damaging them morally and physically. It is a bewitching evil. It has a soothing and quieting effect on the nerve centres, and hence to the user seems to do no harm. And the fact that its use follows the law of increase, makes it much more damaging than if the law were otherwise. Besides, it retards the change of tissue, so necessary to young people. Its check on virility has not been made sufficiently plain."

TOBACCO AND CANCER.

The following is from the *British Medical Journal*:—

" As to whether smoking may be the immediate cause of cancer, surgeons are not agreed; but there is a condition of the tongue which is, in many cases, the precursor of epithelioma, namely, ' leucoplakia;' and this disease is more generally considered to be caused by smoking. Mr. Barker, writing on this inflammation, points out that among seventy-five recorded cases, seventy-one smoked, and only four were non-smokers. Buzenet used the term '*plaques des fumeurs*' for this disease, because he was convinced that smoking so often gave rise to it. Mr. Hulke has more than once shown that ' leucoplakia' may be the starting-point of epithelioma; and out of the above-mentioned seventy-five cases, forty-four developed epithelioma, and in one only was there a family history of cancer."

THE VICTOR VANQUISHED.

Since the above pages were in type, Ulysses S. Grant, our greatest American general, whose deeds have won the admiration of both continents, has passed from earth. His marvellous physical endurance, in spite of his ceaseless smoking, has been a standing argument with tobacco-votaries as to the innocence of the weed. But even the indomitable soldier could not forever "*fight it out on this line.*"

It was early admitted by his physicians that General Grant's disease was epithelioma, or epithelial cancer. In his March statement to a *Tribune* reporter, Dr. Douglas remarks : " Smoking was the exciting cause of this cancer, though there have been many contributing causes." Since Grant's death, Dr. Shrady, in his closing summary, says : " It is quite probable that the irritation of smoking was the actual cause of the cancer ; or at least it is fair to presume that he would not have had the disease if his habit had not been carried to excess."

The sorrowful end so long looked for has finally come. The grand old hero, to whom our country was immeasurably indebted, and whom she has delighted to honor, — whom not tens nor hundreds of thousands in hostile array could intimidate, — this dauntless soldier surrenders at last to a foe which, approaching him in the guise of a friend, he cherished, alas, with his own hand. And the whole nation is clad in mourning.

A few confirmatory testimonies are given as to the relation between cancer and tobacco.

Professor Bouisson, of France : "Tobacco, which answers no natural want, is the most common cause of cancer in the mouth."

Dr. William Hardwicke, coroner for Central Middlesex, England : "Certain forms of cancer in the lips and tongue are clearly traceable to the use of tobacco."

Dr. Charles E. Drysdale, of London : "Cancer of the lip is rarely seen, except in men who smoke."

Professor Lizars, of Edinburgh : "I have had under my own treatment several cases of ulceration of the lips, tongue, and cheek, some of them incurable, all of which occurred in persons greatly addicted to smoking."

Dr. John C. Warren, the well-known Boston surgeon : "The irritation from a cigar or a pipe frequently precedes cancer of the lips."

The "Medical Times and Gazette" mentions a hundred and twenty seven cancers cut from the lips, nearly all the lips of smokers.

Dr. Brown, of Manchester, England, "communicated to the Clinical Society of London a very remarkable observation on an 'ablation,' almost entire, made in two operations on the tongue, affected by neoplastic indurations succeeding an old *ichthyose* of the organ. The only cause to which it could possibly be attributed was tobacco."

Rev. A. Sims gives the case of a banker in Philadelphia who was an inveterate smoker. "The roots of the tongue rotted and the throat sympathized until he could not swallow, . . . and death from starvation and suffocation finally closed the scene."

Mr. Fenn, of Suffolk: "I have seen very mild attacks of typhoid fever rendered fatal from the excessive use of tobacco."

Professor Miller, of Edinburgh, surgeon to the Queen: "In plain language, tobacco tends to paralysis."

Dr. Solly, F.R.S.: "Smoking is one of the causes of paralysis."

Dr. Maillot, Chief of the French Army Board of Health, found among numerous cases of paralysis, many patients who were immoderate smokers.

Dr. Stephenson: "It impairs the functions of the brain, clouds the understanding, and enfeebles the memory."

Dr. L. G. Alexander of Kentucky, in "Good Health:" "The rapid increase of nervous people, nerve pain, neuralgia, and obscure nervous disease is seen by the physician every day, and it is my belief that tobacco, as well as alcohol and opium, is the most prominent cause. It is from this class that drunkards are mostly recruited."

"Journal of Science:" "The temporary stimulus and soothing power of tobacco are gained by destroying vital force. Nor is the poison easily expelled from the system, . . . indeed, nicotine has been detected in the tissues of the lungs and liver after death."

The wonderful pervasiveness of nicotine is illustrated by a singular case related in a recent journal. A lady in one of our western towns being brought very low from illness, her physician recommended transfusion of blood, which was accordingly taken from the arm of her son. The young man was a smoker, and soon after the experiment the mother complained of the taste of tobacco in her mouth! The result, as a wise man might have foreseen, was unfavorable.

Dio Lewis, in "Dr. Holbrook's Hygiene of the Brain and Nerves:" "If a man wishes to train for a boat race, his trainer will not let him use tobacco. If he wishes to train for a long walk, his trainer will not let him touch a cigar. If he will train himself to graduate from a college with honor, he must not use tobacco. It is a powerful poison and the brain cannot escape it if it be used in any form."

Dr. Warren P. Lombard, in an article entitled "*Some of the influences which affect the power of voluntary muscular contractions*," that appeared in the "Journal of Physiology." Among the influences treated of is tobacco. "Smoking was found to have a very depressing effect upon the strength of the voluntary muscular contractions. This was seen when a light cigar was smoked just before each test of the strength during a number of days,

and the amount of work possible on these days
was compared with that done at the same hours
on other days, when no tobacco was used. A
loss of strength was likewise observed when a cigar
was smoked before one of several observations of
a day. The result was unexpected to the subject,
who, though aware of the depressing effects of
large doses of tobacco, thought he could do better
mental work when smoking, and supposed that
moderate smoking tended to excite rather than
depress both mental and muscular activity."

Rev. E. O. Pigott, of England, one of the Cambridge University eight in 1864 : "I am perfectly
convinced that smoking greatly decreases the power
of endurance needful in sustaining physical effort."

Extracts from a paper by Dr. Jay W. Seaver,
college physician and professor of athletics at
Yale : "A record of the users of tobacco has been
kept at Yale for the past eight years, for the main
purpose of determining the number of men who
began the habit while in college."

Omitting certain statistics, the extracts are continued : "If this growth be expressed in the form
of percentage, it will be seen that in weight the
non-users increased 10.4 per cent. more than the
regular users, and 6.6 per cent. more than the
occasional users. In the growth of height the
non-user increased 24 per cent. more than the
habitual user. In growth of chest girth, the non-
user has an advantage over the regular user of 22

per cent., while in capacity of lungs the growth is in favor of the non-user by 77.5 per cent. when compared with the regular users, and 49.5 per cent. when compared with the irregular users. It has long been recognized by the ablest medical authorities that the use of tobacco is injurious to the respiratory tract, but the extent of its influence in checking growth in this and other directions has, I believe, been widely underestimated."

Dr. Seaver also finds the smokers inferior in scholarship: "Of those students who, within a given time, have received junior appointments above dissertations, only five per cent. were smokers, and very few smokers received appointments of any kind."

The setting forth of these facts has not been without results. Dr. Seaver reports that seventy per cent. of the senior class do not smoke, and not a single candidate for the rowing crew is a smoker.

Dr. Bilroth, of Vienna, an eminent surgeon: "The colossal increase of nerve and mind disease in our day is undoubtedly the result, to a great extent, of the tobacco and alcohol habit, and the straining of the nervous system caused by these poisons."

Dr. Amos Twitchell, of Keene, N.H.: "It produces its most pernicious effects by paralyzing the action of the nerves of involuntary motion. Among the diseases it occasions are palsy, inveterate nervous headache, palpitation of the heart, disease of the liver, indigestion, ulceration of the stomach, piles, and many others."

W. A. Axon, in "Popular Science Monthly:" "By causing irregularity in supply of blood, it degrades tissues."

"The Lancet:" "Dr. Chadnovski published in the 'Ruskayer Meditsina' an account of a series of observations made on twelve soldiers in a military hospital, who were perfectly well with the exception of slight injuries. Six of the men were smokers and six non-smokers. In the former the time required for digestion averaged seven hours, while in the case of non-smokers the mean period of digestion was only six hours."

Dr. Copeland, F.R.S. : "Smoking weakens the digestion and assimilating functions, impairs the due elaboration of the chyle of the blood, and prevents a healthy nutrition of the several strictures of the body."

Dr. Mussey: "Physicians meet with thousands of cases of dyspepsia connected with the use of tobacco."

Dr. McAllister, of Utica : "The habitual smoker weakens the organs of digestion and assimilation, and at length plunges into all the accumulated horrors of dyspepsia."

Dr. Darwin, of England : "Tobacco produces diseases of the salivary glands and the pancreas, and injures the power of digestion."

Dr. Rush, of Philadelphia : "It impairs appetite,

produces dyspepsia, tremors, vertigo, headache, and epilepsy."

C. B. Purvis, Freedman's Hospital, Washington, D.C. : "Tobacco prevents in a great measure assimilation of food, and produces a variety of disorders of a permanent character. Smoking causes debility of the stomach, irregularity of the heart, bronchial irritation and partial or entire paralysis of the optic nerve."

Prof. Edward Hitchcock, of Amherst College : "The use of tobacco may seem to soothe the feelings and quicken the operations of the mind; but to what purpose is it that the machine is furiously running and buzzing after the balance wheel is taken off?"

Dr. Woodward, of the Worcester Lunatic Asylum : "Tobacco is very deleterious to the nervous system, producing tremors, vertigo, faintness, palpitation of the heart, and other serious diseases."

D. R. Hagner, M.D., of Washington, D.C. : "Many cases have fallen under my notice of minors suffering from nervous diseases and general impairment of the powers of mind and body from the use of tobacco, and more especially from cigarette smoking."

Says a recent writer : "It has been proved that lunacy has kept pace in France with the increase of the revenue from tobacco."

Dr. Hassock : "Tobacco is one cause of the

alarming frequency of apoplexy, palsy, epilepsy, and other diseases of the nervous system."

"Phrenological Journal:" "Half the old tobacco users are in a state of semi-imbecility. Their memory is leaky, moral sense blunted, general disposition impaired, and tone of both body and mind let down."

Hon. Charles Steele, of Illinois: "When given to the excessive use of tobacco, I was prostrated by a well defined attack of delirium tremens, and from that time found it necessary to abstain entirely from its use."

Dr. Boerhave, of Germany: "Since the use of tobacco has become so general, the number of hypochondriacal and consumptive complaints has increased."

Liebig, the celebrated German chemist: "Smoking is prejudicial to health, as much gaseous carbon is injuriously inhaled that robs the system of its oxygen."

Dr. L. E. Keeley, Keeley Institute, Dwight, Illinois: "Tobacco enfeebles digestion, produces emaciation and general debility. It lays the foundation of nearly every nervous disorder now common to the people of America. It produces amaurosis and color-blindness, insanity, epilepsy, bronchitis, rheumatism and asthma, dyspepsia and catarrh, 'tobacco-heart' and cancer of the stomach."

Dr. Stille's "Therapeutics:" "It impairs digestion, induces constipation, irritates the throat, rendering it habitually congested, induces sense of nervousness, epigastric sinking, or tension, palpitation, hypochondriasis, and neuralgia."

M. Mouzon, director of the Professional School at Bruges: "Without mentioning cases of epilepsy and aggravated nervous maladies, we have three young men who have been almost entirely blind since the age of twelve, from smoking."

Dr. C. S. Jeaffreson, senior surgeon at the Eye Hospital, Newcastle, England: "Tobacco amblyopia — incipient amaurosis — is a very common malady in this district; there are few weeks that I do not see one or two such cases."

Dr. Chisholm, a distinguished oculist of Baltimore, on examining the eyes of a woman was puzzled. "If you were a man," he told her, "there would be just one thing that I should say." "What would that be?" "That you had tobacco eyes." "Then that is just it." It seems that her husband had allowed her to smoke in his company, and this was the result of the privilege.

Dr. J. H. Kellogg, Medical and Surgical Sanitarium, Battle Creek, Mich.: "From the use of tobacco comes sudden or gradual impairment of vision; a blurring of objects; ability to see better in twilight than in full daylight; difficulty in distinguishing colors; and after a time partial or complete and permanent loss of vision."

In a publication by the "Société contre L'Abus

du Tabac," Dr. Galezowski gives the history of an immoderate smoker who lost the power of distinguishing colors, regained perfect sight on abandoning tobacco, had a relapse on frequenting a club where was continuous smoking, and was entirely cured by ceasing to go there.

Dr. Chalmers : " Smoking leads to drinking and drinking leads to the devil."

Dr. Pennoyer, of the Pennoyer Sanitarium, Kenosha, Wis. : " The tobacco habit is one of the things I most inveigh against, believing it to be the most important factor in inducing the liquor habit."

Lord Palmerston at an agricultural meeting at Romsey : " The first step in the downward course of the laborer begins at the tobacco shop, for thence he goes to the alehouse."

Dr. Brochard, on a visit to a French nursery where the mothers employed in the tobacco manufactory leave their little ones during working hours, inquired of the directress whether she had noticed any difference between these and other children. "They are easy to recognize," she replied. "They are weakly, emaciated, undersized, with faces old looking and wrinkled."

Mr. J. II. Hoose, State Normal and Training School, Cortland, N.Y. : " Suppose the law places the boy under the ban for smoking, who will complain of him? A smoker! Led to the office by an officer, smoking! Fined by a justice, smoking!

The pulpit, in many cases, 'smells to heaven' of smoke!   The problem is one of gravity."

Principal Hill, Cook Academy, Havana, N.Y.: "The harmful effects of tobacco upon boys cannot be overstated.   I have personally known many students whose capacity for intellectual work has been well-nigh destroyed, and who have been brought to the verge of idiocy by tobacco.   I am amazed that the church, that society, that parents treat with indifference this menace to all that makes life worth living.   I do not hesitate to say that I believe the 'tobacco curse' is as threatening as the liquor traffic."

Principal Sheldon, Normal and Training School, Oswego, N.Y.: "The tendency of the tobacco habit is to undermine both the health and morals of the young.   It is the direct road to intemperance in the drinking habit."

D. Webster Prentiss, M.D., president of the Medical Society of the District of Columbia: "I cannot express too strongly from a medical point of view my opinion of the grave deleterious effects of the use of tobacco, especially of cigarette smoking, by young persons."

The only son of the proprietor of a French restaurant in New York recently died from excessive cigarette smoking.   He began to smoke when six years of age and the habit grew so upon him that, his father says, with all his efforts to break from it, "In three years I never saw him night time or day time without a cigar in his mouth."

President Barnard, Columbia College, New York: "The free use of tobacco in all its forms, but especially in the form of cigarettes, is doing much to undermine the health of the rising generation, and is nearly as noxious as the giant evil, drunkenness."

It has been shown that throughout the United States during the past year, 1891, there have been about one hundred deaths of young men, mostly under sixteen years of age, from the effects of cigarettes. In some cases there has been an analysis of the stomach, and in most instances there have been found phosphorus and arsenic, which are largely used in the manufacture of cigarette paper. About a hundred have also been consigned to insane asylums for the same cause.

Henry C. Spencer, principal Spencerian Business College, and Sara A. Spencer, vice principal: "In our thirty years' experience in teaching more than fifty thousand young people, we have found the effects of this narcotic to be precocious development of evil passions, premature age, shattered nerves, mental weakness, stunted growth, and general physical and moral degeneracy, and therefore now decline to receive into this institution any who use this noxious weed."

Rev. A. C. Amaron, president of the French Protestant College in Springfield, Mass., tells me that the students are forbidden the use of tobacco in any form.

Bishop of Kansas : " The enormous consumption of tobacco is one of the crying evils of the day. It is destroying the health of our youth, and vitiating the powers of early manhood."

Bishop Grafton, of Fond du Lac, Wisconsin : "I have known the influence of many a clergyman injured by the tobacco habit, and sometimes their health seriously impaired, even their lives lost by it. The late Bishop Whittingham, of Maryland, spoke most strongly against it. The Methodist ministers have given a noble example of discipline to churchmen in making, since 1850, total abstinence and the disuse of tobacco a condition of entrance into their ministry. It would be well if we did the same."

Bishop Gillespie, of Western Michigan : "I abominate the filthy weed. It is especially a grief to me that the clergy will use it. I think our theological seminaries should expel any student who perseveres in chewing or smoking. I know clergymen whose usefulness has been as thoroughly ruined by tobacco as it could have been by drink."

Bishop DeWolfe Howe, of Central Pennsylvania, the oldest bishop in the American Church : "Tobacco is not a specific — as far as I am informed — for any human ailment; it is revolting to the natural taste ; it occasions the loss of much precious time ; it unfits one for attendance on the

sick ; it impairs the health which it does not de-
troy ; its use in any form is uncleanly ; it demands
of its devotees a constant expenditure of money ;
its culture occupies rich arable lands which otherwise would yield wholesome fruits for man and
beast.   I have been grieved by the extent to which
the vile habit of smoking and chewing prevails
among the clergy."

W. H. Wakeham, field secretary of the International Health and Temperance Association : "I
believe tobacco is doing more harm physically and
morally than alcohol."

"New York Medical Journal," November, 1888 :
"When Europeans first visited New Zealand, they
found in the native Maoris the most finely developed and powerful men of any of the tribes inhab-
iting the islands of the Pacific.   Since the introduction of tobacco, for which the Maoris developed
a passionate liking, they have from this cause
alone, it is said, become decimated in numbers,
and at the same time reduced in stature and in
physical well being, so as to be an almost inferior
type of men."

Sir Benjamin Brodie : "If a generation should
arise when both men and women should take to
using tobacco, the deterioration of the next generation would be insured."

Again he says : "I cannot entertain a doubt that
the value of life in inveterate smokers is consider-
ably below the average.   Nor is this opinion con-

tradicted by the fact that there are individuals who, in spite of the inhalation of tobacco smoke, live to be old, and without any material derangement of the health; analogous exceptions to the general rule being met with in the case of those who have indulged freely in the use of liquors. Nicotine occasions death by destroying the functions of the brain."

Dr. Curvengen cited the case of a gentleman to whom he was obliged to administer strong coffee to arouse him from the nervous depression occasioned by long smoking.

Dr. Laycock, Medical Professor in Edinburgh University: "I have not known any good from tobacco that might not have been obtained from less objectionable means."

Abernethy, the great English surgeon: "Tobacco stupifies the moral sense."

A gentleman, it is said, once asked Abernethy if he thought the moderate use of snuff would injure the brain. "No, sir," was Abernethy's prompt reply, "for no man with a single ounce of brains would think of taking snuff."

Horace Mann: "Tobacco should not only be denounced, but the student who uses it should be expelled on the ground that the practice is unfit for a scholar and a gentleman."

"The Christian:" "The smoker more than any one else is a selfish man. No matter how poor he is, no matter how hard the times are, he must have his cigar.

Timothy Titcomb: "I have never seen a slave of tobacco who did not regret his bondage; yet, against all advice, against nausea and disgust, against cleanliness, against every consideration of health and comfort, thousands every year bow the neck to this drug and consent to wear its repulsive yoke."

The president of one of the Cambridge colleges, England: "Smoking demoralizes people more than drinking; when young it makes them skulk, and when grown up it makes them rude and careless of the feelings of others."

President John Bascom: "Ugly and unclean! An indulgence that holds in its right hand a stinging curse."

Rev. Dr. Dexter, of the "Congregationalist:" "I never in my life used tobacco in any form except to burn it on a hot shovel with malice aforethought towards certain bugs which infested my conservatory. Were I to live my life over again, I don't think I should alter it in this respect, except to try something else on the bugs."

Madame de Stael: "Smokers cease to think."

Dr. Nichols, in the "Herald of Health:" "Tobacco makes man selfish, unmannerly, and in certain ways what is called brutal. A smoker will carry his disgusting odor into any company, and show himself utterly callous to the rights of others.

. . . There is no doubt that thousands of delicate women and children are seriously, if not fatally, injured by this stupid selfishness of men, which is the direct result of nicotine poison."

Ruskin, "Queen of the Air:" "It is not easy to estimate the demoralizing effect on youth of the cigar. Tobacco is the worst natural curse of modern civilization, and belongs to a tribe of venomous plants, having the deadly nightshade for its queen, and including the henbane and the witch's mandrake."

From "The Resources of Siberia:" "Among the Buddhists in this country tobacco is strictly forbidden, the priests affirming that it is conducive to indolence, and tends to waste the hours which we are able to spare from the serious occupations of life."

"Tobacco, like alcohol, is a nerve stimulant," and, as Rev. Dr. Munger says, "stimulated nerve means at last irritated nerves, and irritated nerves clamor forever. And being unnaturally irritated and strung into undue action, they lose their force, which is a loss of vitality."

Prof. Montegazza: "It takes ages for ideas of justice to become prevalent, even in the most civilized states; it has taken only three hundred years for a fetid herb to conquer the world."

From many recent letters on this subject sent the writer, the following extracts are given:—

Dr. John Blackmer, Springfield, July, 1892:

" That the nervous system which was blunted by nicotine is not so keen and sharp for mental work as it otherwise would be, is abundantly established. The habitual use of tobacco is weighted in the intellectual race. It accelerates the respiration, produces morbid changes in the blood-corpuscles, disturbs digestion, occasions defective nutrition, lessens the power of the heart, impairs nervous energy, not only in the special nerves of seeing, hearing, smelling, and touching, but also in the ordinary nerves both of sensation and of motion, inducing in some instances partial or complete paralysis, and also insanity.

" The strongest indictment, however, against tobacco is that it makes one a slave. A man of forty-five came to me one day with serious disease of the heart. After an examination I asked, ' Why don't you leave off smoking?' 'Oh, I wish I could.' 'Do you mean to say that you really cannot do it?' 'That is just what I mean; I am a slave, bound hand and foot. I could have broken away once. I cannot now.' And he went to an untimely grave. What a slavery is that which holds a man to the very doors of the sepulchre and will not let him go till the grave closes over him ! "

Dr. J. H. Kellogg, Sanitarium at Battle Creek, Michigan, September 8, 1892 : "In my opinion the tobacco habit is the worst vice of civilization."

Bishop Coxe, of Western New York, April, 1892 : "I feel strongly on the subject and am pained that so many men much better than myself look at the matter in a very different light, arguing that the abuse and not the use is blameworthy, and that a moderate indulgence is an aid to some constitutions. It is hard for me, with due respect for such men, to express all I feel about this dirty smoking habit."

Rev. Mr. Southgate, Worcester: "I dread the crop of suffering and sin which is yet to be reaped when this generation of smokers has shown itself and its penalties to the world. It is a tremendous fight, but reinforcements must come. I hope all Christian people, and especially parents and teachers, will go at the curse."

Rev. S. Robert, a Catholic priest, St. Boniface College, St. Boniface, Canada: "Tobacco is a bad tree which produces bad fruit, and the worst of these bad fruits is the destruction of the reasoning power in man. Paralyzing as it does the tissues and the muscles in the human body, it necessarily follows that the brain and the heart become more or less paralyzed. Hence the weakness of the intelligence to reflect and of the heart to take any determination against tobacco. Therefore, I am very much afraid of breathing the poisoning tobacco smoke for any length of time. But my consolation is for the future life, for I am confident there will be no such smoke in heaven. On the contrary, I am very much inclined to believe that hell will be the smoking room of eternity."

Dr. M. Hammond, Baltimore, Md. : "As a physician of forty years' practice, I give my decided opinion that tobacco has killed ten men where whiskey has killed one. This, no doubt, will be disputed by physicians who indulge in the weed, but I believe it can be demonstrated that many of the chronic diseases to which the male population are subject owe their origin to tobacco. Thousands of boys to-day are suffering from the use of the cigarette, as will be seen by the rejection of so many by the Naval and Army Boards."

Dr. C. M. Culver, an oculist of Albany, September 3, 1892 : "I occasionally see a patient who has the choice between discontinuing the use of tobacco and becoming blind. I have known some such patients stop the tobacco and recover vision, because of such abstinence. Many, however, unhappily choose the tobacco and become blind. I have had much experience with the weed, having used it myself intemperately, as well as studied its effect on others. For more than five years I have been a total abstainer. My experience and study lead me to oppose the use of tobacco."

Dr. Hiram Orcutt, Boston, July, 1892 : "There is but one place in the wide world where a man can properly smoke, and that is the desert of Sahara."

Hon. Neal Dow, Portland, June, 1892 : "There is no doubt that the tobacco habit deadens the moral sense in every one who is its victim ; many of them are not aware of it, but it is certainly true. It is a gross, vulgar habit, without the excuse that drinkers have. Liquors can be made good to every beginner, but the tobacco slave acquires the habit only after a desperate struggle with loathing and disgust, more or less prolonged."

Dr. William B. Hidden, Baltimore, August, 1892: "The heart is the *engine* of the human body. The arteries are the *hose*. To increase the power of the engine and not strengthen the hose correspondingly means disaster. Tobacco lessens the frequency of the heart's action and increases its force, so that any excitement or a hearty meal is liable at any moment to burst the arteries of the brain where they are least protected; hence the tobacco devotee is liable to sudden death."

Dr. Anderson of the McAll Mission, member of the Royal College of Surgeons, England: "All the cases of cancer of the mouth that I have come across, and they are pretty numerous, have been started by the pipe, cigar, or cigarette; and almost all the male neuralgic patients that I have seen in the London and Paris hospitals, as well as a third of the cases of heart disease that have come under my notice, were smokers. As you are aware, at the McAll Dispensary, I have the opportunity of seeing over a hundred and fifty fresh patients each week."

Dr. Charles E. Drysdale, senior physician to the Metropolitan Hospital, London, May, 1892: "The majority of medical men here are anti-tobacco; but there is, I regret to say, a minority who set a very bad example in this respect. For I have always maintained that as it is particularly disgraceful for clergymen to be untruthful, so it is a disgrace to any practitioner of the healing art to make daily use of what is injurious to health, and thereby invite others to do the same. My opinion, based on a prolonged study of diseases of my own sex, is that one of the most common causes of deteriorated health is to be found in the practices of smoking, chewing or snuffing. Among the diseases resulting from the tobacco habit are cancer of the lip and tongue and even of the larynx, weakness of sight, sometimes ending in blindness, functional diseases of the heart and nervous affections. Mr. Goschen, our Chancellor of the Exchequer, has just informed us that the consumption of tobacco per head in the United Kingdom is double what it was fifty years ago. Some of our ladies indulge in cigarettes, and at a new ladies' club, recently formed, there will probably be a room set apart for smokers as there is in gentlemen's clubs. This smoking habit is one of the greatest hygienic delinquencies of modern civilization."

Dr. Benjamin Ward Richardson, London, a physician of the highest authority, July, 1892: "My views expressed many years ago respecting the action of tobacco on the human body have been confirmed in every way by later and continued

observations. I have no doubt that smoking interferes with the proper development both of the
physical and mental powers of the young and that
it injuriously disturbs the same powers in persons
of mature age."

Dr. Jay W. Seaver, Yale University, May 26,
1891: "The evidence regarding the influence of
tobacco on physical growth is, I believe, incontro-
vertible, and seriously against the tobacco user.
I continually have advised against its use both as
a teacher and physician, and I now feel as though
I had an argument that was conclusive and scientific, and that would appeal to growing boys. This
matter has long been recognized by athletes, and
met in a practical way by absolutely forbidding
tobacco to persons in training."

Prof. Edward Hitchcock, Amherst College, September 20, 1892: "I send a scrap on the tobacco
question:" "The matter of tobacco smoking as an
influence upon the physical development of Amherst students has been studied in the history of
the class of '91. Of this class, 71 per cent. have
increased in their measurements and tests during
their whole course, while 29 per cent. have remained stationary or have fallen off. In separa-
ting the smokers from the non-smokers, it appears
that in the item of weight the non-smokers have
increased 24 per cent. more than the smokers;
in height they have surpassed them 37 per cent.,
and in chest girth 42 per cent. And in lung capac-

ity there is a difference of 8.36 cubic inches in favor of the non-smokers, which is 3 per cent. of the total average lung capacity of the class."

President M. H. Buckham, University of Vermont, Burlington, October 20, 1892 : "The use of tobacco is much less prevalent here now than formerly. Free scholarships are conditioned on the recipients' agreement not to indulge in 'the use of tobacco and in other expensive habits.'"

President Warren, Boston University, October 18, 1892 : "Since the year 1880, by authority of the General Conference of the Methodist Episcopal Church, every minister, when taking the vows required for admission as a full member of the clerical body, is publicly asked, 'Will you wholly abstain from the use of tobacco?' and is expected to respond in the affirmative. Some of our ministers in middle life and beyond make some use of the weed, but I know of none in the younger generation. Even such of the fathers as are addicted to the habit find it necessary to be very circumspect that they may not give offence, or be understood to set a bad example. In a few years, I think the whole body will be in this respect the cleanest ministerial body of like numbers in the world. For this we will thank God and take courage."

Among the General Rules of the School of Theology in the Boston University is the following :

" 3. No user of tobacco is considered a candidate for membership in this school."

President Eliot, Harvard University, Cambridge, October 16, 1892 : " The latest statistics as to the use of tobacco by Harvard students which I have seen are those relating to the class which took the degree of A.B. in June, 1891. This class numbered 293 members. To the question, 'Do you smoke?' 125 replied, 'No;' 123, 'Yes;' 19, 'Occasionally,' and 13, 'Rarely.'

President William DeW. Hyde, Bowdoin College, Brunswick, Me., October 2, 1892 : "In reply to your inquiry, permit me to repeat what I have said in a little book on 'Practical Ethics.' 'The use of tobacco is the exception with scholars at the head, and the rule with scholars at the foot, of the class. Shortly after we began to take statistics on this point, I asked the director of the gymnasium what was the result with the freshman class. 'Oh,' he said, 'the list of the smokers is substantially the same as that which was reported the other day for deficiencies in scholarship.' . . . No candidate for a college athletic team, or contestant in a race, would think of using tobacco while in training. Every man who wishes to keep himself in training for the highest prizes in business and professional life must guard his early years from the deterioration which this habit invariably brings."

President Franklin Carter, Williams College, October 3, 1892 : " I believe that the use of tobacco by young men is a form of self-indulgence, greatly hindering the best physical, intellectual and moral development; that as self-indulgence it is always likely to break down the proper sense of proportion in values and to lead to other more pernicious habits. Its banishment from our schools and colleges would, in my judgment, effect a great increase in the usefulness of educated men and give new tone and power everywhere to those who work for the best things."

President E. B. Andrew, Brown University, Providence: "Too many of our young men smoke, but I am inclined to think the number less and less from to year to year. My influence against this habit I make as strong as possible."

President Rankin, D.D., L.L.D., Howard University, Washington, D.C., October 11, 1892: "We do not allow the use of tobacco on the university premises, and no student can have help from the Aid Fund, who indulges in the habit. I regard it as the most selfish and ungentlemanly habit a young man can form."

Rev. George A. Jackson, Swampscott, Mass., October 10, 1892: "Setting forth as you do the facts, your appeal to the chivalrous instincts of young men to give up that which brings such discomfort to others will not be in vain."

Rev. B. Fay Mills, the Evangelist, April, 1892: "I am deeply interested in your efforts to promote cleanliness and practical righteousness. I formerly used tobacco myself, but was forced to abandon it entirely when I realized that it was simply a question of how godlike a man I proposed to be."

Prof. Ruggles, of Dartmouth College, Hanover, N.H.: "All those receiving aid from college funds promise to abstain from the use of tobacco. Several scholarships have been founded on this basis."

Rev. Edward A. Lawrence, Baltimore, October 3, 1892: "The æsthetic abhorrence which most of those who do not use tobacco feel for the weed is usually more deep than loud. The many mute sufferers, therefore, have reason to thank you for voicing their protest in such form that it expresses in emphatic words both the discomfort which it brings to the innocent victims and the disrepute which it brings to the offending victims."

Rev. Dr. J. H. Ecob, Albany, September 29, 1892: "To give *carte blanche* to one bad habit is to make easy the entrance of the next comer. For there seems to be a sort of free-masonry among bad habits; no sooner does one get possession than it invites seven others. Tobacco is the enemy within who secretly conspires to pass the keys of the castle to the invaders without."

FRANK CONFESSIONS.

A friend in the Revenue Service who is an inveterate smoker has given me one of his experiences:

"In the summer of 1878, while at Charleston, S.C., I was attacked with malarial fever, and sent for a doctor, who put me to bed, giving me medicine that caused profuse perspiration. At the end of three days the fever was broken up and I was able to leave my bed. On calling the doctor's attention to the *brown sheets*, he remarked, 'Oh, that is nicotine,' as, indeed, the strong tobacco odor indicated."

. In answer to the inquiry "Does smoking tend to make one selfish?" the same man frankly replies, August, 1892:

"All smokers are selfish. The mother has to hear the boy's lessons, to drive nails, — pounding her thumb, of course,— and do many things that belong to the father, because his 'smoke' must not be interfered with. He declines to make calls, pleading that he is tired, or that he doesn't know the parties, while the true reason is that it may deprive him of a 'good smoke.' From the cigarette to the mild cigar, from the mild to a stronger one; this is the way the habit grows, and *continues* to grow by the increased number of smokes and the use of stronger tobacco, although a new and strange brand will sometimes make the head swim even of the old veteran."

Remember it is a smoker who gives this picture!

" Does smoking promote sociability, and in such a sense that it may be regarded as a tobacco benefit?" To this question he again responds: "Smoking does promote sociability, but it is rarely helpful or instructive. In smoking-cars, it promotes the telling of stories of sometimes doubtful import, and brings one into contact with gamblers and toughs."

Another reply to the same question comes from Port Huron: "Yes, I must admit that the use of tobacco tends to make men more social; while on the Pacific coast, I saw that kind of social life in car-load lots; in fact, it was to be obtained by the train-load. The bulk of this kind of sociability consists of gambling, profane and obscene language, bawdy yarns, sensuous nonsense, and ill-timed repartee."

And another from Chicago: "Of course smoking encourages sociability; so does gambling and drinking. A company of men smoking in a room are very sociable, and there is generally, besides politics, an almost invariable flow of profanity and obscenity, and an excellent chance for smutty stories, and when once started, the earth is raked for material, each trying to excel the other."

TOBACCO AND CRIME.

From "The Criminal," by Havelock Ellis, p. 120: "It is worthy of note that criminals begin to use tobacco at an early age. Thus, among a population which normally begin to smoke before the age of thirty in the proportion of 14 per cent. (and the insane 7.2 per cent.), 22 per cent. of criminals smoke before the age of thirty, and nearly all (279 out of 300 males, and 32 out of 32 women) before entering prison.

Venturi* found tobacco used by 14.3 per cent. of criminal men, 15.9 of criminal women.

Marambat† concluded that the love of tobacco was the first passion that rooted itself in the youthful criminal. Out of 603 juvenile delinquents between the ages of eight and fifteen, 51 per cent. had acquired the custom of using tobacco before their detention."

In the Auburn state's prison, five hundred out of six hundred convicts confessed that they began the career which brought them there, by the tobacco habit.

TOBACCO STATISTICS.

Total tobacco crop raised in 1888, as estimated by the United States Department of Agriculture :

Area, 747,326 acres.

Product, 565,795,000 pounds.

Value, 43,666,665 dollars.

Report of Internal Revenue Department gives the following amounts of tobacco on which taxes were paid in the year ending June 3, 1892 : —

Number of cigars, cheroots and heavy cigarettes, 4,548,797,417.

Number of light cigarettes, 2,892,982,840.

Total, 7,441,782,257.

Pounds of snuff, 11,164,351.

* " Studio sultabacco nei pazzi e nei criminali."
† " Revue Scientifique," 1889.

Pounds of tobacco for chewing and smoking, 253,962,139.

Total, 265,126,490.

The taxes on this tobacco were $31,000,493.07.

The amount expended annually in the United States for tobacco is $600,000,000, while in Chicago $24,500 are daily spent for cigars alone.

The tobacco revenue which Great Britain received during the last year was 10,135,666 pounds, or 49,056,623 dollars.

CHEERING ITEMS.

In the thick clouds of discouragement that surround this tobacco subject, there are a few rifts through which the light is breaking.

A Senate committee on epidemic diseases has recommended to Congress the prohibition of foreign cigarettes and of their sale in the District of Columbia and in the territories.

LIFE INSURANCE.

There is encouragement in the fact that life insurance companies are coming more and more to understand the effect of tobacco upon the health, and especially the liability to sudden deaths from the "tobacco heart." The following instance is given on the authority of a well-known smoker: "The North Western Life Insurance Company refused to insure an applicant, of whose condition they were aware, unless he would absolutely renounce tobacco. Declining to do this, he applied to the New York Life Insurance, but that company made the same requirement."

Says Dr. L. R. Jerome, La Grange, Ill.: "For twenty years I have been largely engaged in medical examinations for life insurance, and it is astonishing how many men have the 'tobacco heart.' Insurance companies are beginning to see the danger of such symptoms and to reject for that cause."

STREET CAR SMOKING.

The nuisance of street car smoking has become so intolerable that the travelling public, whose patience in all this matter has been amazing, is becoming aroused. Appeals to the officials concerned have proved ineffective from the persistence of offenders and the reluctance of conductors and corporations to displease their patrons. The press, however, has at last attacked the nuisance, and if the warfare is vigorously continued, street-car smoking will certainly be banished.

NO SMOKING ALLOWED.

This salutary interdiction is being posted in some of our factories, owing to the higher premium that our insurance companies are beginning to require of the manufacturers who allow smoking in their establishments. May this wholesome proscription be introduced into every factory throughout the land !

A TOBACCO RESOLUTION BY THE GENERAL PRESBYTERIAN ASSEMBLY.

In the minutes of this body held at Portland, Oregon, May, 1892, it is stated that "The Assembly earnestly called the serious attention of its ministers and elders and students to the very apparent propriety and pressing importance of total abstinence from the tobacco habit."

Although "the resolution was voted upon amidst the derisive shoutings" of many smoking elders and clergymen, yet that a tobacco resolution was adopted by the Assembly is surely a sign of progress.

A CHEERING WORD FROM PRUSSIA.

In consequence of numerous complaints by non-smokers that they receive no consideration on the Prussian state railways, the Minister of Public Works has ordered that in half the second-class compartments, exclusive of those reserved for women, smoking shall be prohibited. A movement has been started also to secure an order against pipe smoking on railway traffic. Some time ago the government ordered that only pipes with covers on the bowls should be allowed, but this concession to non-smokers has not satisfied them, and they are now overwhelming the Department of Public Works with petitions against the toleration of pipe smoking at all.

A HIGH IDEAL.

In compliance with my request, I am kindly permitted to give the following from a private letter by Mr. James MacArthur, of New York, September 24, 1892. Would that I could receive a hundred thousand similar letters !

"I have been a votary of Charles Lamb's ambrosial weed, but have eschewed the practice for the sake, chiefly, of being free from a slavish habit and of having a purer example to set to my companions in life. These motives have succeeded when all others failed."

UNIQUE SACRIFICE.

Away beyond Denniston, England, in a lonely coal-miner's hut upon a hill, is the following curious sign, which was put up by the owner some months ago : —

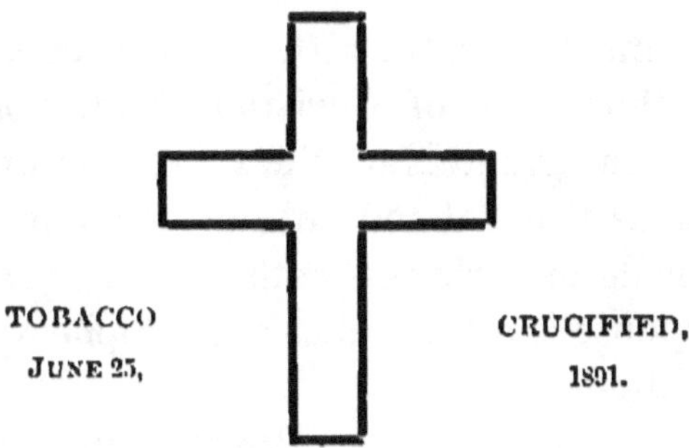

The cross is composed of two sticks of tobacco,

placed crosswise and securely nailed, and underneath is the inscription : —

> "Thou subtle enemy, thou hast held me fast,
> But now I'm freed from thee at last;
> Thou hast cost me £3 10s. each year,
> But I consider thou art far too dear!"

UNFLINCHING PRINCIPLE.

A standing offer of fifteen hundred dollars a month was made to the directors of the grand temperance temple in Chicago for the privilege of placing an elegant tobacco stand in the marble corridor of the rotunda. But in spite of their pressing need of money, Mrs. Matilda B. Carse, chief manager of the temple affairs, without a moment's hesitation, responded: "Never, not if fifty thousand dollars were offered ; we are not poor enough to permit the sale of that vile weed under this roof."

THE GREAT CONVENTION.

The rumors as to the virtuous tobacco abstinence of the thousands of Christian Endeavorers who attended the grand New York Convention were so marvellous that I dared not put them in print till I had made inquiries of Father Endeavor himself. His response is a truly cheering prophecy of future possibilities :

Boston, July 27, 1892.

Dear Mrs. Lawrence :

I think it is safe for you to say that so far as can be ascertained there was no smoking among the delegates at the Christian Endeavor convention. There may have been some who indulged in a cigar, but I did not see any one or hear of any one. There were no smoking cars on most of the excursion trains, and where there was one, I understand it was not patronized. There is no way, of course, of verifying any absolute statement in regard to all the 40,000 young people who were present, but in a general way it would be safe to say that there was no smoking.

Sincerely yours,
FRANCIS E. CLARK.